Chad McClendon

Lipstick Trace

ALL RIGHTS RESERVED

Cover Art:
Michelle Crocker

http://mlcdesigns4you.weebly.com/

Publisher's Note:

This is a work of fiction. All names, characters, places, and events are the work of the author's imagination.

Any resemblance to real persons, places, or events is coincidental.

Solstice Publishing - www.solsticepublishing.com

Lipstick Trace
by
Chad McClendon

Table of Contents

Dedication

Lipstick Trace is dedicated to my children; Annabelle, Evangeline, and Caeden. Chase your dreams using a sports car and a large net.

Book One
Lipstick Trace

April 2003

Quincy Abrams had been in his "new" high school for exactly seventeen minutes before he had earned his first detention. It hadn't been his intention to cause such a ruckus, not as the transfer student, not as the boy who'd only been here two weeks. Quincy just happened to catch a dangling strap of the football player's gym bag, which caused it to fall off the window sill. He also might have just coughed in a way that sounded like he had said something like, "piss brain" as the football player passed.

Quincy had issues. He had no delusions over this incontrovertible fact. So after watching the football player juggling footballs, and attracting whistles from the cheerleaders, Quincy reacted badly.

He had talent, but he never really expressed it, mostly because nobody was there to compliment him. So, anyone who could express themselves he considered to be a show-off. He reflected on this complexity as the football player introduced Quincy to his fist.

It was a quick brawl, and Quincy's first in this school. The Anatomy teacher who heard the scuffle interrupted it before it could get too anatomically intimate. He was given a slip that was to be returned with his parent's signature. This slip soon found a new home in the boy's bathroom and was promptly forgotten. Not like his parents would sign it anyway.

Entering his homeroom for junior year, he heard his teacher, Mrs. Flegler, lecturing someone at the other end of the room. Quincy rolled his backpack from his shoulder and flung it towards the general direction of his desk. The brown haired boy who sat behind him stared at him inquisitively. Quincy didn't make eye contact, but instead slumped into his desk and pulled out his prized binder. He caressed it softly and opened to a fresh page.

He heard the chirping of teenage gossip from behind him, and turning his head slightly, he noticed the blonde haired girl on whom he was currently crushing. Alice Mendell was her name, and he committed her name to memory the first time he had heard roll called.

Quincy often admired her from around corners. Alice wore a light blue spaghetti strap top and a form fitting black pair of jeans. Her blonde hair was pulled back in a simple pony tail.

Around her were her best friends, Valerie Fallon & Jenna Tillman. Valerie's hair was red and slightly obstructed her heart shaped face. Jenna sat in a desk that seemed far too small for her; Quincy was reminded of a giraffe.

He suffered through the morning announcements and focused on his writing, it was his morning exercise to remain sane. From the cobwebbed sleepy corner of his eye he saw a wrinkled hand grab his paper. His throat constricted as he fought back the urge to curse.

"Well, let's see what type of Magnum Opus Mr. Abrams has for us today."

Mrs. Flegler cleared her throat and read aloud. "Not today. I don't want it to be today. If I could just stop you, why do I let you guilt me into this stockade? I believe it is, and will always be, the end of my day. Knowing you. Wanting to teach you too. Just let me do it.

Oh, but not today. It's not going to be today. It's always going to be tomorrow. That'll be my day, tomorrow. Tomorrow it will rain for me, the day after I'll be the bitter regret rotting between your teeth. I can always hope for that can't I?

To be the better end to the story, that's what I hope for. But not today. Today I'm just the reassurance of your own superiority. It'll be sunny today, I hope it rains soon. But remember, not today; today I savor ridicule." She finished. "What contrived self-pitying melodrama is this

Abrams? Certainly this isn't your homework!" She crumbled the paper and threw it into her wastebasket. Several students laughed, Alice among them.

Quincy held his hot face and made a mental note to steal his entry from the garbage on his way out. He listened as she began talking about a special group project. His eyes bore into her, his face burning, and he envisioned her lips being sewn shut.

"Back on to business now. Drop that rubber band Jamison and team up with someone. Should you not find a partner I, personally, will partner you." She gravitated back to her desk.

Quincy got a tap on his shoulder and turned around. His eyes popped, he wasn't entirely sure how he had managed to not admire this oddball more closely before. His face was lightly tanned, and from behind chestnut colored hair peered inviting brown eyes. The boy wore necklaces, crucifixes and pentagrams, and he had multiple piercings. He smelled like his father's cologne cabinet, and the boy chose to smile at Quincy.

"Hey, I'm William! Wanna team up?"

Quincy stared at William's eyes, judged his posture, and came to the conclusion that he was serious in his inquiry. Quincy gave him a quick nod. "Cool!"

Quincy stared at the rubber band bracelets that were around William's wrist. "I'm Quin."

"Oh! I remember a TV show a few years back, it was called ... lemme think. Oh yeah! Dr. Quinn, Medicine Woman. Are ya talkin' that kinda Quin?" William bounced in his seat.

Quincy felt his tongue stick to the roof of his mouth and he tilted his head to the side. "What?" He had to blink several times before continuing. "What the heck are you doing? Did you just compare me to a medicine woman? Don't know if you noticed ... but I'm a guy."

William raised his eyebrows and quickly put on a serious face. "Oh, well, of course I knew, I was just making a comment."

Quincy never broke eye contact with William while he tapped his pencil against his desk, completely unaffected by Quincy's gaze.

"Ya' going to the homecoming dance, Quin?"

Quincy squirmed in his seat and shot William a questioning glance.

He did not answer immediately. When he did his voice dripped with unease. "No. I'm not. Not with you. Not with anyone."

"Jesus dude, I didn't mean with me. Just generally speaking. Whoa, I just kinda got turned down by a guy. I didn't even know I was swingin' that way. Wild. Totally wild, ya know? Guess I have some things to sort out." William scratched his chin thoughtfully.

"No, William, I am not going with anyone."

Well that's kinda a bummer." William nodded. So this project … I was thinkin'. Why not do something like, really impressive, that way any girls we *might* like will like us."

"I was actually thinking about doing the report on the iron maiden. It was a totally revolutionary device in its own time. I was thinkin' we could, maybe, give it some glamour. Bring it back, so to speak." Quincy tapped his fingers on his lap.

William was now the one staring. "So like … what would people use it for nowadays?"

"To drain tomatoes, genius, or make wine or some shit. Jesus Christ, what do you think we'd use it for?"

Quincy rolled his eyes at William.

"Whoa, whoa dude. Why the negative energy? I'm getting some really bad flow from ya." William held up his hands.

"Negative energy? Bad flow? What kinda hippie bullshit slang is this?"

"No way dude, hippie slang … that's totally off. But really? Why so hostile?" William rested his chin on his hands."

"With a name like Quincy Abrams wouldn't you be pissed off?" he cocked his head, his black bangs covering part of his face.

"Why would Quincy Abrams be a bad name?"

"Hmm, let's see. Let's start with Quincy." He smirked. "Yeah, there's a real strong; no, a powerful name. Then your previous comment about 'Dr. Quinn Medicine Woman.' Let me tell ya I got no end of torment over that one in my old school."

"Well…That's not so bad. Dr. Quinn was a hot chick in her own time. I'd go steady with her." William smiled with a faraway look in his eyes.

"See? There's that hippie slang again. How about this; my initials are QAA. Do you know how many times I've tried asking questions only to hear "You should know that answer Mr. Q & A. Shit gets old really quick."

William gave a profound nod. "Ya know I can kinda see where you would come off with that feelin'. My name is bad too."

Now it was Quincy's turn to be interested. "What do you mean?"

"People can honestly call me *Bill*."

Quincy considered appeasing him by jumping out of his desk, but then decided that he wasn't in a good enough mood for that.

"Do you know how bad that is? Look at how many bad people have been named Bill." William threw his hands up as if possessed.

Quincy tilted his head back, his hair falling in front of his face.

"Bill O'Rielly, for example. That cat got in trouble for that sex scandal."

"Well at least he was getting some female interest."

"And Billy Ray Cyrus?"

Quincy paused. "Yeah, you got me there."

"He had a rat tail. 'Bout the only thing going for him." He said, twirling his shoulder length hair.

"You're strange, dude."

William shrugged. "So, Quin, let's get to this project. I know you're thinkin' the iron maiden sounds good. I've noticed that you like those big hair bands from the day, judging by those pictures on your binder."

"Yeah." Quincy smiled, holding his binder to him proudly.

"Well I don't think chicks dig that sorta thing, they're into that whole living thong."

Quincy raised his eyebrows. "Living thong?"

William looked over his shoulder at a group of girls, Quincy was almost certain he was staring at Alice.

"Alright, Sisqo, what do you recommend?" Quincy inquired.

William looked thunderstruck; his mouth was opened, inviting every fly to take up residence. "Sisqo … nobody has called me that since 4-H Camp, Quincy! But anyway! Let's do this. I know girls are crazy over shows like 'What Not to Wear' and 'Queer Eye'." William counted off on his fingers.

"Right." Quincy could hardly keep the fear out of his voice.

"And we don't wanna seem like we're totally endorsing fashion, makin' it sound like we're not into them, or make it sound like we're not interested. We need to sound cool. Ya dig?"

"I guess?"

"No dude, I need you in this one hundred percent. We've come too far to have second guesses now. Let's do a report on how the fashion styles of Iron Maiden have influenced the scene long after their career reached their high point."

Quincy's eyelids lowered until they were little more than slits. "Ok, *Bill,*" he said mockingly. "First of all, Iron Maiden's career is still at its high point. Secondly, I like the idea of the iron maiden. Finally, what do I care if this project impresses girls? I don't need their acceptance.

"I've noticed that no matter where you go to school that there are different social classes around here. Girls who I like are in student government and they'd never like me because of this project. For example, I admire our class representative, maybe she'll go for Senior Representative next year. I'd like to be her prom king next year too. I don't think it will ever happen." Quincy tilted his head back and looked at the ceiling.

"Well that's not a very good attitude. Maybe you'd like this self-help book I've been reading. It tells all about –" William began to sort through books in his backpack, "different strategies on improving your –"

"What kind of weird hippie are you anyway, William? Christ. Self-help books, and your clothes would scare most Goths away." Quincy reached over and turned William's collar down, and straightened his crucifix necklaces. "Those pants though, do they get any tighter?"

"Whatever man. I don't know about the hippie thing, but ya know what I *do* know?"

"Enh?"

"I know how to make girls like you." William winked at Quincy.

"Doubt it."

"Nah, it's true. Just follow me in on this project and if you don't have the girl of your fantasies by the end of the dance next week, I'll um … I'll let ya have all my Roxette cassettes. So do ya dig that idea?

"Ya know, I do *dig* that, those cassettes would fit nicely on my shelf." His voice rose in excitement. "When do we start?"

Quincy and William spent the evening at Will's house. Quincy was petrified when he entered Will's bedroom for the first time.

"Will, tell me that isn't an autographed picture of Men at Work."

"And just what is wrong with Men at Work?"

Quincy threw out his hands and shrugged it off. They spent the next several hours hammering down ideas, and went through all of the band pins in William's craft box.

The boys worked late into the night, discussing their common interest in girls, and ways of attracting them. It was decided that William was going to be dancing with Alice Mendell by the end of homecoming. It was also decided that Quincy was going to come clean with the name of his dream girl by homecoming, too. This was only accomplished after William had promised to stop singing Tiny Dancer.

***

Quincy arrived home that night at a little past ten. Light shined through the dingy curtains of the living room. He closed the door and dropped his book bag in the entryway, then frowned at the infectious voice of Jacky Beezar as it wafted from the television and through the air like a dead skunk.

Quincy walked into the family room and saw where his parents were sharing a bowl of chips that sat between two armchairs in front of the television.

"Sorry I'm home so late. It shouldn't happen again." Quincy offered to the room at large, while Jacky was going on about some haunted hotel in Asia.

Quincy took their silence to mean he was heard, it was as their usual '*I heard you,*' silence. There were varying degrees, and Quincy knew them all. Parental silence, female silence, the silence that could make a guy go nuts.

"I, um, had a good day at school. I made a new friend."

"Mmhmm." His father said, breaking his steady intake of chip consumption long enough to draw a breath.

Quincy looked at the television screen for a brief moment. Jacky was preparing his audience for his next witless guest, who would wow the crowd with some talent that Quincy only wished he possessed. Maybe then he would gain his parent's attention for at least half an hour.

"Yeah I had a great day." Quincy rapped his fingers on the archway of the pass-through, his mind searching for a new topic of conversation.

"Yup." His Dad said, and then clapped his hands loudly as Jacky's guest came on, Quincy wasted a few seconds of his precious existence and saw a tattooed man take the stage. His body was covered in tattooed and he wore very little clothes. He thought William might like him.

Quincy started rolling his head slightly from side to side. "Ya know, I think I'll go shoot some heroin now, you guys wanna join?" He left the question hanging in the air on a very thin thread that his father cut nearly at once.

"He's got a forked tongue! I wonder how that would do ya Denise?" his father laughed derisively. Denise, eyes focused on the television, didn't respond.

"So, gone." Quincy said, as he abandoned all hopes of communication and scaled the steps up to his room, where he was greeted by his poster of Jim Morrison.

He locked himself in, surrounded by the protection of the posters that covered the walls. He delved into his music, his true friend. Pressing the power button on his radio, Kiss pounded out of the speakers. He cranked the volume and hoped it was as fully unwelcome to his parents and neighbors as the plague had been to Europe.

He sat down on his bed and kicked off his shoes. Leaning back, he took out his wallet and looked at the black and white picture of Alice, compliments of the school newspaper archives.

Staring at the photo he said "Why must I always be tortured, oh ambivalent creator? Is that the only reason I was spurted into existence?" Quincy rolled in his bed, not finding a comfortable position.

"Stupid William Denslie." Quincy tried lying to himself. "I could have been fine without him." But, having someone to talk to overpowered jealousy and personal desires.

Quincy put the picture back into his wallet and placed his wallet on his bedside table. He flicked off the light with his finger, and wished his thoughts could be as easily turned off.

He spent a long time that night thinking, pouring over the change of routine that had been brought to him. He finally heard his parents walking up the stairs, and for the first time that evening, thought they might be coming to talk to him.

"Turn off the music Quincy, it's past your bed time anyway." His father said from the other side of the hickory door.

"Your. Face." Quincy said boldly as he yanked the power cord from the socket.

There was no bidding of good night, or pleasant dreams, not even a reprimand for using *foul* language. Just another Kodak moment in the Abrams household.

"And to think, if not for William, that could have been the longest conversation I would have had all day." Quincy shook his head, and returned to his former quandary. He wondered which was more valuable, having the girl of his dreams and losing a potential friend, or simply settling for having two really good potential friends. Finally fed up Quincy rolled over. "It's too freakin' quiet."

***

William decided to enter Mrs. Flegler's classroom on Monday morning by means of the Cha-cha Slide. "Slide to the left, cheka chikuh, slide to the right. Criss Cross. Criss Cross. Everybody clap your hands!" This entrance gained scattered laughs and applause from his peers. "Four hops this time!" He clapped his hands in time with his hops and landed at his desk, red faced, sweat dripping from his forehead.

"I hope you show that much enthusiasm on your presentation, Denslie." Mrs. Flegler's cheeks inflated like red balloons.

"Oh yes Ma'am!" He hopped to his feet and saluted as his teacher flashed him a disapproving frown.

Quincy moseyed to his desk, took a dull pencil out of his bag, and sharpened it.

"Ya got a pointer for me Quin?" William laughed at his own pun.

"Yeah, lay off the perfume, it's overdone."

William looked surprised. "My Mom said nobody would know the difference!" He said looking genuinely distressed.

"Dude, I had no idea it was perfume. I was just messin' with ya." He paused. "Are you seriously wearing perfume?"

The bell rang.

"Saved!" William whispered.

"What?" Quincy asked.

"Nothing. Pay attention." William pointed at the front of the class.

Their presentation went off without a hitch. In Iron Maiden form, William had come to school wearing a blue jean jacket, tight leather pants, and temporary dyed black hair which he had spiked backwards.

Quincy made full use of an electric pointer to show the finer points of proper stud patterns. They even aired a mini-documentary in the fashion of "What Not to Wear Iron Maiden Style" to smattered applause from the females.

They received a 'C' despite much protest from the other boys. Mrs. Flegler seemed to think it lacked gusto. But all the same the two smiled at each other as they returned to their seats, confident in themselves. Attempts to get a date might not completely end in disaster.

***

It was the night of the dance and Quincy made himself look as respectable as he could. He worked aggressively to make his hair lay flat, and he was convinced his face would burn for days from all the cleanser he used. He exited his house without saying anything to either of his parents, after all, he had mentioned this to them. It wasn't his fault, he rationalized, if they chose not to listen.

The evening air felt cool against his sore, hot cheeks; he kept a brisk pace. As he approached the school auditorium he could hear the low throbbing pulse of the music, or rather, the sounds that were playing through the school's speakers. He hardly considered modern hip hop music. He curled his lip in displeasure.

It was easy to spot Alice once he entered the dance. Her beautiful dress seemed to pulse with a soft light of its own. Into the shadows of a corner he blended. He felt his eyes burn as he watched William come up and say a few things to Alice & her group.

Quincy only realized his fists were clenched after they began to feel like pins were pushing into his knuckles. Making an effort to relax, he got a glass of punch. William made talking to Alice look so easy. He would have traded all of his albums to have a tenth of the bravery William seemed to possess.

The strobe lights danced across the walls and floor as Quincy's third glass of punch entered the trash can. He visualized going up and introducing himself to Alice. They would dance, sure, maybe.

But doubt gnawed at Quincy's self-confidence. What would they talk about after the dance? What if he smelled bad? Doubts didn't so much creep into his mind, they more burst the door down with a battering ram. Quincy folded into uncertainty and briefly considered leaving all together.

He was a footstep from the door when he heard Judas Priest's "You've Got Another Thing Comin'" in his head. He thought of the lyrics. "Why should I just give in? Why not just go with it? Let them dance, and work my way into Alice's life? It might be a tad underhanded, but if nothing else, I'll have a friend in William instead of the jack shit life I've had so far in this town."

Steeling himself for what must come, he turned on his heel and boldly approached the two of them as the song ended. Quincy tapped William on his shoulder. William and Alice turned to face Quincy. He tried his best to make his emotions clear on his face.

"Quin, what's wrong dude? Are you okay?" William asked, a worried frown on his face. Alice looked him up and down and seemed to smile out of politeness.

Quincy looked to the ceiling and kicked his foot out. "Lilia turned me down. She said I looked like something the bus ran over." Quincy raised his eyebrows and frowned. The lie would save him the awkwardness of pining after Alice so much.

"Nah dude, you're lookin' like a million bucks. You're just too rich for her blood." William paused. "Lilia Harcourt? Dang."

Quincy turned red. "Yeah. I didn't need to dance with her anyway. My obsession with her was killing me.

"Murder is illegal dude, ya should have called the bulls on her."

"Hah! You and your hippie slang!" He sighed and William clapped him on the shoulder.

"Ya wanna dance with us Quin?"

"You had best watch out for this guy Alice, I think this makes the second time he's asked me to dance with him."

Alice laughed as Quincy explained the joke, and William brought punch.

"I spiked this." William said as he handed a glass to each of them.

"No … that was me." Quincy said.

Alice laughed. "You're both full of it."

"So, Will," Quincy started as he downed his punch. "You still owe me those Roxette cassettes, ya know."

William blanched. "Well, um. Oh."

"I can't wait to start listening to them. How many Roxette albums do you own? Or excuse me … how many *did* you own?" He laughed.

William laughed uncomfortably. "You weren't um, serious about that, were you? They're totally not your style, Bro. They were um … Not at all like Kiss, or Judas Priest … or any of those rock bands! You wouldn't like them."

"Oh. But I *do* like them. I've always had a soft spot for glam rock. It's my guilty pleasure."

William stood there, drinking his punch quietly. Quincy laughed hard and gave William a light shove.

"I'm only kidding Will, don't lose your cool, you can keep Roxette. Now how about this dance you keep talking about? Aren't we all going to dance?"

"Yeah, Yeah! That would be righteously kick ass! Let's do it!" William said lively. He was relieved to know he wasn't losing his cassettes.

William took Alice's arm, and Quincy's, and the three of them began to dance wildly to "Cotton Eye Joe" as the infectious tune blared over the school's speaker systems.

The three of them danced, Abba even came on once. "My DJ came through!" William laughed and he jumped up and down.

Quincy sighed with resignation as he watched William and Alice share their first kiss, and felt no shame in imagining he was William, if just for the night.

He didn't dance with anyone else that night, but at least he had a friend, and hope. Hope that maybe one day he would be close enough with Alice to be able to confess how he truly felt. If nothing else, there was always "Cotton Eye Joe" during which Alice had interlocked her arm with his. A guy could dream.

Book Two
The Bitter Aftertaste

June 2003

Alice Mendell was sunbathing beside her pool in her two piece, marinated with sunscreen like butter on a lobster before the big boil. Her tiny body didn't take up much of her fold out chair. She had plenty of space to turn and stretch.

Her hair smelled of chlorine from the pool, and within two weeks' time her pale skin would be a fine bronze to make even a penny envious of her tone. She reached for her CD player turned down the volume of Joan Jett and the Blackhearts. She was certain she had heard someone calling her.

She turned around in the chair and saw her two best friends walking towards her. Jenna Tillman, a curiously tall and tan seventeen-year-old with slender shoulders and long legs approached her. Jenna carried a small red bag with her, which held a swimsuit, sunscreen, designer shades and a fashion magazine from the New York fashion district.

Valerie Fallon walked side by side with Jenna. Valerie's hair was as beautiful as the summer's setting sun and as long as the equinox. Her penetrating green eyes were distinctly focused on Alice.

Her voice split the silence, as crisp as an apple's skin. "Allie ... you, Jen and I need to have a talk." She sat on a lounge chair across from Alice. She began to compulsively tuck her hair behind her ears.

"We're a bit worried about you Alice. You're *dating* that Denslie boy?" Jenna accused more than asked, her tiny lips curled in a timid smirk.

Alice gracefully sat up and nodded at her friends. "He and I are together. Officially, at least, as of last night."

Valerie tossed her sandals underneath the chair and stretched out lazily, reaching into her bag and pulling out her sunglasses. "Can I ask why you're dating *him* and not someone more on your level?" She pulled off her shirt and revealed that she was already in her bathing suit, a festive bright green that reminded Alice of a watermelon.

Valerie let her shirt drop next to her sandals and pulled her glasses down to cover her eyes from the blinding light of the sun. "Here Jenna, do my back quickly before you get changed." Valerie said, handing Jenna a bottle of sunscreen.

Jenna sat behind Valerie and began to cover her friend in SPF 30. "I agree Allie, he's soooo not your usual."

Alice could appreciate her friend's interest in her love life. "I love that you two are concerned for my sanity, but really, William's got a spark in him. He's fun."

"So are most guys until they get in your pants, honey." Valerie said with contempt, taking the bottle of sunscreen from Jenna without offering to return her friends favor. "You're Alice Mendell, what is he … in the AV club or something? I just can't help but think that he's out to date you to increase his own popularity."

Alice frowned. "Think someone's a tad jealous that I have a good guy for once, instead of some ball grabbing sleaze that's my usual."

"That's not it at all Allie." Jenna interrupted before Valerie could go forward. "We're just worried that he's going to let you down. Think of it, you'd probably have to dump him yourself, and you know how much work that is."

"Especially when they know right where your locker is … have you thought of that Allie? You'd have to pass him *every day* once school starts up again. This is our last year, you sure you don't want Zach?" Valerie asked.

"The fullback?" Alice rolled her eyes. "After what he pulled that last game under the bleachers … I think not."

"Still claiming you weren't ready for that?" Valerie asked.

"Yes. Still claiming. Remember Mick? Not ready for anything like that either again anytime soon." Alice twisted her hair habitually.

Valerie's cheeks flushed and Jenna seized control of the silence. "Well, what's this William guy like really? Is he always so... outdated acting?" Jenna said, falling back into a more shaded region of the back yard.

Alice considered her request and deemed it appropriately respectful. "He's a great kisser, never would have guessed that though from the looks. He's got some good hands."

Valerie burst into laughter. "Oh really?"

"He does. Makes me go all tingly when he touches the back of my neck." Alice grinned, teasing her friends. "If you're lucky, and I do dump him, maybe he'll rebound to you, Val."

Valerie scrunched her nose up, resembling a Pug. "No thanks, I don't want your leftovers."

"Think she's gonna be sick Allie." Jenna giggled, pushing Valerie slightly so that she nearly fell out from her seat.

"Well, it would certainly make me feel better about having so much to eat at lunch." Valerie commented aloud, walking over to the pool and gazing into its depths.

Alice frowned disapprovingly at Valerie and caught Jenna's timid eyes. She had caught the meaning also, and Alice thought that maybe Valerie had more important things to worry about than *her* boyfriend.

"Valerie?" Alice spoke louder.

Valerie turned, stared Alice in the eyes, and dived into the pool with a big splash.

"She's over it Allie, we don't need to worry." Jenna said comfortingly, sitting next to Alice and hugging her.

"You saw her last year. We've come far since then, but I'm not going to rest easy over Valerie for a while Jen."

Alice said, sliding her CD player under her chair and walking over to the pool.

"Alice," Jenna said, pulling her back and speaking so low even that Alice had to strain to hear her. "I am happy for you, if you're really happy for yourself." Her China doll face looked fragile in the bright light of the sun. "What Zach did...I'm sure William wouldn't do. He doesn't seem...forceful."

Alice broke into a wide grin before she fell backwards into the cool water.

***

Alice hurriedly buried her can of soda into the depths of her simple black purse next to her pack of cheese crackers. She had the whole evening ahead of her with William and this was technically their first date. They'd been together at school, but this was their first time out as a *couple*.

Soon, she was at the local movie theater, and there under one of its pillars was William. *Does this boy know the phrase 'Dress to impress'?* She cringed as she noticed his attire.

He wore purple jeans and what looked to be a band t-shirt, with his chestnut brown hair styled down in a simple way. The square specs he wore made him look more intellectual and for that she blew him a kiss. He was unintentionally cute in that stray cat sort of way.

She closed the distance between them and he drew her in for a hug. As she breathed in the smell of his questionable cologne, she thought to herself *what do my friends know?*

They walked inside and approached the ticket desk. She watched appreciatively as he reached into his pocket and pulled out a twenty for their tickets. She walked with a spring in her step as they rounded the corner into the main movie theater atrium. Her last boyfriend hadn't paid for very much during their time together. But he got his money's worth, Alice thought spitefully.

They approached the snack counter, and she recognized the guy working behind it as one of William's friends, Quentin or something of the like. The guy turned red as she and William approached.

"I could go for some popcorn, you game?" William asked. "I've got a hole in my gut for some saltiness."

"I could pick it up," She offered, "You did pay for the tickets after all." She tested him, curiously awaiting his response.

He waved his hand. "Heck no. It's a date you know, that's why I'm wearing my good jeans."

Then again, maybe my friends do know something. She bit her lip as she glanced again at the jeans. *Course, I can always omit what he was wearing when they ask.* If nothing else, he was a gentleman.

"That's very sweet of you." She said, nodding to him.

William waved at his friend who sneered slightly, and Alice gave him an obligatory smile as they came up to the counter.

"Evenin' Quin." William said, and Alice noted his name.

"Hey, lovebirds." He jibed.

Alice thought she heard a crunching noise nearby. She studied the boy's face, long and pale, with dark hair covering his eyes. He had random holes in his ears from piercings that had yet to completely close, and an acne-scarred sort of complexion. He didn't seem like he enjoyed being in his maroon work uniform, his beefy arms seemed like they were about to burst the seams of his sleeves, and his shoulders seemed to be bearing Atlas's burden.

Will ordered and soon they were on their way to their dark and mostly deserted theater. Will took his seat next to her and she watched as he took a sip of his drink. Calamity struck in that the cup soon parted ways with the lid by which he was holding the beverage. Sugary sticky soda saturated his pants and he was soon padding himself thoroughly with napkins.

Alice laughed harshly and felt badly for doing so. She saw William shrug and laugh uncomfortably.

"I'll be um, back." He said, walking awkwardly out of the theater.

Alice composed herself and waited in the dim theater. She ate a few pieces of popcorn without feeling too guilty over it and she reached into her purse and rummaged around until her fingers felt an icy coldness. She coughed loudly as she opened her can of contraband cola.

She got a tap on her shoulder and gasped as she saw the pale face of that friend of William's. "Outside soda isn't allowed in the theater, Miss Mendell."

Alice crossed her arms mentally and prepared to overcome the boy with her winning personality. "You won't let little ole me get away with one infraction of your very high laws, Mister Movie Man?" She tilted her head and stared at his impassive face.

"I could have you thrown out for this. It's a pretty serious violation and …."

"Make me leave." Alice didn't want to listen to his prattle, didn't *have* to listen to his prattle. "I know you're my *boyfriend's* friend, and I'd hate to see him have to fight for my honor."

She watched him as his lips started to tremble. She thought that maybe she'd been too hard on him, she was used to getting her way with her peers and this guy seemed to be breaking with no resistance.

She felt slightly uneasy as he began to stifle a deep and erratic laughter. His hair bounced from side to side, she could nearly see the slimy product falling off his strands. She resisted the urge to gag.

"Denslie? Fighting? What a joke!" He reached down and grabbed hold of her soda.

Alice burned inside, she was not one to be laughed at. "Fine. Take your drink. I'm senior representative in our class, a cheerleader and captain of the dance team. Also known as *popular*. You have your fun now, but this fall, your social life is dead."

Now the boy looked intrigued, his eyebrows arched and his lips parted into a distantly attractive smile. Alice re-situated herself in her seat and took a firmer hold of her soda, determined to win the battle of minds with this brute.

"My social life? Please sweetie, maybe you didn't notice but I have no social life. I have only my pain and my music."

Alice shook her head, wondering where the hell William was. "What's your name again? I know you were at the end of the year dance, but I can't remember much else except you were nearly to tears because Lilia turned you down."

He rolled his eyes. "I'm Quincy Abrams, remember?" He looked at her hopefully. "The transfer student?" He prompted.

"Hmm. No sorry, the name doesn't ring a bell. All I see is the sad little boy with William during *his* presentation." She yanked the soda and yet he held on with a grip death would envy.

Suddenly, she got a devilish idea and with a smile, she released her grip and watched as her soda spewed up and coated his face. Dark liquid dripped down his face and fell onto the movie theater's chairs.

"Well." She shrugged. "I no longer have the drink, so I suppose you can go now. I'll be no further hassle."

Quincy shook his head wildly.

"Ugh, *dog,* stop coating me with your second hand soda wash."

Quincy seemed about to say something else, but with a jerk of his head he walked away. Alice heard a string of curse words and giggled silently.

Alice felt victorious. Boys usually didn't stand much chance with her, and this one was no exception. Just before the feature started William returned. His pants were as dry as best as could be expected. He looked little worse for wear and his shoulder was fairly comfortable compared to others she had rested her head upon.

***

The film let out and William walked with her to the food court, where he was determined to get another drink. His friend wasn't working at the snack bar, and she was actually a little disappointed. Part of her wanted to cause a scene, she was feeling a little roguish tonight and she desperately hoped that William would continue to entertain her.

They walked outside once William had his new drink, and there was a little stretch of forest not far from the movie theater. She watched his hands as they walked, waiting on him to make a move and take one of hers as his own.

She had decided he wasn't nearly as bad as Jenna and Valerie had made him out to be, she was actually fairly impressed with his kissing caliber.

As the silence stretched on into uncomfortable continuance, she looked over at him. He was smiling at her. He nearly tripped over himself and she grinned as he fought to catch himself without spilling his drink for the second time this evening. "Careful Will. It wouldn't do to break your legs, summers only started."

"Breaking my legs would be a drag, suppose I'd be put up for a while." He frowned, taking a long sip of his drink.

She saw his hand clench and release; it swung like a pendulum slowly onward towards hers. Their skin met for the briefest moment and she thought he was going to hold, yet the connection broke.

She exhaled loudly and looked at him with resignation in her mind. "Did your other girlfriends like to hold hands with you?" She questioned.

His eyes widened. "*Other* girlfriends? Well yeah, that's mostly all we were comfortable doing back in 7th grade. Course, we kissed a little, maybe got a grab on the toosh but that's it."

"As we're both seniors, I think I'd prefer a little more hand holding, if not the occasional hand on back motions." She pushed him verbally, willing him to catch on to her needs.

"Oh, okay sure, that'd be peachy with me." he put his hand in hers.

There we go. They continued walking, the stars were becoming clearer the further away from the theater they walked.

"So what were your other boyfriends like?" He asked.

His hands were quickly becoming sweaty; she thought it cute yet slightly off-putting as he had to be nervous. Yet with his question of her past she was suddenly the one feeling anxious.

"I had a few guys, none quite as…" She considered her words carefully, she didn't want to offend him, and he didn't deserve that. "…innocent as you."

"Innocent huh? Your other dudes were guilty then? What crimes did they commit?"

She shook her head. "They weren't criminals; I just meant that you seem to have a pure heart as opposed to the animals I've dated."

He dropped his drink. "You've dated animals?" He ripped his hands from hers and started retreating into the woods.

"I didn't mean I've dated animals, I just meant…"

He lessened the distance between them and she felt his lips upon hers. His hands stroked her hair and she felt herself relaxing. "I know what you meant, I'm not totally unaware. I probably could have not dropped the drink though."

She leaned into him and let herself hide in his embrace. "I dated some real bastards if you want to know the truth, William." She confessed to him, feeling unusually open in this moment. She peered up superstitiously at the full moon and shook her head.

"Oh."

She heard him swallow and his hands clumsily held onto her, yet she didn't mind as much as she normally would have. He seemed to be a different kind of guy, at least remotely in touch with his feelings as opposed to…

"What kind of guys? Like, you're a fine gal, who wouldn't appreciate you?"

"I can't go into details, not really, I wouldn't want you thinking badly of me."

"Nah, that's impossible. I like to know the facts and I never think badly of someone unless they really deserve it. Like the guy that burned my stamp collection when I was at summer camp. *He* deserves my unyielding scorn."

She laughed, and wondered what there was to be afraid of; she felt a kinship with him. "There have just been a handful of bad decisions since my sophomore year Will. Some rude jocks and some private school cocks as I like to say. None of them really wanted to know anything about me; all they saw was a pretty face. Especially the last guy I was with. He was probably the worst guy I ever was with."

William patted her head, and she looked up into his eyes. "I'm not a cat, please don't pet me."

He nodded and simply held her against his chest. "I'm sorry you've had some bad dudes, I know you might already know this, but I'm not going to be one. I'm solid."

She conceded that this probably was true, and so she felt comfortable going on. "He was a college guy, a freshman who had been given a sports scholarship. He was beefy, in a muscular sort of way. He could lift me up and run with me like I was lighter than air."

"What was wrong with him?" William asked.

She frowned, remembering his tan face smirking at her in a way that drove her mad. "He had one thing on his mind, and after months of trying, he got it. The next day, he had another thing on his mind with a new girl."

She looked into his eyes and watched him put the story together, she watched for the usual glint of lust that she so commonly saw in guy's eyes when the topic of sex was brought up; yet she never saw that demon peek out from his eyes. She did see his eyes close slowly and she did hear a sigh escape him.

"I'm sorry." he whispered, and she felt his hands start to leave her.

"Don't." she said, unaware that she had given her tongue permission to speak. She felt him hesitate, and felt relieved as his hands came back to her. She felt so exposed, yet with his touch he eased her anxiety.

They moved only when she felt comfortable again, and even then, they walked slowly hand in hand. "Do you want to know why I stayed with him for so long?" She waited for a sign from him, yet not daring to meet his eyes, she detected none.

"He seemed willing to wait for me until I was ready. He convinced me that he wouldn't run off once he had gained what he wanted."

"Karma's going to write him a big check one day, and that sucker's going to bounce." William leaned down and kissed her forehead.

They walked back up to the theater and found Alice's father waiting. They were unnoticed, so she gave him a long kiss and sighed into his chest. "I don't tell many people what I've told you William. I don't want you telling anyone else what I've shared tonight. But I do want you to know that I feel very safe with you."

He tilted his head and smiled at her. "You don't have to feel threatened with me, I won't ever hurt you."

She let his hand slip from hers and she couldn't be more fascinated by him. She walked back to her parent's car and felt a deep pang for William, though he had only been gone less than a minute. There was something so remarkably different about him. She felt a mixture of guilt as she realized with horrifying clarity that she didn't think she deserved someone like him.

***

The next afternoon Alice had just gotten in from a run when her mother hailed her at the front door with the cordless phone. Alice's calves burned as she ran up the walk to her front door.

"It's Valerie; she's been calling all morning." Brenda Mendell said shaking her head amusedly.

Alice pressed the phone against her ear and shoulder and greeted Valerie breathlessly.

"Where the hell have you been? It's been over 12 hours since your date with that boy. I want the details, you know, seeing as were best friends." Alice heard her speak with a slice of sarcasm.

She walked into her house and slowly took her stairs one by one to her bedroom. She closed the door tightly, turning the lock to ensure privacy. "Sorry, I was a bit busy today. I went for a run to think about some things."

"Well, great. I went swimming, it was cold. Now tell me about the date."

"What's there to say?" Alice said as she untied her ponytail and placing the hair tie onto the plastic hook that hung on the side of her bookshelf. She placed it directly behind the black hair ties, as that's where green ones belonged. "I mean, he was very sweet, and just slightly under-dressed for the occasion."

"How do you under dress for a movie when you're a guy?" She laughed.

"Beats me, but somehow he *did* pull it off. It was cool though Val, he's like…incredible."

"Well, that's cool then." She said, sounding disappointed.

"Are you upset that I had a good time?" Alice took off her shoes and sat them in her shoe caddy.

"Of course not, don't be stupid. I'm just a little pissed that you didn't call me right away. I mean, it was your first date with the guy…first real date, and I wanna make sure he's not screwing you around."

"I appreciate that." Alice said, a little moodily, still not sure that she believed Valerie. "Cuz I—"

"I still think you should date somebody else."

Alice stopped removing her socks and left half of one dangling off her foot. "What?"

"Date somebody else because that freaks not worth your time."

"What makes you say that?" Alice felt herself getting hot, and not just from running.

Valerie didn't respond immediately. "He's got that little skittery thing with his eyebrows all the time. His face…it's like an avalanche. You don't wanna be caught near it."

Alice sputtered out a laugh, like a dying car's last effort to turn over. "You sure do pay attention to him for not thinking he's worth much."

"I do not. I am just observant. He's under you."

Alice bit her lip, and felt a crazy comment pop into her head. Usually she could think of nothing clever when the time desired it, but it was as though she was possessed by a coy deity, and she was not one to deny the inspiration. "Whether he's under me or on top of me is none of your concern, Val."

The line went quiet again, and Alice felt herself revel in the victory of that silence. She usually wasn't so *dirty minded* like that, and wondered what her Mom would have thought had she heard her just then. Her frown was fading, and her lips were stretching into a smile. *I think I kind of like being crass.*

"Well that was uncalled for."

"As is your attitude, chicky." Alice removed her sock and put them in her wicker laundry basket. "Think I'm getting off here."

Valerie laughed. "Okay, you go ahead and *get off*, I think I'll give you a few days to get this boy out of your system. He's already changing you; you never would have talked to me like this before *him.*"

"Fine. Take some time off, I'll be here when you get off the rag." Alice said on impulse, clicking the *off* button with haste.

She pondered Valerie as she went into her bathroom, ready to get a good shower. As she was climbing beneath the hot water, a little voice in her head that told her Valerie paid a bit too much attention to her boyfriend, and she wondered if that was purely as innocent as she claimed.

***

Quincy was working late that night, a quiet night but an okay one all the same. There weren't many customers, but he did feel a surge of interest as two girls came walking in. He stared at them and realized after a few moments just who they were. It was Alice's two best friends, or at least the girls he always saw with Alice. He swore his ears were deceiving him, but as they came closer he heard the dirty words rolling off at least one of their tongues. His hands were shaking at a 0.7 on the Richter scale as their words became clearer.

"How *dare* she not call *either* of us after her date with that slime ball? Doesn't that just piss you off Jenny?"

The other girl, Jenny he noted, swayed and shook her head. "Not really. Seems to me Alice was just real busy."

"Well you can bet she was *busy*. Told me she was *getting off* as we hung up on the phone. Can you believe that vulgarity from her? I mean...really, that guy is just rubbing off on her in all the wrong ways."

Quincy had been chewing bubble gum before that sentence. It soon took a trip down his esophagus and was steadily heading towards his stomach. He pretended to clean the glass countertop. He kept wiping in the general direction in which they were walking, and he nearly upset his packed lunch of grilled cheese sandwiches, an apple and a pack of chocolate donuts. He repositioned himself and his lunch until he was able to hear the angry girl still badmouthing Alice.

Being close to them well...the angry girl was almost too much to tolerate. He watched them walk off towards their theater. He noticed their fancy clothes, their designer jeans and label purses. He cocked his head and thought of a fiendishly clever plan for defending Alice's honor, though it seemed highly juvenile.

"I'll be back in a few minutes Marissa. Got to check something." He reached in his lunchbox and carefully concealed the pack of donuts in his pocket.

Into the blackness of the theater he walked, imagining himself to be a vampire who was forced to walk in darkness; lest the light reveal his true nature. He listened carefully, trying to gauge the whereabouts of his prey.

He heard Jenny address the angry girl as *Val.* Quincy smirked. He was a firm believer that names have power, to know a things name is to conquer it.

The preshow glow of the advertisements had not yet faded before he was crouched behind Val's seat. With a skill born of necessity, Quincy reverse pick-pocketed Val's purse and snuck the pack of donuts within.

He got up slowly, not trusting his bones to be silent and not pop. Away from their aisle he skulked, not breathing until he was at the opposite end. He took a moment to make sure that he hadn't been noticed by them, but they were engaged in conversation. His lip twitched.

He took his slender silver flashlight from his pocket and he walked with purpose into their aisle. He heard them clearly carrying on with their conversation.

When he was within spitting distance he turned on his flashlight. "Excuse me," Quincy began in a whispered tone. "You shouldn't be talking during the show, it's kind of rude." He nodded his head dramatically, as if he was encouraging a toddler to do the right thing.

"Sorry, we'll be quiet." Jenny said, bringing her fingers across her lips and making a zipping motion.

He nodded gratefully, and made a show of looking down at the floor, after a moment he made a confused expression. "Miss, I'm sorry to ask. Are you aware outside food is not permitted in the theatre?"

Jenny looked up at him and held her purse out to him. "There's nothing in here, just my phone and wallet, well my makeup too, but no food."

Quincy shook his head. "I wasn't speaking to you, but to your friend."

Valerie looked at him like he was bubblegum on the bottom of her shoe. "I didn't bring any food."

"I'm afraid I will have to check your purse, just to ensure that fact. Can you empty it out for me?" He shone his flashlight on it, just so that she could have no doubt of where it was. Valerie stared at him, challenging him silently. "What if I say no?"

"Then according to the rules of the theatre, I have every right to escort you off the premises. Why don't you just make with the opening of that thing so the rest of these people can enjoy their movie?"

Valerie sneered and Quincy wondered briefly how any boy could ever find a girl with a face like that to be beautiful. She reached down and opened her purse, and her eyes lit up as a pack of chocolate donuts fall out.

He picked them up and made a show of looking at them. He looked at her and shook his head.

"Those aren't mine." She said staring him right in the eyes.

"Is that your purse?" Quincy asked.

"Yes."

"Donuts fell from your purse. And I really am usually a nice guy, but to be lied to like that...I'm afraid you're going to have to come with me."

"I don't think so. I don't eat that *crap*. I care what goes into my body." Valerie said loudly.

Jenny looked confused, as she looked from the donuts to Valerie. Quincy wasn't paying a whole lot of attention to her, for in his mind, she was the more loyal of the two.

"Moot point. They were in your purse, in the theatre. Ergo, you come with me and I give you a lovely escort to our parking lot. Get up." He was through discussing the issue, and he felt his victory falling into completion.

"No." She replied.

He tilted his head and smiled. He enjoyed the customer who had the nerve to engage him in open debate. Because then he could employ choice words against them, he could fully show just how ignorant they truly were. He might have felt a little bitter aftertaste as this girl didn't bring in the food, but she had committed a crime of disloyalty to her friend.

"Want an armed escort off the premises? I can arrange that too. The boys in blue like girls like you, a little firecracker in their seemingly boring day of delinquents and hooligans. They'll give you some real fancy bracelets maybe if you talk to them like you're talking to me." He lied.

"I don't give a—" Valerie started before she had a hand clamped over her mouth.

Jenny had turned in her chair and silenced her friend. "Valerie, let's just go. I don't want you to get in trouble." She looked into her friend's angry eyes and shook her head. "Please?"

Valerie looked at Quincy and he saw her resolve break for the moment. He knew that she would remember him henceforth, and he invited the opportunity to further make her life hell if she continued to insult the girl he was crushing on despite everything.

"We'll go. You don't need to walk with us." Valerie said, getting up and picking up her purse. She looked at him, as though about to say something. She instead snatched the donuts from his hands.

The two walked off, and every other patron in the theatre looked at Quincy with a bit of respect mingled with fear. They all held their purses close to their chests; one man tried hiding his can of soda. Quincy nodded directly at him before leaving, not making any attempt to seize his illegal drink.

By the end of the night, Quincy was whistling.

***

A few days passed without Alice and Valerie talking, yet best friends have a way of getting back in company with each other. Valerie invited Alice and Jenny over on Saturday night for one of their traditional sleepovers, which usually meant a good time. Tonight was going to be no different, Alice was determined.

She arrived at Valerie's at a quarter past nine with her backpack full of fresh clothes and a few mutually favorite movies. The night stretched on and with each burst of laughter, it became easier to talk again.

"So you were really thrown out of the movie theatre?" Alice asked as she grabbed another handful of popcorn.

Valerie nodded, looking at the popcorn hungrily. Alice pushed the bowl towards her and Valerie took a handful. "He looked familiar, course, maybe it was just because he was a freak. All freaks generally look alike. Long hair, bad breath, tweaky little eyes."

Alice grinned. "You should be a profiler for the cops when we get out of school Val, I can almost see the wanted posters now."

Jenna rolled onto her stomach and propped her head on her knuckles. "He was just doing his job Val."

"But the freaking donuts weren't even mine. I don't eat donuts."

"So what? You think he smuggled the donuts into your bag? Maybe he's got a thing about girls with fancy purses." Alice winked at Valerie and tossed a piece of popcorn into her mouth. "And you used to love donuts."

"I have no explanation." Valerie admitted and put her popcorn down. "Grr. Let's not talk about him anymore."

"I'm alright with that." Alice tugged a light blanket towards her with her feet.

"Alice, you're so classy." Jenny snickered, watching as the blanket crept towards her friend.

"I know. I'm one high class dame." Alice poked Valerie. "You look distant, chicky. What's wrong?" Alice asked. Valerie did look pretty pale, almost shaking at times even. Alice had noticed it since she'd arrived.

"I'm fine. I'm just on some new medicine that's making me a bit queasy." Valerie said while she turned up the volume on the TV.

Jenna tossed her a piece of popcorn.

Alice wondered if Jenna was thinking along the same lines as she was currently. "For your focusing issues? Your ADD?" Jenna inquired.

"Yeah. That."

"But it's summer silly, why are you still on it? Shouldn't you only take it during the school year?" Alice asked, probing.

"Gotta maintain continuity, don't want to be off it and then go whamo once fall arrives." Valerie smiled.

"I guess that makes sense." Jenna nodded, staring up into the TV.

Alice wasn't sure what to believe about Valerie anymore. It had been a long time since Valerie had had her *problem*. Alice wanted to believe that she was really okay, and deep inside she knew that's why she didn't pursue the topic any further.

The night wound on, until they all ended up doing each other's hair. They did tight little mini braids that night, the kind you could easily sleep in.

Alice rolled onto her stomach, smiling. She loved these girls, and was glad they were in her life. She whispered to Valerie after Jenna had fallen into slumber. "Val, you don't really mind that I'm dating William do you? I hate to bring it up."

Valerie took some time in answering. "I honestly don't think he's right for you. He seems to me like a guy you get a little from, but then you leave him wanting more. If you do it right, you'll make that boy think about you and long for you his whole life. But if you're happy, then sure. Do your thing."

Alice fell asleep shortly after; at least, she was asleep for a little while.

Alice awoke to the invading glow of the red lit alarm clock that was on Valerie's bedside table. There was a low light coming from under Valerie's bathroom door, and water was running.

It was just after two AM, and Alice looked to her left to see if Jenna was still in her sleeping bag. She was. Alice's mind was a bit slow. *What's going on?* Alice sat up and looked in Valerie's bed; the covers were strewn across it in a jumbled heap. Alice stood up and tried to be as quiet as possible. Up until she heard a crinkling sound, she had been successful.

Next to the garbage can were several wrappers strewn about, Alice knelt down and picked up the remnants of several high carb snack bars and the infamous donut pack wrapper. *No. No those aren't all from tonight; they've just not been cleaned up.* Alice walked over to the bathroom door and listened closely.

It was silent, save for the water. Alice began to feel cramps in her legs the longer she knelt beside the door. She was just about to get up and return to her sleeping bag when she heard a sound more painful than anything a boy had ever done to her.

Alice shook her head and felt her eyes water up, she clasped her hand over her mouth and snuck back into her sleeping bag. She wasn't prepared for this; she had thought Val was better.

She should have known, she told herself. *She's not taking ADD medicine. She's using that* crap *again. See the signs Alice, be the friend. She refused your damn popcorn, candy wrappers, mood swings and anger. Just like last time.*

Alice heard the bathroom door crack and the light get switched off. Alice feigned sleep as best she could. She heard Valerie get back into her bed, she imagined Valerie taking comfort in the night, believing that nobody could see her deeds.

Alice smelled her sickness however; she smelled it in the bitter air, as pungent as the smell of a slow death; which was surely what was going to happen to her friend unless she acted.

Last time she and Jenna had been able to nearly kill her obsession. This time, they couldn't tackle it alone.

Alice wrung her hands together whenever she was not massaging her temples. She hated making adult decisions. She frowned and rolled over, burying her hands under the cool side of her pillow, willing morning to hurry up and arrive.

***

William sniffed his father's coffee which was brewing and hissing loudly in the kitchen. "Sneaky snake, hissing and sputtering as you stutter along." William said, peeking at the brownish liquid that was emerging from the spout.

"Sure, you smell good, but are you gonna stunt my growth?" William grabbed a ceramic mug with bright purple orchids on it. The coffee pot continued to give him the cold shoulder as best as any electronic device could. "It's okay, I know you can be shy, we'll take this slow. This will be my first time."

He brought the coffee pot out and poured himself a full cup of coffee. Its tiny wisps of steam slithered up his nostrils, tempting him to down it without a breath.

"You smell really good today; your perfume is intoxicating." He held the mug close to his cheek and felt it warm him. "Would you like some sugar from Daddy perhaps? That is to say, my Daddy has sugar I can give to you. He won't have to know, it can be our secret, okay?"

He sat his cup of coffee down and forestalled it with a finger as he reached into the pantry. He brought out the sugar cubes and dropped four or five into it, watching with mirth while they slowly spun around as he stirred his beverage.

He could feel the tension building, and he finally gave into his desire. He brought the cup to his lips and tilted back the mug.

"Oh wow." He said. Not so much sitting down, but more like collapsing into the chair as if just being told he's expecting triplets.

He felt his head spin as his throat burned savagely, yet he welcomed the pain. He thought he had just started a very serious relationship that would last a lifetime. "I'm William by the way, you can call me Will." He kissed the cup and froze in place as he heard a knocking on his back door. Fearing that he had been discovered lip locked with his coffee he hastily put his mug on top of the counter and went to the backdoor.

He peeked through the blinds and saw that it was Alice. "Eek!" He looked at his coffee. "Play it cool, I got this."

He opened the back door and Alice immediately wrapped her arms around him. He felt okay because he hadn't been discovered drinking coffee on his own, but he felt certain heaviness in Alice's embrace as though not all was well.

He smelled her hair as she was pressed so closely against him, and he looked down at her. "Alice, you okay?"

She looked up into his eyes, her eyes were wet and she reminded him of one of those sad puppy dog sympathy cards he got when his grandmother had died. "Oh gosh, you're not okay. Here, sit down."

She let him lead her to a barstool in his kitchen and he jumped up onto the table to hold her hands.

"Will …." She looked away, and then looked back.

"You seem conflicted. You can look at me if you want, or I've got some paper bags in the drawer if that'd make it easier." He suggested.

She sniffled a little and patted him on the leg. "Will, I don't know what to do. I need to talk to you."

"Well, okay I can help. What's wrong?"

He listened as she told him about Valerie's past, about the struggle to help her get back to a normal weight. He frowned as she told him about the sounds she'd heard last night, the smells she detected, and the empty bottle of laxatives at the bottom of Valerie's bathroom waste-bin.

"Gosh." *I don't know what to say.* He ran his hand down her long soothingly. "I'm sorry to hear all of that."

"I want to help her again, but I don't at the same time."

"Well, that's kinda difficult to do one way or the other."

"Will, do you think it'd be wrong of me to go straight to her parents?" Alice's cheeks were wet and red now.

William wiped away her tears with the cuff of his shirtsleeve and shook his head. "I think if she was as bad as you said then you should do whatever is necessary to save her life. Though, this is really heavy stuff."

She grinned for a second. "Yeah, it is heavy. Like a Mack truck."

"You'd have to be really brave to do something like that, Alice." He fumbled over what to say next, he wanted to make sure it sounded genuine. "You're brave though, I know you can do this."

"I wrote the letter already, explaining everything. That was hard, and I just really know that actually *giving* them the letter, the physical act of it will be the hardest … you know she's gonna find out who did it."

He shrugged. "So what if she does? Won't change the fact that you care for her and want to make sure she lives past thirty." William took a few deep breaths. He could hardly imagine going through this on his own had it been his friend.

"I'm going to go deliver it, I know I have to. But that's not all that's up." She said slowly.

"Okay, well I can hear more. I'm a good listener I think. I learned a lot of song lyrics by listening."

"Promise me something William." Alice kept almost meeting his eyes, but then bashfully looked down; he loved her eyes, and so he was happy for the chance to look into them, even if it were for seconds.

"Of course."

"Don't hate me." Her lower lip trembled.

"Hate can only be vanquished by love. I'm all about the love."

"Do you think we're okay for each other?" She spilled out her words in a rush of emotion.

William felt a chill pass through him, and he kinda wished he had his coffee to warm him up. He nodded and smiled, though a little uneasily. "Of course. I dig you. You're a fine gal."

"I don't know if I am, William. I mean, compared to you."

Williams's eyes grew wide. "You sayin' I'm a fine gal? Cuz that's cool and all … but eh … no." He nodded again.

She smiled again; he felt happy over that.

"I mean …William, What I mean is you're very honest. You're very unique."

"I appreciate individuality." He grinned, but couldn't help but feel that there was a blackness creeping into his house uninvited. "This is you ditching me, isn't it Alice?" He frowned with certainty.

She hesitated. "I don't think I like the words you used just there, but they'll be suitable. I'm not so much *ditching* you as I am saving you from me."

"What do you mean?" He asked.

"I'm not the kind of girl who can have a guy like you William, does that make sense?"

He partially closed one eye and scratched his head.

"I'm saying, Will, that I'm afraid I'm going to end up hurting you. You're a sweetheart, and I'm just … a blackheart."

"You're in Joan Jett's band?" He nodded.

She shook her head. "You know I love them, so it was kinda lame to use that phrase. I guess I'm trying to say, that as awesome as it's been getting to know you, I don't want to hurt you, and I would. It's soon to say this, and exceptionally awkward considering the nature of this conversation. But I want to say that I grow attached to some people very quickly. I love who you are William. I love you."

"Groovy!" His face burst into a smile. "I mean it's a bummer that you and I aren't gonna be together anymore, but I feel the love. It's stronger than all the bad vibes rolling through life right now."

"You understand why I'm doing it right? I'm underhanded in going behind my best friends back. Val and I have known each other since we've been in diapers. If I can do that to her, what could I do to you that'd be underhanded? I can't trust myself with your heart. It's too fragile."

He took her hand in his, maybe for the last time, and kissed it while peering into her eyes. "I pledge eternal friendship, Alice. So long as you want me as your friend, I am going to be here for you. I'm not stoked about it, but I just want you to be happy. If we never get together again, it's fine."

"I've said it before, and I'll likely say it again. You're not like other guys William."

"I know. I'm a gem."

"Something like that." She kissed his cheek as she got up, and promised to call him later.

"Be strong, Alice." He said, waving until she was out of his line of sight. He felt a little sad over things, but wouldn't be caught down. *Friendship beats everything, and I'm still her friend. Life is good.*

He looked back at his cup of coffee and considered rekindling the romance he had started to engage in this morning. It seemed like a good remedy.

***

When Alice got home from dropping off the letter at Valerie's house, she immediately went to bed. She dreamed about putting the letter in their mailbox, she dreamed of what Val's parents would do when they read it. Her dreams shifted into thoughts of William, and even of that friend of his.

The night had nearly settled in when Alice was awoken by a soft knocking on her bedroom door. She rolled over and rubbed the sleep from her eyes. She opened her mouth in surprise. *Ugh.* She stared down at her shoes, both of which were still on her feet. "I never sleep in my shoes, dear God what a day." She shook her head, as she remembered what had all gone on in the last few hours. Yesterday everything seemed so perfect, yet she had been the catalyst of change.

"Come in." She answered as the knocking started up again.

Alice felt her heart start to race as Jenna came into the room; her eyes were puffy and red. *Never a good sign,* she thought.

Jenna looked at Alice, and fell onto Alice's bed like a sack of rocks. She spoke into the mattress and her voice was muffled. Alice heard a string of profanities and a renewed surge of crying.

Alice put her hand on Jenna's shoulders. "Do you think we hid it from ourselves?"

Jenna nodded her head, and looked up at Alice. "We knew. Both of us did."

"Then why did we wait Jenny?"

"Did you want to admit that we had failed her? We were her best friends, we were supposed to see this coming and stop it before it began. But we screwed up."

Alice patted her back and sunk back into her pillows. "Where is she?"

Jenna curled up on her side and didn't look at Alice. "I was there when her parents found the letter. I was having lunch …Valerie was …" Jenna shook a little and forced herself to speak. "Valerie was in the bathroom of course." She added angrily.

"Gosh." Alice said. *I did this.*

"I wish you would have come to me Alice. You and I, we were never as close as you and Val, but I thought we were close enough to figure this out on our own."

"I did what I had to Jen, I should have included you, but I didn't trust myself to wait. If I didn't go fast, I would have kept ignoring Val's problem until she was finished. It's so much easier to ignore the problem and hope it goes away. You said it yourself, we both knew."

Jenna sat up, arms wrapped tightly around herself. "Valerie's been admitted to a place upstate. Her parents took her earlier. Do you want to know what she screamed out as they were forcing her into the car?" Jenna asked.

Alice cringed, visualizing her best friend in such a sad state. *I have to remember that what I did likely saved her. I can't give hold to her rage.*

Jenna gave up on waiting. "She screamed that she hated you. Her parents read your letter; they confronted her on the laxatives and all the food avoidance." Tears began to fall from her nose. "She screamed she hated me too …."

"I don't care." Alice stood up. "And neither should you."

"I don't." Jenna said. "I know that it's going to help her in the long run, maybe this time she'll get better." Jenna scooted closer to Alice.

Alice put her arm out for Jenna and the two embraced. "She's going to be better. Believe that Jen."

"I can't believe; I can only hope." Her eyes, usually so bright and outlined in eyeliner, were dim, like a Jack-O-Lantern whose candle had gone out.

***

Alice waited on news that never came as the weeks stretched on. She knocked on the Fallon's door, but though the lights were on, nobody was ever home.

She was amazed at how her friendship with Jenna unraveled like a loose string in a flannel shirt. The common link between them was Valerie, and with her out of the picture Alice was horribly low on friends.

William was always there for her of course; his friendship was the life preserver that kept her afloat. She was not expecting to forge a new friendship that summer, and it came from the unlikeliest of individuals.

Her mother decided to take her to the movies one night, in hopes of cheering her up. While Alice was going to the restroom during a lull in the drama, she noticed a particularly recognizable *freak* behind the counter. She approached and didn't see any twitchiness to his eyes, nor did she detect bad breath. But he did have the long hair.

He saw her approach, and she could have sworn that she saw him break out in a small sweat. "You're Quincy. The one William always talks about. I remember you."

He seemed surprised. "Yeah, remember? We were all at the dance together?" He filled his glass full of soda and watched her. "You threw your soda on me."

She felt bubbly. "I hope I don't sound ... weird or anything, but I wanna ask you a question. It's kinda personal, and I hope you're not offended by it." Alice tried to remember the details of the story she had been told by Valerie on the last blissful night they'd hung out together.

Chad McClendon • 52

"Oh gosh no! Why would your asking me a question offend me, after what we've been through." he smiled a little.

She smiled a little also. "Do you remember a girl with fiery red hair and exuberant green eyes? A little taller than I am. She came in here about a month ago with another friend of mine."

She thought that she saw him; if possible, turn paler than he already was. "Yeah. I remember the girl. She got thrown out for having food on her."

Alice walked closer so that nobody could overhear them, should anyone choose to eavesdrop. She reached out and grabbed his collar and pulled him close to her. "Did you sneak those donuts into her purse? You lie to me, and I will rip your earrings out."

His eyes grew wide and his face grew as red as a stop sign.

"Remember." She prompted. "I'll rip them all right out. A guy tried to screw with me once, and I ripped out his damn earrings just like they were pull tabs on a soda can. Don't lie to me."

She heard him swallow, she was clearly getting through. "Yes. I did."

"Let me ask, *why* did you do that?" She felt herself feeling a bit happier than she'd been in a long time.

"Okay. Well," he seemed to be thinking, and he looked up to the ceiling for a moment. "I heard her talking bad about a friend of hers, I didn't think it was very honorable and I wanted to give her some karmic justice."

"What friend?" She peered into his eyes, boring into his brain.

"Rory Matilla. I had a crush on her last year. I thought her speaking like that was a mean thing to do, so I got payback."

She scrunched up her nose and shook her head. "I'll give you one more chance, which friend? You lie to me; you'll be getting stitches in these ears of yours.

Quincy's eyes focused on hers and he pressed his lips tightly together. "The friend was you. Val was talking badly about you. I didn't …."

She released her hold on him and leaned across the counter. She kissed him on his forehead.

"Thank you."

"For getting your friend thrown out?" he scrunched up his face, and touched the spot on his head where her lips had been.

"You saved my friends life by giving her those donuts. I'm not being facetious so don't give me that look. Without those donuts, I don't think she would have … well, let me just say chocolate donuts used to be her favorite thing on Earth."

"I'm glad to have helped?" he shrugged, backing up a few feet, clearly afraid she'd grab him again.

"I'm going to be free tomorrow night, I'd like to talk to you a little more, you seem like an upstanding dude. Are you free?" She curled her lip a little and hoped he'd say yes.

"No. I'm not."

She grinned and took out a pen and paper from her purse. "Great. Here's my home phone. Call me, we can discuss why you defended my honor."

He took the slip and then looked back at her, his face incredulous. "I'll throw this away once you leave, you know that right?"

She smiled as she walked away, without Quincy she might never have realized Valerie's problem had returned. She felt hopeful as she walked back into her theatre, and leaned her head against her mother's shoulder.

She felt okay about herself for the first time in almost a month. Things might not be perfect, but she knew that she'd be able to live with herself. Maybe tomorrow she would write a letter to Valerie, it certainly couldn't hurt anything. If she was lucky, it could be the second best decision she'd ever made.

She wanted nothing more than happiness. When tomorrow evening rolled around, she was determined to start down the path that would hopefully lead towards it. It was a gamble, but she felt that she could handle a little risk.

Book Three
Glitter Wings & Fairy Kings

August 2004

Quincy Abrams held onto sleep as desperately as a drowning man holds onto air. The darkness of the room offered him no clue as to the hour, though it must still be early. He wondered what had drawn him from his dreams. He groggily swung his head away from his reddened arm which, judging from the numbness, was also hesitant to awaken.

He opened his eyes to their fullest possible extent, and was greeted by a wild haired and bespectacled boy he knew as William Denslie, just inches away from his own face.

"Hey, Quin," William said, which caused Quincy to reel backwards, and tumble out of his bed with a loud *thunk*.

Quincy stared up from the crevasse between his wall and bed, as William gazed down at him. He grabbed the legs of his bed and pulled himself up.

"What. Have. I. Told. You?" Quincy panted, from drowsiness as well as fury, "about being that close to me when I wake up?" Then he noticed Williams' stranger than usual appearance.

His chestnut brown hair was tied back, as was his new habit these days, and his brown eyes shone behind glasses that rested on the bridge of his curved nose. There was a long pink rift of a scar which faded into a scruffy brown thicket of beard.

Strapped across his shoulder was a black leather satchel, an insignia patched on the front. His tan vest didn't compliment his hairless chest. His cutlass rested as his side.

Yes, William was in rare form today, and it was still too early for Quincy to assimilate this new character into his head. "And what the hell are you wearing that for?"

Quincy stared at him. "I already told you, if you wanna role-play in the bedroom, then go see Alice."

William laughed, a bright and pleasant sound at any other time of the day - but it was still too early for Quincy.

"Aw, Quin! Don't flip out! Like I already told you, Alice and I are still just friends. And…you know I don't swing that way." He looked at Quincy who started right back at him, a quizzical expression on his face.

Quincy yawned, as he curled his toes up, causing them to pop loudly. "Then tell me, Billy the barbarian, what's with the getup this early?"

Will's jaw dropped, and his hands fell open palmed in front of him. "I'm a *pirate!"* Will declared, his cheeks flushed. "Not a barbarian…" William furrowed his brow, "…and you called me Bill…" he added as an afterthought.

"No." he said seriously. "I called you *Billy,* not Bill." Quin corrected him.

"No need to drop the B-Bomb, anyway…"

Quincy didn't break the silence for several seconds, but he did smile in appreciation of his harassment methods for Will. "Ok, then, William Wave Slasher, what's the deal?"

"Quincy, it's the day before Ren Fair! I totally told you this eight days ago!" Will looked flabbergasted, as he continued to nerd out loud.

"Yeah, I know. You told me last night, too. You said you were going as a fairy, not a pirate." Quincy said.

Will grinned sheepishly. "Well, I had the wings all glittered up, face paint galore, all the stuff a proper fairy would need, and I was ready to go. But I think Alice made off with my stuff, I couldn't find it last night, so I got this outfit instead."

"Why would Alice steal your stuff?" Quin was intrigued.

"When I showed her the fairy costume she said the only person who needed to see me in tights was her." He looked at the ceiling. "She's so repressed." Will bit his lip and walked to the window, to stare out at the street below.

"Hmm, I bet." Said Quincy, a visual of Alice danced in his mind, complete with fairy wings and glittered tights.

William sighed. "Nobody appreciates garbage men, ya know that?"

Quincy shook his head, not certain he had heard correctly, really wishing he hadn't been woken up; if garbage men were outside his house it meant it was still before six.

"I mean, M'lord." William said, as he clasped his hand around the handle of the cutlass at his side. "Were it not for the refuse carriers, the plague might rear its ugly 'ead, again- then where wouldst we be?" William nodded gravely.

Quincy snorted and tossed a pillow in Will's general direction.

"Well, Long Beard Barnacle Ass, your ship's making berth soon, so kindly shiver your timbers out of my room. I'm getting changed."

***

William thanked Quincy for dropping him off at the Corline Park Renaissance Fairgrounds, with the admonition to visit shortly. "And bring Alice; you two will have a really rad time!"

Quin stuck his head out the window of his green sedan. "Really? Rad?" Quin smirked. "Don't you mean a grand old time? Or some nonsense like that?"

William paused, the leather scabbard for his sword tapping against his knees. "Suppose I do, my liege. Let the sun set warmly on your hindquarters." William bowed deeply as Quin peeled away, covering William with a cloud of dust.

"Gotta love Quin." William smiled, as he strolled the stony pathway leading up to the black gates that separated the 20th century from the 16th. He passed between the black metal and stepped back in time.

The first stand he saw was setting up a display for an odd type of oval instrument called an ocarina, and William being a music lover himself, decided that he should peruse the merchandise. As he drew closer to the wooden booth he was pleasantly surprised to see that it was manned by a teen decked out in what looked to be gypsy garb.

He took his time walking to the ocarina stand, making sure to size up the cute entrepreneur. She had slightly chubby cheeks that made her smile more pronounced. She wasn't heavy set but neither was she as lean as Alice. Her charcoal hair occasionally fell across her face, obscuring William's view of her assorted piercings. She wore a dirty white peasant style top with the top two buttons undone. His eyes automatically were pulled to a blood red necklace that hung between her—

"Good day to you, you scoundrel." she said, stirring William from his thoughts. Her voice was as light as the winds that blew her hair.

"Lady, I would choose my words carefully." He picked up his Ren Fair accent, a brutal impersonation of a proper English merchant. "For do you not know, that I am the feared Captain Will Denslayer?" He struck a pose that was meant to be impressive, though it may have come off as more ridiculous than anything else.

Judging by her smile she either thought it was cute, or exceptionally horrid. He considered her. *She has a nice smile though.*

The gypsy girl raised her head in dawning comprehension, and she placed both of her bejeweled hands on her hips. "I say, I had no idea. Fancy that, a pirate captain coming to my shop, the day before I can start selling anything." she sighed.

He was upset; he was rather thinking that an ocarina would set off his pirate persona all the more, nothing like a shanty piped out through wood to set the mood. "Well, as I be merely looking at your wares, might I ask how much one could pay to acquire a fine instrument such as this?" he lifted up an ocarina and tossed it lightly into the air.

"For you Sir, I say it wouldn't cost more than five dollars." she tilted her head and grabbed the ocarina as it fell back towards his outstretched hand.

"Hey, I was looking at that." He fell back into his modern day accent.

"You can look tomorrow, when I open my shop officially. Right now it's just the setup." she replied, her own accent dropping.

"Well, right." he said, looking around the fairgrounds now. "You've got a prime spot for merchandising here, my fair…?" She had not yet revealed her name, and that was alright.

"My name is Lady Roslyn." she extended her hand.

Now, a suave cat would have taken the lady's hand, pressed their lips against it while staring deeply into the lady's eyes. William however, was rarely suave. So, instead of a warm kiss, he gave her a handshake. "Nice to meet you." he answered awkwardly. His face felt hot.

"You're here early, Will Denslayer." she knelt under the counter for a second and brought out an mp-3 player, which she dexterously scrolled through.
"I didn't think modern day items were allowed in the fair." he questioned her, hopping up to sit on the countertop.

"Consider it of the minstrel's line." she said, before the pleasant sounds of Material Girl emerged from the speakers.

William looked at her, never would he have taken her for a Madonna fan. "I. Love. That. Song." William said, jiving where he sat.

Roslyn gave William a strange, searching look, as he hummed along to her music. "You like Madonna?" she narrowed her eyebrows as she watched him.

"Heck yeah!" he started counting off on his fingers. "Vogue... Like a Virgin... Beautiful Stranger... I love that woman. Her influence in the world of pop has been more substantial than any other singular female artist. Though it could be argued that Sinead has—"

She forestalled him by placing her hand against his lips and he felt the cold metal of her rings against him. "Sorry. But I just can't believe that you, a guy of ... what, seventeen—" she looked to him.

"Eighteen actually..." he said, as she took her hand away.

"Ok, an eighteen-year-old guy... an eighteen-year-old *cute* guy." She paused. "I just find it hard to believe that a guy likes Madonna." her lips formed a perfect 'O' shape as she seemed to have stumbled upon a thought. "Wait. Do you keep your sword in a sheath or next to other swords?" she smiled enigmatically.

William raised his eyebrows at her. "Cute, eh? You know, my friend Quincy asked me the same thing when we first met."

"Does he buckle swashes too?" she crossed her arms across her chest.

He paused, before he caught on. "Hey! No, not at all. He doesn't. I don't. We don't buckle swashes... or cross swords." he felt himself turn red all over again. Sweat and leather made an interesting fragrance, of that he was certain. "I like to sheathe my sword. Or ...I would, I'm sure. But being that I've never sheathed my—"

She burst into laughter. "You, are too much. There is no way a straight, eighteen-year-old guy is a virgin. I'm sorry, but I'm beginning to think this is a prank, put on by the Royal Guard." She shook her head.

William was dumbstruck; he just didn't know what was so unbelievable. Didn't everyone want to save themselves for that right person? He thought that was a good defense, so he pressed on with it. "I'm saving myself for the right person." He nodded.

She smiled again. "I notice you said person, not girl." she said, not unkindly.

He breathed heavily, now and repositioned himself on the counter so that he faced her plainly. Now he could look her right in her brown eyes. "I am saving myself for the right girl. But what if I was saving myself for the right guy? I believe that love knows no gender."

"Aw, that was almost sweet. Did you steal that from a U2 song?" she lifted herself up and sat next to him on the countertop.

"Actually no, but I like them too. Does that make you think I'm weird?"

She pondered his question for a moment, before shaking her head. "No. Just a bit stranger than every other guy I've known."

They didn't speak again for several minutes, during which time they were passed by men in kilts, chanting druids and grog drinking merchants. A particularly burly man with a stomach that preceded him by about a foot carried a turkey leg that smelled heavenly.

"I say, Roslyn. My ship is currently far away from me, but I was wondering if your band of gypsies had a horse or mule."

"Now why would you wonder that?" she looked out past the fair gates.

"Well. There are some restaurants just next to the expressway, outside the grounds. If you had some transportation, we could grab some grub."

"Why Captain, is that a proposal for courtship?"

"Nah, just a pirate asking for a companion on the way to have food."

She walked from behind the countertop and nodded. "C'mon then, Captain, take me to the new world."

***

William and Roslyn walked under the gates. Their arms swung back and forth in wide arches as they ambled through the grass leading to Roslyn's vehicle. William thought it silly that he hadn't been at the fairgrounds for more than an hour, and yet here he was leaving. He caught himself occasionally brushing Roslyn's hand with his own, and he had to make a conscious effort to not make it appear obvious.

"That'll be mine, right over there." Roslyn pointed, and Will saw an ordinary green van, dirtied windows and a rusted tailpipe. Being so far away, he couldn't make out any more details, but as he drew closer it came into focus.

"Shotgun." he said as he turned his head to look at her.

She laughed and William thought how unusual it was that she laughed so often, yet he so little. "Shotgun doesn't work on my ride, Captain." Roslyn said as she walked right past the green van. When Roslyn stopped at gleaming chrome covered motorcycle William felt his pulse quicken.

"You never told me you rode a bike." William said. His eyes scanned the bike up and down, admiring its beautiful design.

"I pointed to it, it's not my fault you thought it was that heap." She smiled wryly. She reached into a leather pouch with skulls emblazoned on it, and pulled out a pink helmet.

"Cool helmet." Will said, checking out the little stickers on it. "You're a real Hell's Angel, huh?" he crossed his arms.

"Glad ya like it," she tossed it to him, and he barely caught it. "Cuz you're the one wearing it." she took a black helmet out of the other bag and put it on. She straddled the bike and looked behind her. "Ya getting on?" she asked as she pulled out a pair of sunglasses from an inner section of her top.

"I didn't think you seemed like a pink helmet kinda lady." He swallowed hard, lowered his eyes to the helmet and put it on hesitantly. *I get to hold on to her waist...is that a little fresh?* He swung his left leg over the chassis and settled himself onto the remainder of the cushion.

He put his hands on her shoulders, thinking it was more fitting, and he heard her sigh heavily. She slapped him on his knee and he released her shoulders at once.

"It's the waist or nothing, Denslayer." as she lowered her visor and brought the bike to life.

He took a breath and put both arms around her waist. *Is this too high? Should they be lower? Is that safer?* He breathed heavily. *If I fall off...does that make me the bitch?* He wondered if his helmet was supposed to feel so hot.

***

As the two sat in the off white and extremely uncomfortable benches eating their steamy burgers, they shared stories of life. "I came to fair to have a good time, because for as long as I remember, I've always loved swords and leather." William took a sloppy bite out of his cheeseburger and wondered if his eating habit made him look like a glutton. Smaller bites, he told himself. He remembered when Alice picked on him for taking big bites.

"So you handle yourself pretty well with blades then?" She dipped her french-fry in mustard.

William had seen weirder things; he was sure of it. He just couldn't recall when. He licked the roof of his mouth and then sipped his soda. "I guess I can, I've never been in a joust or anything. Though that would be pretty rad."

Roslyn folded the wrapping of her cheeseburger and nodded in agreement. "I'd like to see you be all knightly. I think it could be pretty *cool.*" she added emphasis to the last word, and William wondered if she was toying with him.

"Cool?" he rolled his eyes. "Who says *cool?*" there was a ringing bell as another couple came through the front doors of the establishment. He caught his thoughts...*a couple...he and Rosalyn weren't a couple...why did it feel like they were?*

She chewed thoughtfully. "I don't suppose anyone in the sixteenth century said cool."

He grinned. "Me neither."

"However, I don't think anyone in the 20th century still says *rad.* I was in a Big Sister program, my sis said *rad*, and she's about 28 now." her tone of voice made it seem as though she had settled the matter by superior argument.

Maybe it was a stroke of inspiration, or perhaps it was just chance, but he found an excellent response, pre-formed in his mind. "I see, so you think I am more mature than my age. I thank you, kind lady." William inclined his head and raised his paper glass in a toast to her good nature.

"You like to infer, don't you William?"

He didn't know if she was being playful or serious. If only he understood her the way, he understood Quin and Alice. Roslyn was an interesting girl, he thought, and was excited to get to know her better. "I do like to infer." he replied.

"I like you, infer what you will from that." She put all of her trash on her tray and sucked the last bit of liquid from her cup, before bending the straw so that it re-entered the cup.

William felt it necessary to respond with something coy, something that would make him seem flirtatious. "I like…" his words clung to his throat.

She waited, her expression patient, yet it eventually gave way to resignation. "Me? Is that what you were searching for? Cuz if you do, I would be very pleased to consider you my first new friend from this season."

He grinned, and nodded his head perhaps a little too vigorously. Her lips became thin, as they were pressed so tightly together. Before she stuck her tongue out at him. "Aye, I would like that." William admitted.

"Alright then." she patted him on his hand from across the table. "I think we can go back to the fair now; likely we'll have something to do tonight. Some big party, or pre-party party. This more likely than not, will be followed by a post-party party."

William had just started to feel comfortable, but at the mention of a party, he became excited. His fingers scratched at his pants, and his scabbard tapped against the tiles on the floor as his leg bounced. He made a bold confession. "I play in a band. I sing, actually." His eyes met hers, he waited for her response. *Please, let her be impressed. I really like this girl, God if you're listening …I'm really sorry about the extra sips of wine during church yesterday…let her like me and I'll never overdo the wine again.*

"Oh really?" she raised her eyebrows, and rose from her seat. "Let's hear it."

His stomach dropped out. "N..n…now?" he stuttered.

"Yes."

William shrugged it off, and looked around the restaurant. "Not the most ideal place to promote Lipstick Trace…that's the band name, by the way." He gave her a meaningful look. "But all the same, I'll do it." He clapped his hands together and stood up proudly. "Attention everyone." the twenty or so people within the restaurant turned to look at him. "I am going to entertain you with a song. If you like it, please let me know. If you don't like it, kindly refrain from saying so."

Roslyn gave him some space and let her hands fold across her lap.

William took a deep breath, placed one hand on his chest and belted out a cracked voice version of one of their latest songs. "Hey you, fairy princess. Let me take your stress, from off your wings, and gimme the chance to sing. Oh oh…"

The tomato that hit him likely came from a cheeseburger. It slapped against his cheek and William took that to mean it was a good a time as any to bolt.

Roslyn laughed raucously as they made their way back to her bike. "Will, Will, Will… my shanty singing pirate. I think it's my turn to hold your waist." She took the pink helmet and handed him the black.

William was feeling rather encouraged, despite his unwelcome welcome to Corline County. So he fumbled the mechanism that started the bike, and lost his breath as Rosalyn's arms wrapped tightly around him. He could get used to a thing like that.

***

Rosalyn pulled the bike back into the grassy field where she had previously let the bike come to rest. Rosalyn patted the hands resting on her sides and William released her. He felt a pang of sadness that the ride home had seemed much shorter than the adventure out.

Rosalyn pulled off the helmet and placed it back in the leather pouch from whence it had come. "I thought you said you had operated a bike before?" she said, her voice accusatory.

William didn't have to think long on where she had gotten such a terribly fictitious notion. "Actually, I had intended to say I had had dreams where I operated a bike. I must not have said the first part loudly enough." He shrugged, placing his pink helmet, acquired after they had sat in the restaurants parking lot for a period of five minutes, back in the leather pouch.

She nodded slowly, a facetious smile on her face as she started walking back into the fair grounds. "Mmm, I mustn't have been listening intently enough."

"That's OK; I think you're still groovy." He swayed his head to and fro; his tied back hair was causing him some level of discomfort, his face contorted painfully.

"I bet you use that line on all the girls, huh? I betcha it wins you many a sexy lady." She paused, her grin mischievous. "Or, maybe you just use it on the dudes, Mr. Swashbuckler."

William's cheeks turned a magenta color, and his eyes rolled in disbelief. "Oh come on, Rosalyn. I do think you're groovy."

"I notice no comment on the dude part of my retort. You're as good and gay as Freddy Mercury." She sighed exasperatedly. "And here I was hoping you would want to hang out some more this merry evening."

"Oh I can still hang out." He decreased the distance between them, as they walked past Rosalyn's booth and further into the grounds. "I mean, if you want to hang out I think that would be awesome."

"Even though you're as gay as Freddy Mercury?" she winked at him, and her necklace flashed in the sunlight.

"You keep talking about my apparent fascination with homosexuals. Dude, seriously. I think you have unresolved issues, something having to do with a misconception of gender roles-...something to do with Freud..." William struggled to remember his Psychology class in high school; he thought he had come off sounding well educated.

Rosalyn laughed.

"Is that laughter a clever cover up for the accuracy of my statement?"

"Come on WD-40, there's going to be a gathering of Rennies this way."

William stopped in his tracks, cutlass banging against his leg as his jaw dropped in astonishment. "Are you for real?"

"Yeah. Real as fairies. Come on, I'm playing with you." she motioned for him, her index and middle finger making little walking motions.

"I can't believe you just called me WD-40." he felt rather disgruntled. She seemed to have an odd way of showing friendship; if that's what the last few hours had been the start of. He hoped so, Rosalyn made him feel pretty rad. "What's your last name?" he asked.

Her face screwed up in an odd fashion, eyebrows raised and lips curled. "Where did that come from?" She stepped onto a wooden bridge that ran over a small lake.

"Well," his hands went into his pockets, and, feeling nothing within, he removed them, "you know my last name, hence the WD comment. I just don't know yours." He felt like he might be hovering on the creepy side, he needed to make his curiosity sound normal. "So I can…you know, make up a clever taunting name for you."

She let out a low whistle, and looked sideways to him. "It's Lyden. Rosalyn Lyden. I'd like to see you make a taunting and clever nickname for that, Sir." she said, poking him on his bicep.

He returned the poke; his heart fluttered. His hand went too far west and he touched her in a place he had never dared touch Alice.

Her hand slapped his with the haste of a charging paladin. "Virgin my ass!" she cried uproariously, a giggle just detectable in her voice.

"I…" he looked her in the eye. "I…" he looked at her chest. "I…it was an accident?" He knew he was grasping at straws, maybe she was aware of his desperation as well.

"I'll let you have that one, grace. Do it again though, and I may have to shove an ocarina up your ass."

"Oh." was all he could manage, his imagination flying hazardously. He ran his hand through his hair, applying all of his strength to a particularly irksome itch he had come to know in the last few seconds.

Rosalyn and William walked through the fairgrounds, a good majority of the establishments were still closed up; a few people were sitting outside shooting the breeze. The owners smoked cigarettes boldly, with their cans of soda resting not too far from their hands. In the morning, William thought, all of this would be gone. It would be all old world. "I can't wait for tomorrow," he said, as they passed a jewelry booth.

"You gotta appreciate the now William. Otherwise tomorrow is gonna be nothing but regrets." Rosalyn looked to her feet, William did the same. He missed the sounds of the fairy bells on his ankles, but pirates never wore bells. It would give up the secrecy aspect of the career. "That was deep. This one time, I had a teacher in high school tell me something like that. Life's like a coin, you can spend it any way you want, but you can only spend it once." William tried to sound wise.

"That's almost kind of right." she said, kicking a clump of mud out of her way; it went flying. "I heard there were these coins you could cut up and get different values from them. A nickel could make five pennies, like that."

"Wow. You have a way of over analyzing things." William shrugged. "It's ok, I admire that."

"Well, how do you want to spend your coin tonight?" she nudged him; her feet carrying her a little too close to his side.

"Hmmm, I've already sung today, so that's out. I've already eaten a little, so I'm not too hungry. We could—"

"Get a portrait drawn in renaissance style." she interrupted, pointing at the booth occupied by a balding man who was looking lonely. He had a large pitcher of grog, or rather, a large pitcher. The grog was nearly all gone.

"I could lay down a coin or two for that. But I don't know if I'd really want a picture of myself in Ren garb just yet. I want to get a few paychecks built up and really improve my look."

"You've got the look, Willie D. You're a juvenile scam if I ever saw one." She said wistfully with a glint of amusement in her eyes from beneath those black locks.

William had to stop in his tracks; he was making sure he had heard correctly. "Did you just," he looked at her, certain that he was going loopy, "quote Roxette?"

She nodded. "I like 'em. I think they're pretty rad, as you would say."

He resumed walking, by her side as wonderful possibilities found a comfortable home in his head. "I love Roxette. They are like, my favorite band …ever." He added emphasis; he had to make her know how he felt about them.

"Well, that's just fine with me. You've earned some brownie points; it's not every eighteen-year-old cute, *straight,* guy who would admit to liking them."

"Totally." he mustered.

"Oh, and Will." she added, her voice dropped to a light whisper, he had to lean in close to hear her.

"It's going to be a picture of both of us, which I will keep until such a time that I no longer desire it."

William was glad to have an honest reason to look into Rosalyn's eyes. "Oh. OK, just promise not to do anything weird with it."

She scoffed. "Like masturbate?"

William paled; she certainly had a tongue on her. Of course, he scolded himself, her tongue shouldn't be on his mind. They had just met. "No," he said awkwardly. "Well, yes!" his voice raised before he knew it.

Her eyebrows furrowed and she looked insulted.

"Well, what I meant to say is that's well within your rights... if you wanted to... I couldn't stop you..." He thought of Rosalyn in ways that he hadn't really thought of Alice. *FOCUS! DENSLIE!* He ordered himself. "What I meant was like, don't draw me with a mustache or anything after it's been completed...I don't really like mustaches." he ended weakly.

***

The two had their portrait drawn, after which, they walked the grounds of the fair. There was a castle resting at the edge of the fairgrounds lake. Its pointed towers spiked into the air like foreboding fingers. There was a jousting court tied off with yellow ribbons. All around them people were preparing for opening day tomorrow.

Rosalyn and William took the aged looking charcoal drawing back to Rosalyn's tent, a yellow worn looking thing. William stood outside waiting; he waved to a man who looked startled to see William. "It had to be my outfit, cool." William said as the man walked away, snacking on a packet of peanuts.

Rosalyn emerged from the tent and she told William about the party they were about to attend. "Will you be my escort, Denslayer?" Rosalyn asked him.

"A male escort?"

"Well, you've already been one to me all day today, I can't see a reason why you shouldn't continue on as such tonight. You've taken me to dinner, you've walked with me through the fair." her hair swayed as she shrugged.

"Oh." William's hands were hot, and he felt like dancing. "I suppose when you put it that way." He agreed. "I would love to be your escort tonight."

She smiled imperiously up at him. "Good."

The sun had begun to set as they made their way to the pre-opening night party, a trickle of people meandered toward an amphitheater. Benches sat in a circle around a fire pit, which had a small fire, over which hot dogs were being made.

"Get me a hot dog please?" Rosalyn asked him, as she walked around the crowded aisles of benches, seeking out a spot for them. "Chips, too." she called out.

"Hmm." William grabbed two plates and loaded them with hot dogs. He warmed Rosalyn's over the fire, but left his own cold. "I like 'em better this way." William said to a portly man roasting three hotdogs on one stick, as he left his own hot dogs on his plate.

He joined his new friend under a large tree where Rosalyn sat cross legged. "Right here, buddy." she patted the ground next to her.

William ate his hot dogs and was quite happy. Yet every now and then a potato chip crumb would tumble from his mouth, as he took to talking to his companion.

"Nah, hot dogs...I just don't do it. I like 'em a little chilly."

Rosalyn took a bite. "Cold wieners worry me. Eating raw and or undercooked meat can result in a heightened susceptibility to food borne illness." She said with an exaggerated wave, with a grand wave of her free hand.

William was floored. "You know, not even I have taken the time to memorize that. You're kind of a nerd." William stopped chewing at once. "I've never been able to say that to anyone before!" He seemed to have stumbled on an idea. "Cold wieners worry you? Doesn't that sound provocative?"

She smirked. "You'll have quite a story to tell once you go home on Monday, then, won't you? You were able to tell Quincy you called me a nerd." She flicked a piece of heated hot dog his way, it landed in his beard. "And yes, cold wieners worry me. But you'll just take it any old way won't you?"

He dropped his hot dog onto his plate and picked out the projectile. "I resent that statement. And why do you think I'll just tell Quin? I've got other friends. I've got a band; we've got fourteen fans."

She raised her eyebrows and made a fluttering motion above her heart. "Because *Quin* is the only friend you've told me about. But I wouldn't mind hearing about this band a little more. And fourteen fans? Be still, my poor heart."

"Yeah," William said importantly. "It's awesome. We've actually got a show this coming Thursday back home. Some real nice place Quin says'll get us a lot more exposure."

"There ya go with the Quin talk again."

"I am unaffected by your interruption." William said, not stopping even when she mocked being insulted, her eyes watering and her lip trembling. "I sing, we're called Lipstick Trace, and it's just awesome. Alice, she's my ex, she plays guitar and sometimes keys. She's gotten pretty good in the last few months. I sing, you heard that earlier, though I'm better at a show. And Quincy, he plays the drums."

"An *ex,* huh? And here I was thinking you were a total newbie to the dating scene. I'm proud of you, Denslie. And what was the name of your band again? I missed it the first three times you mentioned it."

"Yeah. Anyway," he disregarded the Alice comment for the moment, he was talking to a girl like he never had. "We're playing a show this coming Thursday, and...and... where do you live?"

She slapped his hand. "Stalker much? We met today and already you want to know my addy."

"Do not!" he held up a finger, then reconsidered. "*Do.* But it's only because I want you to come to my show. It'll be awesome. You could be our *fifteenth* fan."

"What, do you keep a registry of your fans?"

"No. I'm nowhere near that anal." There he was with the Freudian references again; *I hope I sound intelligent.*

She blushed. "Whatever you say."

"So, will you come to the show?" He sat his dinner aside, excitement overtaking him.

"I'll make the descent into your territory. Sure. Question, though."

"Ok."

"Why are you called Lipstick Trace?"

He stared right back into the eyes that peered into his. He was hoping this question might just come up later, but with his luck, it hadn't. Now was a good a time as any to let her get to know him just a little better. "I was at a dance, in high school. It was my first real dance, and the first time I really got dolled up. I got kissed there, anyway, and um…" he looked over his shoulders for eavesdroppers, finding none, he continued. "I got kissed, and Alice was wearing Sassy Vixen Violet Lipstick."

Her face fell, looking as though she had expected more. "So you named your band after a *freaking* kiss with your ex? That's lame dude."

"It wasn't for the *kiss!*" his voice rose. "I named my band Lipstick Trace because I like the feel of lipstick on my lips!"

There was a cacophony of laughter all around William, as his co-workers came to realize they had quite a character on their hands. William felt himself growing hot, he was sure his cheeks were flushed. "Well…that didn't …" his eyes traveled to Rosalyn, who was silently heaving with silent laughter. *Way to mess it up William. Maybe Quincy can come get me now, he shouldn't be working.*

William started to get up, ready to leave, when Rosalyn stopped him. Both her hands reaching outwards for his and clasping hold on them, those pointed fingernails almost digging into his skin.

"William," she said serenely, eyes scanning him. "I entreat you, stay."

"Can't."

"Oh but you can," she stroked his hands with hers. "I too like the feel of lipstick against my lips."

"Sure. That's a pretty normal thing for you, but now everyone knows it about me. It was only supposed to be you."

"Nothing about me is normal, William. But all the same, please, stay with me. I won't hold it against you. Plus, I think Sassy Vixen Violet would look great on you."

He did like the feel of her hands on his own, so he sat back down. The people around him had gone back to their meals. "You wanna head out of here? I'm not really digging this scene, right now. You understand...?" He felt her hands slipping out of his and he wondered if he should hold onto them.

"Let's go for a walk." Roslyn reached for his hand.

***

The approaching nightfall meant that the newer people to the renaissance fair were heading to bed, whilst the veterans were just getting started with their festivities. As Rosalyn and William walked the grounds, minstrels played and drunkards fulfilled their destinies. There was a pig roast, William could tell from the smell wafting throughout the air.

They had reached the castle, with its darkened windows and drawbridge canvassing the chasm beneath. Rosalyn's eyes had a mischievous radiance as they were illuminated by the waxing moon. "Ya ever been inside? It's great, there are all these old torture chambers and weapons."

"Not me, but I wouldn't mind going." William said, half paying attention to the conversation, half still wondering if he should have held onto Rosalyn's hands at dinner. His hesitation had consumed him as they walked, her hands dancing alone at her hips. But as they stepped onto the bridge, he made a decision, and his hands found hers, and she did not break away.

The castle was barely lit, the flickering lamps casting odd shadows on the dirt richened walls as they breached its chambers. William found himself feeling rather proud of himself, not only was he holding Rosalyn's hand, he also sounded very well educated on the iron maiden display. "People nowadays probably use it to drain tomatoes, though." William smiled.

She screwed up her face, almost laughing. "No." she spoke in a matter of fact fashion. "People use it these days for sado-masochistic pleasure."

William blanched. "Is that what he wanted one for?" William whispered, more to himself than to Rosalyn. "Wow."

They reached a chamber decked out with long reaching curtains, embroidered with ancient looking crests. There was a certain something in the room that seemed to drain William, and it wasn't long before he saw the tower of wood known as the guillotine.

"Ooh," Rosalyn applied pressure to William's hand, and she stepped over the red rope barricade, pulling him forward.

"Hey," William sounded deflated. He wanted to maintain a respectful distance from the shiny blade. "Maybe we should stay back a little. That thing looks sharper than my duds in my junior pic."

"Oh no, we're going closer." Rosalyn went so far as to sit down on the platform of the device, as if it were a glorified bench. William felt his grip on her hand slackening as she motioned him forward to join her.

"Come on over, William, keep me company." her head inclined his way, her shoulders followed.

"No thanks."

She shrugged, and he let her hand go, a sense of horror welling up within him as he watched her lay down, neck resting in the grooves where the blade could very likely fall. "Ok, seriously, get out of there. You're making me really nervous."

"Come lay down with me, there's room for two." she motioned him over, with the hands he had so recently held.

William was petrified, unable to move, not even to run for help. His throat felt as though it were stuffed with cotton. "Look, Rosalyn," his voice cracked, she giggled. "I'm sure that guillotine is really the cat's pajamas but please, get out from there!" he stamped his foot, and watched in horror as the vibrations caused the rope holding the blade to fall.

The blade fell with the speed of a sack of bricks, and William was motionless unable to react as the blade raced toward her neck…and stopped before hitting it. William dropped to his knees, dumbfounded. Rosalyn's wonderful sounding voice rang through the air, like music to Williams' ears.

"It's a rigged gag, you ass." she got up, red in the face from laughter. "We always trick the newbies!"

"Well thank God!" William felt his throat returning to normal. He got to his feet and took Rosalyn's hands, taking her away from the guillotine.

"Aren't you sweet?"

"No. Just terribly unnerved." William directed her into the next room; nothing could be far enough away from that beastly device.

William saw the light dissipating as they progressed further into the next room. "What's this room, I wonder."

"It's supposed to be the exit. The doors are over there."

He felt her gesture in the darkness, and it was then that he decided to do it. He moved in the darkness without need of light, and he pressed his trembling lips to hers. At first he felt tension in those supple areas, but it was overtaken by a restrained ferocity he had not yet known. The exit might have been five feet from William Denslie, but he was miles from it.

The kiss ended as every kiss must, but it left William feeling very happy.

"That wasn't expected so early." She spoke into the blackness, her hands in his.

"I wasn't expecting it either, if it makes you feel better. But I don't regret being impulsive, not this time." He wondered if she was smiling as much as he.

"I'm going to walk back to my tent now; you should probably get to yours, too. They've got them setup near the amphitheater, towards the forest if you didn't bring one."

She permitted him to walk her back to her tent, and even treated him to another kiss before sending him off to bed. His head was full of fanciful ideas, and he decided, as he lay in his cot, that he was very glad he stayed tonight.

***

Quincy refilled a thirty-ounce cup for the stupid looking customer who made meaningless comments about the weather.

"Enjoy your film." Quincy's lack of enthusiasm seemed to unsettle the customers smile, it faltered.

Once two o' clock came, Quincy hung his uniform shirt in his locker and left Mega Cinema behind him. The sun was shining brightly outside and on his light blue four door station wagon with real oak exterior.

"Come on Ning, work with me," Quincy turned his key again and willed his car to life. It grumbled as it stirred from its sleep, Quincy roared appreciatively.

"Thank you!" he exclaimed. He turned up his radio dial and switched to Slayer. He was in a good mood, and even more so because he got the pleasure of picking up Alice Mendell today. He sang along to the soundtrack and pulled up to her driveway.

Alice's mother answered the door when he knocked. "Quin! So good to see you again." her mother said, welcoming him in.

"Hi, Brenda." he said casually, as usual.

"Alice is upstairs, and I'd keep you company, but I've got my sister on the phone."

Quincy took the stairs up to Alice's room two at a time. At the end of the hallway he knocked on Alice's door, which was covered in posters of Joan Jett. Quincy heard Alice from the bathroom.

"Quin? That you?" Alice called out.

"No. It's his good looking twin brother." he said sarcastically.

"Oh, good. I'll be in the bedroom in a few minutes."

Quincy sighed, and wished that her statement had one bit of sincerity. He went into her room and sat at her desk, its usual tidiness bothered him. He rearranged her stuffed animals, knowing that it would pester her just a little bit.

He looked around, bored, the minutes were inching by. He got up and walked around, then decided to collapse on her bed. It smelled of flowers, and Quincy smiled. "It smells great, every time." He felt a stirring of desperation as his heart beat heavily in his chest. He looked up at her ceiling, and saw various pictures of her, himself and Will. Their first practice, their first show, and various senior pictures covered her ceiling. He also saw a few pictures of

Alice's old girl friends, though there were far fewer of those.

Quincy sat bolt upright as the bedroom door opened and Alice walked in.

"Hey Quin."

"Wow." Quincy marveled. Her face was dusted with glitter and her green eyes sparkled. She had silver shimmering wings on her back, and pink tights made Quincy pay close attention to her beautifully shaped legs. "You went all out."

"Kinda." she said, sitting at her desk.

"I suppose that was Williams famed fairy outfit?" His eyes roved over her body hungrily.

"Well, the tights were always mine." She chuckled. "Imagine walking into your room and seeing your ex-boyfriend rummaging in your underwear drawer."

I hate you, William. He cursed, wishing that he could be so voyeuristically bold. "I can't imagine having an ex-boyfriend. It's gotta be that whole straight issue I've been dealt."

"I'll believe the whole *straight-issue* when I actually see you with a girlfriend, buster." she jabbed at him, and he smiled uneasily.

"You could be my girlfriend, you know. Help squash an urban legend." He titled his head to move his hair from his line of vision. It wasn't a serious question, but it was good practice for when he finally would ask her.

"I might consider your proposal if I knew you were serious." she said.

"Oh, yeah?" he joked right back with her.

"Put on this outfit, glitter & all and I'll date you."

"Chyeah. Right. Whatever you say." Quincy laughed, but eyed her outfit, wishing it were so easy.

They went downstairs and left the house. Quincy got into his car and let Alice in. They started down the interstate towards Corline County. The soundtrack switched to Quincy's favorite song, and he sang along with Tom Araya.

Alice looked at him. "Why are we listening to this...this...*song?*" She sounded unsure of herself, her mouth was agape.

"I'm in a good mood." he responded simply.

"You're in a good mood...equals Reign In Blood? Slayer is not what I would call good mood music."

"You're entitled to be wrong." he left it at that.

Quincy sang loudly as they drove on.

"I'm kind of glad William's our singer, Quin. Your singing voice sucks." Alice laughed.

"Your Mom sucks." he lied, he secretly felt that Brenda was the coolest Mom he knew, far cooler than his own.

"Sucks my Dad." she smirked.

"Gah." he feigned vomiting. "Have you no shame?"

"Gimme a break."

"Hmph. And Will called you repressed," Quincy slipped, not sure if he was supposed to say that last part or not.

"Oh, really?" she was interested, he could tell from her red cheeks.

He grimaced. "Yeah. He said you'd never let him tie you up."

Alice muttered, and he wished his music hadn't been so loud, as he might have heard something deeply interesting. "What did you just say?" "Nothing for your ears, Mr. my-cars-about-to-fall-apart."

Quincy ignored it, he didn't care if his doors were rattling. "Now leave my car outta this, if it weren't for Moore we'd be nowhere. So what if he can't go sixty."

She sighed. "Was that really the best you could do? Aren't you supposed to be the clever one? Moore, Ning, Wood?"

He slapped the steering wheel. "What would you suggest, Woody Allen?"

"No, that's not even near clever."

"We've been through this," he said exasperatedly. "I'll push you through the looking glass, Alice." he snickered.

"That was funny the first time *William* said it." she reminded him.

"I still think it's funny."

"Yeah, and you also think that Iron Maiden is popular. So that's pretty funny in my opinion."

He rolled his eyes. "Little miss I loved the Backstreet Boys."

"I'm not going to let you get to me, Quincy Abel Abrams. Mr. Q & A, my endearing little medicine woman."

"That was below the belt, dude. I am not even kidding."

"But I was kidding. You know you love me, Quinnie the Pooh."

Quincy pulled over into the emergency lane, his cheeks burning. He stared at her, shaking. "Never. Again. Please. God." he touched her cheek, red from laughter. "Promise me, I don't think I could endure that again."

"Do I win?" she smiled.

"Yes. You unbearable woman."

He merged back onto the highway, as Alice smiled triumphantly.

***

William kept his eyes focused on the main gates to the fair, ever vigilant for Quincy and Alice. A child came up to him, and held out two dollar bills, his wide smile expectant. "How fares your day, lad?" William said as he opened his side bag, which was full of sugar coated almonds and peanuts.

"Are you a pirate?" the child's voice was high pitched, and his eyebrows were arched.

"Aye, son. I am the fierce William Denslayer, scourge of the seas." William contorted his face to a predetorial scowl. "Arrrr." He said fiercely.

"Why are you selling nuts?" The child said unaffected, taking his new packet of nuts.

William's heart leapt, he saw Quincy and Alice coming through the entrance. Alice was wearing *his* outfit, William was shocked. "I sell nuts in my spare time, the high seas aren't so high anymore." He waved to his two friends, who waved in recognition.

"My older brother says you guys are like my Uncle Henry, but just a little better." The child said, ripping the corner off the pack of almonds and popping one into his mouth.

"Oh?" William was losing interest as his friends approached. "Why would your brother say that?"

"Yeah, he says you guys at least get paid to dress funny. Thanks." He said, walking off, leaving William feeling a little offended.

"Oh, well!" he exclaimed. William ran over to Quincy and Alice, his sword bounced against his leg. "Hail, my lord and lady!"

Quincy had his hands buried in his pockets, his hair messily styled across his forehead. He gave William a cursory look, and smiled halfheartedly. "Nice nuts ya' got there, Will."

"I agree Will, I don't think I've ever seen finer nuts on you."

William smiled sheepishly, trying to figure out what to say in character to his two teasing friends. "Your garb is strange, my lord, have you had the displeasure of having your caravan sacked by vagabonds? Is that all you have to wear? I hear our pelts have been recently cured, should you need something more fitting to your form. Aye.

"And you, Lady, I do believe I've seen yonder wings before, they suit you well." William finished.

"Sure. Insult my *garb*," Quincy smirked, "and compliment hers." Quincy shuffled his feet. "Though, he's right, they do make you look nice."

"Thanks Will, and you too, Quin." Alice bit her lip. "Though it seemed like you were just trying to one up your buddy."

"No. I wasn't." Quincy focused on Will, who smiled back at him.

"Aw, I'm very gay over the two of you being here, your journey must have been epic."

"You just don't get this mid-world speak, do you Will?" Quincy asked.

"Nay, I say." William said, putting his arms around each of them. They walked through the fairgrounds as William peddled his wares. William pointed to a large clearing and they walked toward it.

"The stables are over there, with real horses." William said, sneaking off into speaking regular English.

"Awesome. So when does the fun start? Real horses? Whew, boy. I dunno if I can handle it, Will." Quincy said lowly.

"Oh come on, this'll be great. Follow me."

William walked over to the stable man, and handed him a handful of bills. "What say ye to allowing my friends and I to have a turn?"

"I'd say you're barmy, me son." The burly man said, his mustache twitching.

"I can ride, tis true." William nodded, and offered the man a pack of coated almonds. "What's more, I'll give ye this pack of nuts, who can resist their charm? A sultry sea wench? Nay, my friend. What say you?"

The man took the nuts and waved William on. William motioned Quincy and Alice to follow him. They approached a pair of brown horses, and William pumped his fist. "Do either of you two wanna race me?"

Alice looked down the tracks and nodded. "I'll do it Will, but I didn't know you could ride a horse." she said warily, as she gracefully swung herself onto the saddle.

William was startled, for he didn't know Alice could ride a horse. She mounted the steed and looked so at ease, stroking the horses' mane.

"Well, I bet you didn't know I could drive a motorcycle either."

Alice stopped petting the horse and Quincy cackled. "You can't drive a motorcycle, you liar." Quincy said as he kicked at some grass.

"Well, I rode on a motorcycle, it was great."

"That's nice; now let's see if you can best me on this beast." Alice said, waiting on William to mount his steed.

William sat down his satchel of nuts and clumsily got on his horse. It neighed, and its call seemed to be unnaturally loud to William. He felt the horse's mane, imitating Alice, and wondered if he would be able to get this one started. He supposed he could just kick it.

"Ready?" Alice asked.

Quincy snickered.

"Yes." William said, and he kicked the horse in the ribs, and the next thing he knew he was falling. He was falling fast and screams were heard before he lost consciousness.

***

"Can't drive a bike or ride a horse." William heard a voice he thought belonged to Quin.

"I think he'll be okay." That was Alice, he was sure of it.

"Well, these smelly sticks ought to do something." William suddenly understood why a foul smell had taken to his nose.

"Roslyn?" William asked.

"Yeah, he's waking up. He remembers my name too, that's a great sign."

William opened his eyes. They met a chestnut brown pair. "Hello." he said thickly.

"Welcome back to the fair, Denslayer." Roslyn said, one of her hands cradled his head against her legs.

William sat up quickly, too quickly, and he almost fell backwards, his head felt like it was bobbing in the ocean during a typhoon. "I feel like I got stampeded." he rubbed his head.

"Well…you weren't," Alice said darkly, "but you scared us all half to death."

"Sorry." William was.

"Will, you're lucky that sword didn't go up your ass. Which reminds me…what did medieval devils use as lubricant?" Quin asked.

"Horse feces." Roslyn spoke up, as she stood, facing Quincy.

Quincy blanched. "Are you serious?"

"Yeah, it's right there. You could try it if you wanted to, but, this isn't the time or the place for experiments. We need to get William something to eat I think."

"Is that usually what you do when someone falls off a horse?" William asked.

"No, but it's what you could do when one's friends show up and they've not been properly introduced to me. For the record." she sounded like she was reprimanding him, but her smile was warm enough.

"Right!" William said, shakily dusting himself off.

The four walked to the picnic area, where Alice brought them turkey legs and soda.

As the four sat around a table William cleared his throat. "William, I am. This be …"

"Can you stop talking like that William? It's not working towards your goal." Alice asked.

"Yeah, sure." William nodded. "Quincy, Alice, this is Roslyn…my …" he searched his head for the right title. *Was she his girlfriend? Was that too forward? Oh boy…*

"This is my, lady friend?"

"Please! You make me sound like a female escort." Roslyn said. She held out her hand to Alice and then to Quincy, while her other hand held her turkey leg. "I'm William's girlfriend."

Now that felt forward. William was astounded. *And I thought she said she wasn't expecting the kissing so early…boy, I should…hey! I've got a girlfriend!* "Yes. This is my girlfriend." William nodded excitedly.

Alice's jaw dropped. Quincy gave Roslyn and William a dumbfounded look. He looked Roslyn up and down, then looked at William. "Here I was thinking she was just some nice medic girl. Shows what I know."

"Wow, did you two know each other, before coming here I mean?" Alice bit heartily on her turkey leg. "Seems kinda fast…" Alice said softly.

"No. But I discovered quickly that I liked him a great deal, he's got quite a voice." Roslyn said.

"Agreed," Alice gave Quincy a joking look as she stuck her tongue out at him. "William does have quite the voice. I'm Alice." Alice said, and then pointed to Quincy. "This is Quincy, he's *my* escort today." Alice laughed.

"I had thought so, you two seemed like the type of friends William here had described." Roslyn said.

"Aren't they awesome?" William felt the food and drink strengthening him from the fall.

"Well, now that we're all introduced, what all you do think we should do today?"

"We should be working, shouldn't we?" William questioned Roslyn.

"Should be, but I talked to the Guard, they said since you fell off a horse in record time, they'll give you the day off. My stand is not doing so hot today anyway, so I'm taking today off. My Mom will never know."

"Cool." William said, and he thought it was very cool indeed. He was sitting at Ren Fair with three friends. He nearly choked on his drink. He corrected himself. Two friends & his *girlfriend.*

"Roslyn?" he asked, as Alice went off to the bathroom with Quincy in tow. "I was wondering."

"Why your two friends are going to the bathroom together? I wasn't going to mention it, but maybe Quincy's androgynous."

He felt his smile flat line. "I've never thought to check, truth be told. I think he's got parts."

"What's your question Denslayer?" she poked him in the ribs.

"I was wondering, actually, when we decided to date each other." He rubbed his side.

"I said I was your girlfriend, and you didn't argue the matter. As I see it that was me asking you, and you accepting." She twisted a strand of hair behind her ear.

"I can hold your hand then?" William asked, his heart swelled as she nodded.

"I would love you to."

Alice and Quincy came back, and William felt his mind reel. Quincy & Alice were holding hands. Quincy Abrams and Alice Mendell were holding hands. It was a neat development, it seemed as though love was in the air. "Whoa, are you two together too?"

"No," Quincy admitted dejectedly. "Alice and I just wondered what you would think if we came out holding hands."

"Your reaction was less impressive than I thought, so unfortunately I owe Quinnie five dollars."

"What did you think he would do?" Roslyn asked.

"Fall out of his seat."

"Spill his drink."

Quincy and Alice spoke simultaneously.

"He did neither, I guess he's over you." Roslyn said, gazing at Quincy.

"Why are you looking at me like that? It's unsettling." Quincy turned his head away from Roslyn.

"You've lost your boy toy Quincy; his heart belongs to another." Alice giggled.

"I never considered William to be my boy toy. It's wrong to suggest it and I resent the comment."

"Oh come on, you know it's my goal to get you and William together." Alice suggested, her hand found its way back to its other.

Quincy looked crestfallen, having no hand to hold. "Why do you suggest we're gay? We're not. He's got a girlfriend, he's had you, he's...I'm not into William."

"Well, yeah, of course you're not into him, Quin. As I said earlier, there's a time and a place for experimentation." Roslyn chimed in.

"I had to ask about the lubricant, didn't I?" Quincy rolled his eyes.

William wanted to hold Roslyn's hand very much as the four of them set off towards the shops. So he boldly took it and found holding it was about as nice as it could be. She didn't seem to mind when their palms got sweaty from contact, as Alice had, and she also liked to massage his inner palm with her thumb. He had a good afternoon, and Quincy and Alice seemed to enjoy theirs as well.

At least, that's what he could assume from their flirtatious acts.

"Hey, Quin." William took him aside briefly outside a jewelry shop. "Talk to me for a few seconds."

"Just don't make it look like we're having sloppy seconds and I'll be fine."

"Alright, look. I think Alice is into you, have you been *flirting* with her?" he asked astounded.

Quincy breathed heavily, and looked over his shoulder. "Yes."

"Well, listen. I'm sure you two are gonna be great together, really I do. But ya gotta know something, if our band breaks up, not that it should ever do so, but if our band ever breaks up, you guys have to stay together."

"I'm not following you." Quincy looked at a poison ring.

"Well," he put his arm around Quincy's shoulders.

"I thought I told you not to make it look like we're having sloppy seconds. That includes you putting your arm around me in an *oh so sexy* way. Please, I really do not want Alice to think I'm into you. And yes, I just said *oh so sexy.*"

"Horse feces, Quin. Horse feces. Now shut up and listen to me."

"Did you just tell me to shut up?"

"That's inconsequential. The facts are these Quincy."

"Quin."

"The facts are these Quin, it's known universally that if any two people in the same band date, they break up and the band likewise breaks up."

"Yeah."

"So stay together if the band breaks up, I mean, that's a whole new ball field. What if bands started breaking up, but the people in the relationships still stayed together? Logic could suggest that if you want to save your relationship, you should break up the band."
"You hit your head too hard earlier."

"No! Well, maybe! But think of it! Maybe, it's kinda like John Lennon & Yoko. Yoko thought their relationship was going to end, so that's why the Beatles broke up! John wasn't gonna be having any of the separation blues, no way he was gonna be on a bummer. He knew all you needed was love, so he broke up the band and boom! His relationship was saved."

"I promise you, if our band breaks up, Alice & I will stay together…if we get together."

"Do you swear on the honor of your father, child of Denise and Bradley?" William asked, his voice taking on a British accent.

"Don't remind me of what I am. But yes, I promise, we'll stay together."

"Cuz if you two break up, then our band would be broken up. It would have to be that way. So remember that Quin!" William patted him on the back.

"Remember…what exactly?"

"If you two break up, then the bands' lost, and if the bands lost …I can't think of it. But if you wanna date Alice, just know, you might have to marry her. I just want you two to be happy, but remember, we could be the next Beatles. Yeah."

"Will, I have no idea what you're talking about, or trying to say. But know this, I'll break up the band before I break Alice's heart."

"Cool."

"Also, isn't that generally the reason you date someone? You believe you could marry them?"

William nodded. "You're one hundred percent correct, so that means I could marry Roslyn. How far out!"

"Well, you are dating her." Quin said.

"Yeah." William felt like he had just beaten the high score on all the video games at the laundry mat. "This feels pretty awesome, I like being in a relationship."

"Yeah, well, as I'm still not in one, let's not gloat."

"Sure Quin. Sure."

***

William and his band of friends visited the booths that looked interesting. William came across a duck pond and felt compelled to stop. He watched wide eyed as little plastic ducks were propelled along in a circular tub of water. Their little yellow bodies bobbed up and down.

"What's the point of this game?" William asked the proprietor of the stand.

The proprietor looked at William, assumed him to be serious and answered plainly. "Thee picks up a duck, on its belly is writ a number. Find said number twice, ye win a prize, so ye do." the man said rolling a cigarette with nimble fingers.

"I would play." William said, looking to Roslyn, hoping within his heart to win her a prize.

"Righto. Well, it'll cost my lord one slip of green. Make haste with it, I find myself needing something to cool me throat."

William handed him the dollar and rolled up his shirt cuffs. The water felt cold against his arms as he grabbed a duck, this one had a white spot on its neck so it was special. He turned it upside down, and saw fifteen written on it.

"So I need a fifteen?"

"Aye." The man said, striking his match across his front teeth, causing it to ignite. He spat bitterly and lit his cigarette.

"What would he win?" Quincy asked, with only mildest amusement.

"I bet it would be one of those bears behind the stand, unless this guy has a weird obsession with stuffed bears with eye patches and cutlasses." Alice said as her wings blew in the wind.

"I bet he keeps the good prizes under the counter." Roslyn stated, scrupulously watching the proprietor.

"I think I'm going for …" William bit his lip, "this one." He pulled it up and frowned, *two.*

"Aww, that be too bad. Care to try again?" the smoking man asked, his smile wide now.

"Yeah. I do." William said, determined.

As he handed over the dollar Quincy went into his own wallet and pulled out two singles. "Add me in. Next."

"The gambling man's money has no home." said the master of the duck pond. It sounded Confucian coming from this gut heaving man of about forty.

Quincy was not to be outdone by William, who drew a three and a seven. He frowned and watched as Quincy drew two sixes, followed by a one and a thirteen. The owner nodded to Quincy. "Well played M'lord. Care to double your chances and go for a bigger prize?"

"Nope." Quincy said coldly. "I'll have that brown one, the one that looks like he's got a sword up his *hindquarters.*"

"My, we have learned a little verbiage haven't we, Quin?" Rosalyn smirked.

"Mayhap." Quincy accepted the bear, and sniffed him curiously. "Here, Alice, hold him for me. Imagine the way my image would be hurt if I was seen walking with him.

"I'm naming him Quinnie, regardless of what you have to say about it." Alice said, taking the bear and clutching him to her chest.

They made their way through the fair, the delicious smell of roasted chicken permeating the air. "I hate chicken." Quincy held his nose.

"Why?" Roslyn asked.

"Personal reasons." Quincy said.

"Yet not so personal that you chose to voice some comment? I don't think so, out with it." Roslyn demanded.

"I had an issue as a child, a petting zoo field trip gone horribly wrong."

"Oh?" William was intrigued; he stopped walking to rest under the cool shade of a tree. Roslyn stood next to him, her hand weaved into his.

"Tell me more. I've not heard *this* particular story yet." Alice said, sitting crossed legged on the grass.

"You've seen the running of the bulls, or heard of it I suppose?" Quincy asked, accepting his fate as a hanged man would two seconds after the noose was laced about his neck, knowing the inevitable was upon him.

The friends nodded, waiting.

"It was like that, only with chickens..." he grimaced. "And I was the only one in my class lucky enough to be in the pen...yeah. I didn't learn to tie my shoes until fourth grade." He frowned in remembrance of that day. "I tripped, a lot. It was like," he paused, "a really bad day."

"I have a new appreciation for you Quincy." William said, placing his hand on his best friend's shoulder.

"I've got a new appreciation of chickens. God love them!" Alice laughed.

"Alice, I need to go to the privies. Come with me." Roslyn stated a moment later, jerking Alice along with her.

"That wasn't obvious." Quincy said.

"Think they'll talk about me?" William wondered aloud.

"I just told a story about me being overrun by chickens. They're going to talk about me."

"You had to steal my thunder somehow." William kicked a tuft of grass.

"I can steal your thunder any day."

"Steal my thunder as well as my ex-girlfriend." William smiled.

"I thought we were cool, supposing anything happened."

"I am, I just wanted to say it. It's crazy, you and Alice getting together."

"How are you and Roslyn? Did you know she was going to be working here this year?"

"No." William said. "I didn't even know her before this week."

"Have you kissed her yet?"

"Alice? Oh yeah, we kissed a lot. Like, every time we saw each other. It was great."

Quincy looked grave, his eyes turned to slits and his lip upturned. "I meant you and Roslyn."

"I know exactly what you meant; I just wanted to get back at you a little. Ya know, stealing my thunder and all."

"Whatever. Answer my question. Man."

William felt color rush to his cheeks, and grinned like a child. "Yes, we did. It was so fantastic! I don't say this to ruin your first kiss."

Quincy glared at him, his lip trembled a bit with suppressed swear words.

"I mean…your first kiss with *Alice*! Yeah, I didn't want to ruin your first kiss with Alice by presenting this as a comparison…but yeah! It was nice."

"You aren't taking it a little fast? I mean, you guys could be married by next Tuesday at the rate you're going."

"Nah, we'll be just fine. I feel like I know her pretty well, actually."

"That's good, if you feel that way, then. I just don't want her finding some other scallywag and breaking your heart, dude. I don't wanna have to play sappy break up songs at our shows."

"I could write sappy love songs."

"Point made, write sappy break up songs if you have to."

"Noted Sir, most noted."

***

The smell of the privies was about the most realistic Renaissance element in her day so far. *Alice, wash your hands. No. Don't look through the door, wash your hands.* Alice was feeling distracted or maybe ill at ease by being in the same confined space as William's new heart throb. She kept bumping her wings into people, most of whom didn't seem to care a great deal, but it bothered Alice all the same.

She touched the slimy looking metal faucets and was surprised to see that water did actually flow from them, as opposed to her original thought: sludge. Roslyn came to join her a second later, letting her stall door squeak shut on its poorly oiled hinges.

Alice dried her hands on what was advertised as 60% post-consumer waste hand towels, much to her surprise. She had thought that they wouldn't be using paper here, much less recycled paper. She had been expecting crude towels, or nothing at all, save for maybe the fabric of whatever she had to wear that day.

They left together, Alice was trying to walk at a normal pace, but kept finding herself speeding ahead of Roslyn, perhaps it was self-preservation. Questions were bound to come soon; it was the way with girls.

She paused, stumbling across a thought that had put itself in her path. *Shouldn't I have questions of* my *own?* She looked at Roslyn, and started to compare the two of them. *I really don't have any questions about the two of them, but shouldn't I have questions? She is dating my ex.*

"What's on your mind, Al?" Roslyn asked, pulling a blue colored ocarina from her pocket.

Al. We're already to nicknames. "I don't know. Nothing really."

Roslyn blew quickly into the ocarina's mouthpiece, and sniffled thereafter. "My new ones always smell weird. Kind of like that lie you just told." Roslyn turned her head to look at Alice.

"I didn't lie, I just said I don't know what I'm thinking about."

"Is there a central trend to your thinking? I might be able to help; it has to do with your boys doesn't it? Your boys and maybe even Lipstick Trace?"

Alice smiled, kind of pleased that William had spoken of his friends so much. "In a way I am thinking of them. The band and the boys."

"See, I'm doing wonders already, aren't I? I've already read your face and seen to your thoughts."

"Was it that clear?"

"Nah. Not at all." Roslyn gave the ocarina a sharp blast and turned red. "Sorry, that couldn't have been pleasant."

"It's fine."

Alice watched Roslyn, waiting for her to continue speaking on the subject she had raised. *I might as well be waiting on William to admit he likes guys; she's not going to bring anything up again.* "I was wondering how William feels about Quincy and I dating, to be honest."

"I thought it might be something like that." Roslyn said.

"Well, what do you think?" Alice wondered.

"I don't know." Roslyn put the ocarina away. "I don't want to say that William will do this or that, being that I don't really know him inside and out."

"I won't say that I do either… but he just seems like you and he talked a lot over a short period of time."

"I won't deny that we did. Williams' a fun spirit, we mesh together." She shrugged. "He might approve, he might not."

Alice frowned. "I was really looking for more of a straight answer."

"A parallel line is a straight answer. I think." she caught a piece of floating dandelion in the air. "Course, math was never my strong point. Maybe it's a ray that's straight. I know that they are two lines running in the same direction, while never touching."

Alice smiled a little. *I may use that line one day, it sounds appropriate.* "I mean; I want to know how I feel about Quincy too. I just want it to be like a light switch. It's either up with a charge, or down with nothing but darkness."

"Okay, we'll move on to science. I feel a little more capable with this answer. Kiss the boy, find out if there's an electron or a neutron."

Maybe I should, I'm sure he and Roslyn have already kissed, and really *why shouldn't they have? I have had Quincy over more often than William recently.* "Oh God." she thought of something, and Roslyn turned to make sure she was okay.

"What's up?"

"I hope Quincy doesn't take to wearing lipstick because of me too." Alice trembled. They rejoined the two boys, neither of whom was currently wearing lipstick.

***

The amber ocean of the setting sun colored the horizon as Quincy opened the car door for Alice, who nodded pleasantly, as she stepped into the car that would take her away from the fair.

As Quincy drove away, William and Roslyn waved from the gate leading into the fair. Quincy noticed the hesitant smile creeping onto Alice's face.

"That good of a day, was it?" Quincy asked.

"In some ways, yes." Alice didn't elaborate just yet.

"I think it was a good day. It didn't rain today." Quincy said, making small talk with himself.

"Drive me home, Quincy." Alice requested, and he did as she asked. He didn't have the radio on, and it was a pretty quiet drive home. At least, in the car it was quiet. In

Quincy's mind, it was a cacophony of questions, all having to do with Alice.

It feels like we're right, this time. He looked at her, her fairy wings off now, they were in the backseat. He considered putting his hand on her leg as he drove, but thought it was just a bad idea. *Haven't I pushed enough barriers today?*

Quincy missed the sound of music, but what he really missed was the sound of her voice. It was a tense quiet, he was waiting for the first bullet to fly, or the first bomb to drop. William was better with these spells of quiet, not he. Quincy had to write his thoughts down, or he would just go crazy. With him having no paper, it was a very bad drive home indeed.

He finally pulled up to her house, it looked quiet within, and she had told him once that her parents usually watched television in their bedroom when they were alone. They would turn it off once their daughter arrived home, where they would pay attention to her for a little while. Quincy frowned, thinking of his parents.

"Here we are Miss Mendell, home sweet home." he said, though with a sarcastic edge to his voice, while reaching over to open her door.

She moved as lithely as a ballerina, pulling her lips towards his, as her hands wrapped around his head. He was a fish, caught by an Angler's glow, as her lips sought out his. He expected to be torn to pieces by her teeth, gleaming from the light of Woody's off yellow ceiling lights. He felt himself tremble slightly under the weight of her lips. *Today is my day, and it's not raining.*

The radio was playing loudly on his way home from Alice's.

***

William sat happily at the bonfire. He was feeling pretty good about the day, even the stars were starting to come out. It was a clear sky and the air held promise.

"Your friends were interesting, William." Roslyn said, taking out a pocket knife and fashioning herself a hot dog spear.

"I think they liked you. Which is good, my friends are usually a good judge of character." he bit into his food.

"They picked you as a friend, it must be true."

William smiled, and leaned against Roslyn lightly, liking the way she felt next to him. If he was to start cuddling, he might want to take his sword off, he thought. So he untied the belt on which it was lashed and laid on the ground.

"I'm a good judge of character, I picked you." he hoped that didn't sound too awkward. He watched her nod once, not making any further comment though.

"How are you getting here next weekend? Is Quincy driving you again?" Roslyn inquired.

"I think so."

"He must get tired of driving you all the time."

William shrugged, he was not thinking along those lines at all. "We're friends, he's good for it. He knows that when we actually start selling our demos I'll give him a bigger cut of the earnings."

"So that's why he does that." she started. "Alice told me something about Quincy, a fear really, I guess."

"Something she's afraid of?" William asked, his eyes widening in wonder.

"Typically that's what a fear is." she pushed him a little. "Anyway, she said she was afraid that if she started dating Quincy, he might start wearing lipstick as well, just like you did."

"That wouldn't be Quin, I couldn't see it happening really. Unless he thinks copying my fashion sense will get him more help with Alice." he bit his lip. "Nope. I still don't think he would."

"How often *do* you wear lipstick, William?"

"At every show, it's a *must*."

"And you cross dress?" Roslyn asked.

"Well, no. I get glammed up, leather pants, glitter, nail polish and eye shadow, lipstick, of course. Black boots and a sleeveless blue jean jacket. Though, I have been thinking of adding fishnet undershirts to the ensemble. Oh, and bells, bells on my boots. Don't forget those. They make the best noise when I dance."

She smiled. "I'll remember that."

"Why do you ask?"

"As we're dating I need to know certain information. I've got most of everything I need."

"Well, you say mostly everything, what else is there?"

Roslyn turned her hotdog over the flames. "How did you do in Biology in high school?" she asked in the most serious tone he'd ever heard her use.

"Umm...I passed. He didn't like me talking to his pet iguana as often as I did, but he gave me a B."

"Will, earlier you told me that 'love knows no gender', you meant that didn't you?" she asked, staring at him in the dancing light of the flames.

William nodded, though he was starting to wonder where the conversation was headed. "Are you falling for Alice?" he asked, saddened at the thought that all of his friends might have the hots for his ex.

"No." she laughed. "I don't want to jump your ex, that's Quincy's business."

"What is it then?" William was starting to worry, she looked cautious, as if he would hurt her.

"Promise me, Will, that you're not going to interrupt me until you've heard me out, okay?" she touched his free hand with hers.

"I promise, yeah. Go on, really, it's okay."

"When you told me that you thought love knew no gender, it was probably the sweetest thing I'd ever really heard in my life. Not because it's the *chick* thing to think, but because it genuinely sounded like you believed it. That sort of thing means the world to a person like me."

William held his tongue, remembering his promise.

"I say, a person like me to prepare you for what I'm about to say. I've been on you all day, throwing jokes, testing you on certain things." she ran her fingers through her hair, pulling it back out of her eyes, illuminating her white face. "I know we've only been together for a very short time, and I normally wouldn't go so word spew on you this early. However, I really think we've got something.

"Will," she cast her eyes down. "Captain Denslayer, I am going to tell you this, I promised myself that I would." she laughed at herself and nodded, steeling herself to go on. "I've got A.I.S., or, Androgen Insensitivity Syndrome."

"So it's not AIDS?" William was relieved. "Thank goodness, you had me bummed out when you spelled the 'A' and the 'I', like, really."

She hit him lightly. "No, not AIDS."

"Then what is A.I.S.?" he knew this had to be hard on her, she looked like she wanted to run away. He held onto her hand tightly.

"It means that I am genetically a guy, William. A female body, with guy chromosomes. I can't have kids, don't have fallopian tubes, no uterus for me. None of it.

"My Mom told me early on, I was five. She said my doctor didn't even want to tell her," she coughed nervously, and he put his arm around her. "Said that it wasn't practical to say anything. Well, my Mom, she was brave. She told me that it didn't matter one bit that I was like this. Said, I'd be the envy of every one of my girlfriends, as I wouldn't have a monthly intruder.

"Do you think I'm strange now?" she took his arm off of her, yet he put it back just as quickly.

There was no hesitation in his reply. "Roslyn, first, thank you for trusting me. No, I don't think you're weird at all, I think you're the cat's pajamas. I don't care what chromosomes are rocking out inside you, I care about you." He kissed her cheek.

She instantly recovered from his words. "You don't care? At all?" she asked, shyly it seemed, as her words were so low.

"I'm amazed that something like that actually happens, but that just means you're special. It's actually pretty cool. Does it have any upsides?"

She laughed, bemusedly. "Yeah, I barely sweat thanks to my estrogen levels. What's more, I don't get smelly, and…I have never had an acne outbreak."

"And no period?" he was amazed.

"Nope. None at all. Of course, all the girls I have known have been extremely jealous over that. But I tell them, at least you can experience the joys of labor. I'd have to adopt if I want a child. Of course, I usually only say that to the meaner ones, the spiteful girls. I'd never say it to my friends for example."

"Of course." he was still processing a lot of the information; he had truly never heard of anything like A.I.S. before.

Roslyn jumped, as did William. His pocket was vibrating wildly, and he was not pleased to be receiving a phone call at this exact time- yet, it must be important. Otherwise, why would they call? He thought.

"Sorry, Roslyn, just a second."

"Sure, Will. I'll be here." she laid her head on her hands.

He looked at his screen and saw *ALICE* scrolling across his screen. William opened the phone and answered. "Hi Alice" he paused, and then looked to Roslyn.

"Well…yeah, she's right here. Um…yeah. Sure. Catch ya later." he handed the phone to Roslyn.

Roslyn took the phone and was wide eyed with surprise. William could hear Alice speaking still, she sounded troubled, which worried him.

"Roslyn, I really need to talk to a girl right now, I hope I'm not interrupting…" and that was when Roslyn stood up and walked away from William, leaving him with his hotdog.

***

"No, you're not interrupting at all, what's happened, Alice?"

Alice walked about her room, wishing that it were a bit bigger.

"Well, Quin drove me home, you knew that, stop repeating yourself Alice." She put her free hand to her forehead, and felt the heat rushing off her. "I took your advice, and I felt a charge, but it was, nearly overpowered by neurons… if that makes sense."

"So the boy can't kiss? Surely you could fix that, all it would take is a bit of practice."

"I think you're right, and I was thinking the same thing too. I just wanted to hear from a female's point of view, make sure it sounded logical. I used to have girls I could go to but… not so much anymore." Alice jumped onto her bed and fell back into the pillows. "But it's just, him. You saw him, I thought he'd be the type to have great kissing experience!"

"Not to pass righteous judgment Ali, but I took one look at you and thought you'd have had more experience."

"I… I'm not really sure how to respond to that. Not to sound like a… a slut, but I'm experienced enough. I'm just, disappointed I guess." Alice said, her voice dropping low.

"I think you should try again." Roslyn said, chuckling a little, and Alice just couldn't figure out why.

"Well, I will bring it up with him, but, ooh." Alice bit her lip. "Maybe I should just, work on it with him, give him some exposure."

"That could work, give him some more face time and he'll be rubbing your lips all the right ways."

"You make it sound so," Alice searched for the word, rolling her eyes, and snapping her fingers, "pornographic when you say it that way."

"What else can I do but offer my voice and insight?"

"Be as omniscient as you seem." Alice smiled.

"Okay, first, let me ask. What makes a good kiss?" Roslyn asked.

"Well, with others and… Will,… oh beans, this won't be weird will it?"

"Go on, I'm here as a friend."

"Well, with William he had a way of, it was…"

"William could kiss you and make your body feel like jelly?" Roslyn suggested.

Alice frowned, and glanced up at her pictures of William. "Yes. That's it exactly."

Alice could hear Roslyn stifling a giggle again. "I'm sorry, but don't sound so put out about it, that was me being omniscient again."

"Sure. I understand."

"So, that's what makes a good kiss. Were they always like that, or was it hit and miss?"

Alice considered it, their last kiss had been nice, but not Williams usual. Then she wondered, maybe it was because she knew the end of them was near that made it less than wonderful. "You know, I think I've realized that maybe, William ruined other men for me. He sets a high standard for a girl."

"Take him on a date tomorrow. Let him go to the movies."

Alice laughed now. "You don't think it would be boring for him, seeing as he works there?"

"Take him to the backseat then, seems to be plenty roomy enough. It doesn't really matter where the kitchen is, so long as the oven works."

"I think you've got a good point." Alice appreciated the subtle innuendo of Roslyn's words.

"Thanks."

"I'll take him out tomorrow, and find out about him."

"Alright. It was good talking to you then."

"You too Roslyn, have fun tonight."

Alice got up out of bed, and went over to her window. To her, nothing was so tranquil as sitting on her roof, so that's where she went. She leaned up against the window frame and stared up at the night sky.

"As far as I know, Quin's kissing could be completely normal. I know he's a good guy, weird, but cute all the same." Alice sighed and looked out at the small pond in front of her house. "I think I like him." She stayed under the night sky until the rain clouds moved in.

***

Quincy pulled into his driveway and exited his car, his lips still felt as hot as his car's hood. He unlocked the door to his home and heard his parents watching television, he knew they would be, but he didn't really care tonight. No, he was in too good of a mood. *Let World War III come, can't bring me down.*

He walked into the room with an almost drunken gait and stood right in front of the television. "Hi." He said, waving to both his parents, who looked confused and slightly put out that their show was being interrupted.

"Hi, Quincy." His father Bradley said, a bit of annoyance detectable in his tone.

"I've got news for you," Quincy said, in a sing song voice.

"Well sit down and stop blocking the TV."

"Late shows aren't the news. But let me be your anchorman for the night." Quincy tried to flatten his hair back to look more professional. "Greetings America, I'm Quin Abrams reporting LIVE for Channel 24.5!"

"Quincy, that is not amusing." His father said.

"I have a girlfriend! Her name is Alice Mendell, and by God's hairy chin, you are going to pay attention to me for five minutes out of your day!"

"Well, that's great son. When fall comes you focus on your studies and not your little girl friend. There's some food for you in the fridge, now I'm going to hear about the Top Ten. Move over." His Dad said, getting up and moving Quincy from the front of the television.

Quincy sighed. "Well, I'm going to sneak over to her house then, might try and feel her up, plant some wild oats. Repopulate the planet." Quincy said, aspiring to head off to his room; knowing his parents would ignore whatever he said anyway.

The TV went silent for the first time in a long while, Quincy couldn't remember the last time it had been turned off during the late show.

"What did you say Quincy?" His Dad got back up, and crossed his arms over his beefy chest.

Quincy looked over at his mother, who had a most unusual look on her face.

"Umm…" Quincy was not expecting them to have paid attention, he had said far worse things in the past and it had never gotten their attention. "I was joking."

"You're a real funny guy then, son. Might want to think about taking over the late shows, you're a real crack up." Bradley stepped towards his son.

"Oh, thanks." Quincy said, turning red now.

"I thought you were more responsible than this Quincy. To joke about something as serious as *sex*. About making some girl pregnant. What kind of mouth do you have on you these days?"

"God, I joke about failing out of school, about shooting up heroin, about robbing a Quickie mart, and I get nothing. I was even partially serious about some of those things. Yet I joke about doing things with my girlfriend and you jump my case? Are you serious?"

Bradley shook his head; Quincy noticed the receding hairline had become more pronounced lately. "To joke about becoming a father at this point in your life, it is very stupid."

Quincy held up his hands. "Excuse me, what's sex compared to me returning to the house at all hours of the night, you know I was the only kid in high school without a curfew?"

"It's because we trust you Quincy." His mother said softly.

"You *trust* me? Then why couldn't you have said something like that earlier on?"

"Do you and your friend, William feel the need to say how much you like one another?" His mother inquired.

"No we don't! But you're my parents, not my best friend. When did we last talk this much? Do you know when?"

"We don't want to see you ruin your life. You and your girlfriend need to think about what's important. Don't do something just because you think it's what's expected of you." She continued.

"Wow, I'm getting advice from my parents. Who'd have guessed?" Quincy muttered.

"You don't need to be a sarcastic mouth all the time, let this sink in! You're eighteen now, you mess up, you're going to be fending for yourself. I can only do so much." His father resumed his tirade.

"Right."

"Get dinner, I don't want to hear that kind of talk from you again, are we understood?" Bradley asked, his tone serious.

Quincy stood there, looking up at the man who hadn't given him advice when he had been sent to a new school halfway through his high school career; who hadn't given him advice on girls until just now. He nodded his head. "Yeah, we're clear."

Bradley nodded and turned back on the TV, his mother remained quiet.

Quincy grabbed a tuna sandwich from inside the fridge and walked up the stairs to his room. All he had wanted was attention from his parents for as long as he could remember. Now he shook. "If they make problems for Alice & me, after all I've been through to get her ..." he entered his room and let his head fall back against the door. "I will go nuts."

He turned on his radio and tried to calm down. Reaching into his dresser, he pulled out a big binder. It was getting kind of shabby now with tattered edges; the pictures of Judas Priest and KISS were a little faded.

He turned to a new page and began to write.

Today is my day. It's no longer raining.
I have what I want, and have need of nothing.
Tomorrow might belong to someone else,
But today is always going to be mine.
Alice Mendell & Quincy Abrams Saturday August 9.
***

The next day at the fair was a busy one. William had to visit his boss twice to refill his satchel full of nuts. At the end of the day William had a good fifty dollars in his pocket after his employer's cut.

He walked over to Roslyn's stand, a red rose in his hand, courtesy of a traveling flower girl.

"Lady Lyden, a flower for thee." William said with his head bowed.

He raised himself and saw her smiling. "Thank you, Denslayer." She reached for the flower, but he pulled away.

William stuck the stem of the rose between his lips and did a comedic eyebrow roll as he walked toward her.

She grinned and took the rose from his lips with her own. "Take you all day to think that one up?" she teased.

"No, a couple seconds actually." He hopped onto the counter and sat. "Business good for you today?"
"I had a lot of families today, I did well."

"I had a lot of customers too."

"So you emptied your sack then?" she said, adjusting a box of ocarinas, placing it on the counter.

"Twice!" he nodded excitedly.

"Careful now, this counter can't take your butt dancing, it might break."

"But I'm excited! Next weekend I can buy something nice, a hat, or something involving feathers!"

"That does sound exhilarating, I would be a keeper of the feather."

"I know!" he felt his face might break sooner than the counter, he was all smiles.

"Come help your girl with this, move these boxes with me to storage."

William took a couple of the boxes and walked carefully to the dusty storeroom with Roslyn.

"It smells funny in here." William commented.

"Ren fair." Said she.

"So, now that I've made out like a bandit with my salesmanship, I was wondering."

"Well, wonder on then." She sat on a crate not belonging to her.

"Thursday, after the show, do you want to do something?" We could bowl, or get food, see a movie."

"Assuming I don't leave the show crying because of the opening acts, sure."

"Nah, no worries there. We're opening, so you won't have to wait long." He leaned in and kissed her head.

"Aren't you cute?" She rested her head against his chest.

"Maybe. I wouldn't know. I'd think you were the expert."

She got up and took Williams hand. "Time to go. Do you have a ride home?"

"Quin's supposed to be coming to get me when he gets off work."

Roslyn looked uneasy. "When is that?"

"He closes."

Roslyn poked his side. 'You goof. I'll give you a ride home. You shouldn't have to stay 'til dark."

"Wow! Thanks Roslyn!"

"Don't mention it. Let me go get changed out from this skirt and we'll go."

"Yeah, I'll get changed too. No swords on the highway, the bulls wouldn't approve methinks."

William slipped into the privies and texted Quin, telling him the ride wouldn't be necessary, he had a better one that night.

***

Quincy was on his last break of the night and was on the phone, hoping that Alice would pick up. She hadn't returned his calls yet and he was beginning to worry. As the ring carried on he looked at his well bitten fingernails, wondering how much more they could take.

"Maybe my fourth message wasn't clear enough." He wondered aloud. He had wanted to tell her about the scene with his parents, but hadn't been able to reach her.
"Hi Quin." He heard at last.

"Alice!" *Finally,* He laughed.

"Been trying to reach me? Was this message going to be just as desperate as the last one?"

He heard her laugh and he smiled. "Why didn't you call me back?"

"Well, you're at work for one."

"Not all day. What about this morning?"

"Church with the family."

"Oh well, I've got you now."

"You sound a little possessive of me. Do you think you've got some claim over me now? Hmm?"

Quincy lowered his voice as a coworker walked past. "Yeah, maybe a little."

"You'd better."

"Hey, Allie. I've got to talk to you about something." He waited for her to respond, which seemed to take longer than usual.

"Yeah. I've got to talk to you about something too."

"Oh, okay. Tonight after work?"

"Can't, I've got to be up early. Dad and I are going to check out another university."

"Thought he was fine with you going to the local one with me & Will?"

"He is," She sighed. "He just wants to make sure my decision is an informed one."

Quincy thought of his own Dad. "Well, I'm here again all day Tuesday. You free Wednesday?"

"I am. Want to make it a date?"

He could nearly see Alice twirling her hair, awaiting his response. "Sounds awesome Alice, I can't wait."

"Better get back to the popcorn and pretzels, Quinnie."

He let the name slide. "Alright." He paused. "I'll see you Wednesday. Seven good?"

"Perfect." She paused also. "Bye."

He hung up the phone and clocked back in, wondering just where you took a girl for a date when you worked for the movie theaters.

***

Quincy knocked on the Mendell's door and waited for it to open. He knew Mr. Mendell would appreciate his button down shirt and black slacks. He seemed to like a clean cut guy for his daughter.

Brenda opened the door and told him to come in. "It's so nice that you and Alice are going out tonight. I'm sure you'll have a great time."

"Thanks Brenda, I hope she will. This means a lot to me, thank you for letting her out tonight." Quincy beamed, feeling great about the night's prospects.

"I can tell it does. I can see your face instead of a curtain of hair tonight. And no torn jeans."

He felt himself flush and was grateful for the distraction presented by Alice. She was in a sapphire blue top and a black skirt. A pearl necklace decorated her chest and small diamond earrings adorned her ears.

At once, Quincy felt underdressed.

"Descending the stairs is Alice the elegant." Said her father, Daniel, from the kitchen doorway. "You look wonderful sweetheart."

Alice reached Quincy and he tentatively took her hand in his. "Sir, I promise not to elope with your daughter, tempting as it may seem."

Daniel gave a short laugh. "I appreciate that Quincy. Have her home by midnight please."

Daniel extended his hand which Quincy shook with his free one.

As he left with Alice he heard Brenda and Daniel talking quietly. "Well, he's certainly tamer looking than her last boyfriend." Daniel said, and Quincy shared a good laugh with Alice as they closed the door.

Quincy walked her to the passenger side and opened the door for her. After he took his seat she touched his leg. "You do look very handsome."

"And tame, don't forget tame." He chuckled, turning his car onto her street. "What did your Dad mean by that anyway?"

"Gosh." Alice began. "William, on one of our first dates wore a Genesis T-Shirt and bright purple pants; on top of his already outrageous jewelry and hairstyle." She shook her head, as if the thought still made her cringe.

Quincy laughed, which helped to ease the anxiety that had started working its way into him. "So I figured we'd go see a drive-in movie. A nice romantic slasher flick."

Alice scoffed. "Better not be taking me to a crappy movie like that. You know the only things involving those words that I like are slash romances." She said jokingly.

"Oh yeah, you and your niche novels."

"What are we seeing?"

"You know that one movie; with the guy in cliché glasses, with really bad hair?"

"Oh yeah. I know that one. It involves some sort of plot doesn't it?"

"Dunno." He sped up a little. "It was the only thing playing and it lasts three hours. I figure if it gets too boring we could crochet or something."

Alice was silent.

He eventually stole a look at her, he saw her staring intently back at him. "Fine, don't crochet with me. I don't need your help."

"Just drive, weirdo." She said playfully, turning his radio to their favorite station. Music filled the air and he hoped it wouldn't negate the need for conversation.

At the drive-in Quincy purchased popcorn and two sodas before returning to the car. "Your food Miss Mendell."

"Thanks!" she took her drink and stole a handful of popcorn.

The movie began and Quincy was paying about as much attention as could be expected of an eighteen-year-old guy.

It took him a little past the first bad joke of the movie for him to get bored with it. He sucked on his bottom lip and looked over to Alice, who seemed to be sizing him up.

"Not your box of chocolates is it?" Alice asked.

"Well, it might have been. But, like I said, I kinda wanted to talk to you about something…I'm hesitant to bring it up on our date, but I feel it's kind of related."

"Well," she crunched her popcorn. "I also wanted to talk to you about something, related to our dating. But," she looked up at his car's cloth ceiling. "You go first."

"You know how I've told you about my parents, and their general disregard for giving me attention."

"Oh yeah, what happened this time? Threaten to burn the house down?"

Quincy groaned. "No, not at all. I actually got a response this time."

"Wow, wonders never cease." She smiled and looked at her fingers. "Butter." She said, reaching for a napkin in the cup holder. "This sure is a weird place to keep these. Hmm. Anyway, go on."

"Yeah. Well, my Dad and Mom got on me pretty bad over what I said." He didn't feel like rushing the point, but knew he was heading headlong for it all the same.

Alice seemed to be waiting for him, but she didn't rush, she did scoot closer to him though.

"I told them you and I had started going out, I kinda said some vulgar things and they didn't appreciate it."

"Oh really?" she looked up into his eyes.

"Yeah. My Dad said you and I should talk about responsibilities to each other and not having sex right away."

"You mean I won't get any tonight? Well there goes my plan!" she giggled.

"I don't really care so much. I don't think I'm ever going to have much of a relationship with either of them. I'm gonna talk to my kids on a daily basis, kinda like your Dad does with you."

"I love my Dad."

"It sucked though, because in the past I'd made serious threats, and they never paid me two seconds of their time. Yet I mention feeling you up and my Dad goes nuts."

She laughed out loud. "You'd like to be so bold Quincy."

"Anyway, said if I messed up, I was fending for myself. I don't care, I'm not going to mess up things with us. I've liked you too long for that."

Alice looked up into his face and he couldn't help but be reminded of a small curious kitten with the way her eyes peered into his. "Tell me more about that." She snuggled in closer to him; he detected a jasmine smell coming off her. She always smelled lovely, and Quincy became self-conscious about himself. *Hmm. Maybe I should wear cologne more often.* Quincy started to feel goofy, his cheeks were tingling and his hands were sweaty a little. "Umm…I've been crushing on you since I moved here."

"Okay."

"I think you've got one of the cutest faces I've ever seen."

"Okay." Her head was right against his now.

"I had a weird feeling the other day on the phone, when we were about to hang up."

"I did also." She admitted.

"It felt like I was supposed to say…" he readjusted his position and she moved in closer to him, "well, I wanted to say I love you, but I don't think that's what people say after only a few days of dating."

Alice was again silent, Quincy was quickly beginning to dislike these silent spells she had so frequently fallen into, and he didn't know what to think.

"That was weird, I'm sorry. I shouldn't have said it. Just, ignore it."

She was laughing now, and he knew his cheeks were as hot as this chick on the screen was trying to be. He moved away from her, as best as he could, but she stopped him.

"I paused too you know."

He did remember her pause.

She went on. "And do you really think that friends can't love each other? You and William are pretty much my best friends now; all the other friends I had are gone now." She took a deep breath. "I think if love exists on a friendship basis, it could be a very fluid movement into romantic love."

Quincy settled back into his seat, but this time with his arm around Alice. It was slowly dawning on him what Alice was saying. He kissed the top of her head, and she moved to look at him. "That simply won't do, Sir." She said softly.

He was thrown off. *Huh?* He thought. *Oh. Oh.* He looked past the tuft of blonde and gazed into her eyes. "I really like you, Alice."

"How much?" she questioned.

He thought of the countless journal entries he had made about her, the thoughts of the jealousy he had felt when William had her, and the pain he felt when he had to choose someone else's happiness over his own. "I love you Alice. I'm not saying that because it's what I think you want to hear; I'm saying it because it's the truth I've been holding inside me all of this time. It's time you knew it."

She leaned in and brought her lips toward his, and he felt her hand on the back of his neck. She looked him full in the face and held his face in her hands. "I love you too, Quincy."

***

William carefully applied his Deep-sea Blue lipstick; his lips were puckered in front of the mirror to attain full coverage. He heard Quincy behind him tapping his fingers in his usual pre-show anxious way. "Dude, your face, it's like…you're the poster child for every Dad's worst fear."

William snorted. "Don't bother me right now Quin, this is delicate work. It always has to start with the lipstick, if I mess it up, it throws off my qi."
William heard Quincy laugh now, and he too decided to laugh it off. "Will, we've got a little over twenty-seven minutes to go, just a kind FYI. You might want to pick up the pace with that pink lace and beautifying."

"You can't rush a masterpiece." William applied his usual cover of glitter, making sure it was covering his face yet not crowding it; he still had to do his eye shadow. "You think a Blue Frost or Chipper Charcoal would look best tonight?" William turned just in time to see Alice enter. Her hair was hanging down tonight, and her guitar was slung across her back. She was in her black pinstripe cutoff vest and her tightest pair of leather pants. William felt a twinge of jealousy as he looked from Alice to Quin.
"I still want those pants." William said.

"Well, get to a size ten and you can try." Alice grinned, placing a kiss on Quin's cheek. "You about ready fashion queen?"

"He's still got to do his *eye shadow*." Quincy groaned, waving a hand at William. "I'm glad you're here, he's asking me for advice."

"I was asking you, I need a second opinion! Alice, what do you think?" He held up his two final choices. "Blue Frost or Chipper Charcoal?"

Alice walked over and took each in her hand, and looked at Williams's getup. "Chipper Charcoal, go light. No mascara tonight either, your crappy kind always runs."

"I know, I need to go shopping with you, we could get some then. You still need new foundation?"

"Okay, this has got to stop." Quincy got up and put both his hands on Williams's shoulders. "Show time. Minutes away. Get done dude." Quincy led Alice outside the bathroom they had all just occupied and left William to do his thing.

"Guess I'm going with Chipper Charcoal." He said as he closed one eye.

***

Alice walked up to the bar and got herself a soda, feeling pretty good about the crowd tonight. She recognized a few of their loyal fans and waved to them, one of them particularly wanted to speak with her.

"Alice!" she heard, and turning around she saw Roslyn.

"Don't you look rocker chick tonight?" She laughed, drawing Alice in for a hug.

"Well, I have to look the part, though I'm pretty sure I'll be overshadowed by William tonight."

Roslyn grinned. "I am so looking forward to that, seeing his outfit I mean, he seemed so excited when he told me about it."

"Yeah, I think he's getting better with it. Still needs some consultations but that's easy enough to do." Alice took a drink, feeling the pre-show buzz.

"I wanted to ask you, how did your date go? Was there a spark?" Roslyn sat on a stool at the bar.

"It went amazing." Alice did a quick dance, and turned back to Roslyn.

"So his kissing improved?" Roslyn inquired, looking around to see Quincy on the stage, behind his drums in preparation.

"Not initially, but by the end of the evening we were able to work it out; I didn't even have to mention it to him. He surprises me; I never would have thought he could be such a good guy."

"What do you mean?" Roslyn had to raise her voice a bit; the music had just gone up.

"When we, we being my friends in high school and I, first saw him, we joked that he was one of those quiet guys who'd one day do something totally insane. I thought he was an asshole; thought he'd slash my tires. Fortunately, though, he never did anything of the sort."

"Didn't even streak?"

Alice blanched. "God no. I'd see that of William before I would Quincy."

"You'd better get on Allie, there's Will coming out now." Roslyn said, getting up to get closer to the stage.

***

William took to the stage, and he stared out into the crowd of eager fans. He recognized a few of his old friends from high school, and some other people they'd won over in previous shows. Alice hopped onto the stage and equipped her guitar, nodding to William.

He breathed. *It's important to keep breathing.* He told himself. He reached out for the microphone and his fishnet sleeves pulled back a little. He pulled it back in place. Then he saw Roslyn smiling wryly as she approached the stage, front and center. William ran his fingers through his hair and felt his hand get sticky; he had obviously used too much hair gel tonight.

Carrying on, he shook his hand off and smiled out at the crowd.

"Hi!" he stamped his feet and waited for the crowd's response, which was a subtle smattering of applause tonight, overpowered by one very loud wolf whistle.

"We're glad you're all here! We're Lipstick Trace, and Spark Substation, get ready to ROCK!" William said, as Quincy led in with the drums, and Alice started up with a powerful guitar riff.

The music was playing and William was dancing, feeling alive as he could ever hope to be. He reached for his tambourine and shook it wildly.

Some of the more dedicated fans started clapping, recognizing the very catchy "Frolicking through the Pheromones" song for which they were best known.

"Rocking with ease and carried on the breeze, I can sense your scent.

Apple in sky, by and by, you are heaven sent.

And sprawled on your lawn I see your smile, as you lay next to me.

This is our cause this is our time, now is meant to be. So let's frolic through the pheromones, tell me you'll respond.

Cuz I can't wait to lie with you, let's make lovely spawn!

I need to know it's you I know; won't you rock with me?

And we'll indulge exclusively in this crazy biology!"

The crowd started to dance, and William caught the gaze of Roslyn, who stared up at him with an incredulous look on her face. He placed the mic in its stand and started hammering away with his palm on the tambourine. Quincy's hands were flying across the drums, William only detected a few wrong beats this time.

Alice was ready to take on her thirteen second solo; all William had to do was keep the crowd entertained. He hopped up and down on the stage like a bunny on a caffeine rush. "Clap your hands! Come on now, you didn't come here to stand there and look pretty! That's my job!"

The crowd started to respond by forming little circles, in which people moshed and danced almost as wildly as William. Alice started her guitar solo and William swung his arms in the air like he was hailing taxis. He saw his skin sparkle with the glitter and waited for Alice's solo to end.

He momentarily lost track of where he was dancing, and he nearly toppled the mic stand onto Roslyn. As luck would have it, his hands were quicker than his eyes, and it was easily rectified. William looked uneasily at Roslyn, who yelled "Less mic, more jive!" As she danced from side to side.

His dance ended sooner than he thought when his foot got tangled in one of the many cords on the stage, and he fell out into the crowd. William had never stage dived before, but his fans were fast in catching him and placing him back on the stage. *Heck, that almost looked planned!* He heard Alice pick back up where she had left off and the music played on.

By the end of the show William was positive they had acquired at least a few more fans. He had to work quickly to clear the stage for the next band.

"Want some help?" Roslyn asked, holding out her arms for something to carry.

"Hey! Yeah, that would be great. This is my tambourine, be careful with it now." He grinned as sweat poured down his forehead.

"That was a funny show. Promise me you'll do that little dance again for me sometime?" she made way for him as he came off the stage with a bunch of cords.

"Anytime you want it. I'm in a great mood." He beamed, placing the final bit of cord into his backpack.

"Clear the way! Pardon me! Very important Quin coming through!" Quincy declared as he took his bass drum outside.

William and Roslyn walked outside with the rest of the band's equipment e, and placed it in the back of Quin's car. "Pretty nice backseat you have in this beast." Roslyn commented.

"It gets its use." Quincy replied.

"Oh really?" Roslyn put Will's tambourine in the back.

"Take that how you want to." Quincy said. "You guys gonna stick around for Rusty Soup Ladles?"

Roslyn looked at Will. "Nah, Quin, Roslyn & I are going for an adventure down Action Boulevard. Thanks for the invite though."

Quincy rolled his eyes. "Action Boulevard? Jesus man, get a back seat and save yourself the trouble."

"Well, you put on a good show Quin, tell Alice I said the same. I'll see you later." Roslyn waved goodbye and William took her arm.

"Gotta love Quin." William said, putting on his standard pink helmet and giggling.

"No you don't. That's Alice's duty."

"I suppose you're right. So where are we going?"

"A little forested lake. It's supposed to be a good night for seeing stars." Roslyn gazed up at the sky, fastening her helmet.

"Sounds wild. Let's do it!" William hopped on and wrapped his arms around Roslyn's waist.

Roslyn kicked the bike to life and drove off with William. He smiled this time on the bike, much more at ease.

***

Quincy had run off to the bathroom to fulfill the call of nature and was in the middle of doing so when he heard two other guys enter. He had always harbored a sick little hobby of listening to bathroom conversations, he didn't quite know why he kept on with it, but sometimes he would sit in the bathroom stall much longer than necessary, just to hear the end of a good joke. The jokes were commonly better than the graffiti, but judging from the stall walls, these two guys had a lot to live up to tonight.

"Not a bad show so far, though that chick's guitar skills were weak at best." A loud and gruff sounding guy said, occupying the stall next to Quincy.

"Yeah, she looks like she'd be more at home wielding a Rusty Soup Ladle than an axe." The second guy laughed.

"Well that's remarkably sexist, dumb shit." Quincy said, maybe just a little too loud, because the guys had stopped talking.

Quincy heard a fist pound on the barrier of the bathroom stall.

"What did you say piss pot?" Said the man in the other stall.

Quincy opened up his door, and walked calmly out into the open, causing the man in the stall to follow suit. The man standing at the urinal looked like he was going to enjoy the next few minutes.

Quincy watched as a well fed man exited the stall. His head was shaved and his arms were densely covered with tattoos.

"I said, that comment was remarkably sexist, you dumb shit." Quincy said, standing tall in front of a man obviously stronger than himself.

"You hear that Mick? He thinks your talking was *remarkably sexist.* Little tool, think we oughta show him some real dirty language?"

The big bald man, Mick, looked at Quincy lazily. "Yeah, Trip, I think it's our civic duty to tear him up a little, let him know what happens when he has a potty mouth."

Quincy scoffed, and held up his hands. "All I'm saying, *Mick,*" he said smartly, "Is that you shouldn't talk about her that way. She messed up because of a cord trip, not any other reason."

"Say, aren't you that drummer too? He looks like he is." Mick said.

"Yeah, I think you're right, stupid hair and stupid beats." Trip chuckled menacingly.

"What, was that your little girlfriend out there on that guitar? Wasn't so bad looking, I might have a bit of her myself." Mick goaded.

Quincy's eyes narrowed and he felt his hands clench. "Now you've gone from being a sexist prick to personal insults. I don't think I'm going to stand for that." Quincy's voice rose.

"Oohhooo, he's not gonna stand for it." Trip said.

Mick walked closer to Quincy. "And whatcha gonna do about it, little fairy friend? Why don't you got no makeup like your singer?"

"You guys, are severely stupid." Quincy said, not believing the ignorance of the two men.

Quincy next knew a blast of pain, He felt his jaw crack.

Quincy dealt a kick to Mick's groin and landed a good punch to his nose.

Mick fell backwards, holding onto his nose.as he groaned. "You punk! Think you're getting away with that?" Trip rushed Quincy smashed him on the side of the face with his fist. A jolt of pain dizzied Quincy as his head banged against the concrete wall., He knew he was in trouble, and in a rush of desperation, reached into his back pocket and removed a drumstick. Grabbing the back end, he whacked it over the top of Trip's head. The man howled in pain and grabbed his head. "That'll teach ya!" Quincy said, almost comically, as he turned tail and fled from the restroom.

Alice was at the band table handing a demo CD to a fan.

"Alice! Time to go! Go! Go! Go!" He yelled, and leapt over the table. He grabbed his jacket and the small box they used for tips.

"Quincy...your nose is bleeding, what the hell?" Alice tried to talk, but Quincy yanked on his jacket and picked her up.

"No time to talk babe, gotta go!" He carried her as a newborn and, tossed her into the front seat of the car.

"Buckle up!" Quincy yelled as he slid across his hood and opened his car door.

He screeched out of the parking lot just as Mick & Trip exited the club, searching for him.

As he drove onto the highway, Alice turned to face him.

"What the hell just happened?" she demanded, her face red and eyes looking terrified.

Quincy looked in the rearview, making sure they weren't being tailed. It was a few minutes before he replied, all the while glancing in the mirror, while Alice's looked more peeved that afraid. "Had to deal with two idiots." He took the exit to his house without really thinking about it. They were paused momentarily at a stop light.

"Okay, so why is your face bleeding? What happened to you?"

He ran his fingers through his hair, wanting to turn on the radio but not daring to do so. "I was in the bathroom, these two dicks come in and start saying how you're crap for the guitar, and then they go on to say how you'd be better in a kitchen. So I call them sexist dumbasses and they get a little upset over it."

Alice stared at him. "It's green, keep going. What happened?"

Quincy turned right and headed down the road. "Then they start insulting you personally. Guy swung first and got me, so I got him."

Alice let out a mirthless laugh. "Seems like they got you more than once."

"Well, I took the first guy down, and then his buddy figures he'll mess me up a little more. He got a hit in, and then I treated his head like it was a cymbal." Quincy's head nodded viciously. His hands were tapping against the steering wheel. "Not going to have them talking about you like that. I'm not having it. No ma'am not one bit." His left food was jerking and tapping against the floor.

"Okay, well calm down." She urged him. She put her hand on his leg, and it calmed him some.

"Can I turn on the radio?" he asked.

"No. I'm not done yet."

"Okidoke!" he said, a little louder than he had wanted to. "Sorry, keyed up."

"Yeah."

Quincy pulled into his street and parked the car. "Want to come in?"

"Let's sit out here for a minute, let you calm down. You don't want to go in there like you are now."

Quincy nodded, as he gripped his keys tightly in his hands.

"Give me those." She said, peeling his fingers back from the car key.

He released them, and looked at Alice. "Guys made me nuts."

"I can tell that." She smiled now. "And I think it was just about the sweetest thing ever that you stood up for me like that." She looked at his face. "Is your nose broken or …anything?" She asked uncertainly, not appearing as though she felt safe in touching him.

He squeezed the bridge of his nose with his two index fingers. "Doesn't seem to be, it hurts but not really bad."

"Well, that's good." She frowned. "You do have a fat lip though. It also looks like your eye's going to be a black one." She sighed and shook her head.

"Well, that's great. I look the part of a skeazy rock dude now don't I?" he laughed slightly.

She allowed herself a smile. "Yeah, my skeazy rock dude." She tenderly kissed his head.

He smiled and reached to his change cup, grabbed a couple napkins, and began to wipe the dried blood off his face. "So is this how I get to meet your parents?" Alice asked. "With you all bruised up and bloody?"

"We could probably walk right into my room, and they wouldn't even know. They've not been speaking to me again."

Alice nodded. "Well, come on; let's get your face cleaned up at least. Maybe I can win your parents over." she smiled, and it was enough to calm Quincy down.

"Doubtful." He opened his door and walked with her into his house.

Quincy looked into the silent living room, surprised that his parents weren't there. He walked into the kitchen and saw it empty also. "Want a drink?" he asked, opening the fridge.

"Whatever you're having is fine." Alice said, looking around the kitchen.

"Cool. Fruit punch for both of us then." He poured them a glass and started off towards his room.

"Your family's not very big on pictures, are they?"

Quincy smiled. "I wouldn't say that." Quincy opened his bedroom door, sipping his drink.

"Oh, well at least you've got a few in here. "She said, picking up a picture of herself, Quincy & William.

"My parents don't suppose I'm worth the exposures I guess." Quincy walked to his dresser and pulled out a fresh shirt and pair of pants. "What a night, he said, sitting on his bed.

She sat down next to him and looked at him closely in the light.

"Do you want ice or anything for your jaw?"

"Nah, coulda gotten it downstairs."

"Oh, yeah you're right." She grimaced. "I'd want it. But, I'll let you get changed." She got up and stepped out of the room.

He took off his shoes and wondered how long he'd get to enjoy having his parents out of the house; it was so seldom they went anywhere.

As he took off his shirt, he heard his door creak and he smiled without looking over to it. He instead looked at his mirror and saw a sliver of Alice's face in the doorway. *Wow, I've got my very own voyeur.* He couldn't resist the urge to tease her, so he also shed his pants. *Just like changing in the locker room, only in front of a girl.* He grinned. He stretched dramatically, still wanting to appear as though he was ignorant of her gaze.

He heard a soft click and was enveloped in darkness. He heard soft footsteps on the carpet and then felt her hands on his shoulders.

He leaned his head back and his eyes met hers, reflecting the light of a nearby streetlamp. "You realize how much trouble I'd be in if we got walked in on right now?" he asked, realizing he enjoyed the rush of the risk....

"I'm just going to kiss on you a little, no harm in that is there?"

"I'm not exactly wearing much." He said.

"No different from your bathing suit." She kissed his shoulders.

He let her continue, he wasn't used to anything quite like this, and he had certainly abandoned the locker room mentality.

She kissed his ear and scratched his back. Then, she kissed him long on the lips. "You had better get dressed; I don't want to push my luck."

He wished they could have more time, but he did what was asked of him.

Alice left and returned with a wet towel. He had just his pants and shirt on. She dabbed his face gingerly. "There was still a little blood. It's all gone now. Though I was right about your eye, it's getting dark."

"The clothes make the man. How do I look now?" he asked.

"Aside from the black eye, you look like a million bucks." She grinned knowingly.

Quincy shook his head. "Yeah, I lied about having another crush at the dance. I never did have a thing for Lilia Harcourt." He admitted.

"You think I didn't realize, knowing what I know now? It was all too obvious. Just like when you tried to say it was Rory."

He brought her close to him and kissed her quickly. "I should get you home."

"I thought we were waiting for your parents?" she looked confused.

"Not tonight, Alice; tonight was too good."

"You were in a *fist fight*." She threw her arms up. "How is that good?"

"I defended your honor and got some nice Alice time. I think that constitutes *good*."

She took his hand in hers and he felt light. "I think your meeting my parents tonight might mar the evening, and I don't want that. I have a black eye; they're surely not going to be happy about that. So…right this way. Your wooden chariot awaits."

***

William and Roslyn were sitting under a large sycamore tree watching the heavens. The dark lake in front of them reflected the twinkling canopy of stars. Hours may have passed, but William paid no notice. It was nice sitting in such a picturesque location with his girlfriend.

They had been exchanging stories like the crickets had been exchanging song. "My parents said they'd wanted to give me a brother or sister, they just never got around to it I guess. So I got a lot of attention growing up." William said.

"And they were flower children right?" Roslyn leaned back against William, and he wrapped his arms around her.

"Yeah, they were born in the early fifties, so they were our age during the swing of the swinging sixties." He listed as a frog interrupted the crickets with a loud *ribbit*. "So what about you?"

"I've got a younger brother, Eli," She looked straight ahead. "My Mom raises Eli & I." she exhaled in a low whistle. "My Dad's outta the picture."

"Oh." He looked out at the lake and ran his hands up her arms. "So what does that mean?"

Roslyn's tone was as cool as the night air. "He's done a lot of drugs, and kept making us pay for it. We sometimes, I mean, my Mom and him would argue. They'd think we were asleep." She elaborated, her hands making a rolling motion "She'd accuse him of taking money that was meant for our clothes and things for my brother and me."

"That's so dishonest." William frowned, leaning his head on her shoulders.

"Yeah, well, just one of his many great characteristics." She snorted. "I don't... care so much anymore. He's gone and I'm grown up. I just wish Eli would have had a better male influence. He's a good kid, but imagine being told how to shave by your Mom."

"I love how open you are. I mean, Alice and I never talked like this." He confessed.

"Not quite sure why you dated her, even." She shrugged. "All that aside though, I think I can trust you with things, Willy Nilly. You're quite the guy."

He grinned at the name. "Well, so are you." He patted her shoulders.

She got up and knelt in front of him, holding out an accusatory finger. "That is *not* even cute!" she waved her finger, though he could see her starting to grin.

"I'm only kidding." He also knelt now, holding her hands in his. "Don't take it seriously."

"You know how few people know about that, and yet I told you in under a week." She smiled.

William loved the way her wavy hair had just fallen across her face, and he kissed her nose. "I'd share anything with you, even my Star Wars figures."

She burst out laughing. "Is that a joke?"

William just shook his head. "It's nothing, just me being goofy."

"Of course." She rose off her knees and helped him get up also.

"Thanks!"

"Thank you for the wonderful night, William." She said, kissing him on his Chipper Charcoal lips.

"Is that the date ending?" he asked a moment later.

"Eli's got a quiz in French tomorrow and I promised to help him with it."

"Didn't know you spoke French."

"Oui, allez viens." She said angelically.

"Ooh, what's that mean?"

She smiled. "Means we're going for a ride." She motioned him with her hand. "Come on."

Arm in arm they strolled back to Roslyn's bike in the dirt lot.

***

Quincy walked back into his house after dropping Alice off at her parents. He heard the TV blaring as usual. He had wanted to bring in the band gear. Therefore, he walked as quietly as he could past the doorway leading into the living room. He had the basement door in sight when he heard his father.

"Quincy, I'd like to see you."

Quincy looked up at the ceiling with his hands up, wondering why him.

"Yeah." Quincy said, turning around into the living room, thinking, the only time I *don't* want attention. He walked in and tried to stick to the darker portion of the room. "What's going on?" he asked.

"Step into the light." His father said.

Quincy looked to his mother who looked somber as his father stood up.

"Found this," Bradley Abrams said, holding up a cloth with red stains, "in your room."

Quincy was stunned. "You went into my room?"

"Your eye is black, there's a bloody rag in your bedroom." Daniel tossed the rag to him. "What are you doing, and why are you doing it?" Daniel took his seat again, propping his feet up.

"You don't seem happy, Quincy." Denise Abrams said, which caused Quincy to laugh despite the look his father was giving him.

"I'm unhappy?" Quincy tossed his hair back with a jerk of his head. "This is probably the happiest I've been since moving here."

"You were obviously in a fight, and you say you're happy?" she frowned.

"Happy as a bird in a bread shop." Quincy employed one of William's phrases.

Bradley shook his head. "A fight and sexual immorality, all in one week. You're really testing me."

"Oh come on! Alice & I aren't sexually immoral. But yeah, I was in a fight and I held my ground."

"*Why* were you fighting?" Daniel leaned forward.

William wondered if honesty was always the best policy. "I confronted two sexist dumbasses in the bathroom. It was exciting." Quincy said in a dull fashion.

Denise looked surprised, but Bradley grew red. "What did they say to make you so aggressive?"

"Said Alice was better suited in a kitchen than on a stage." Quincy said. His voice was still thick with anger over the situation.

Bradley bit his lip and nodded. "This isn't a good way to show me you're old enough for a girlfriend. I knew that band would come to trouble. All those *rock stars* end up dead by thirty or strung out on drugs. Is that where you're headed?"

"Oh yeah. I'm big on the heroin scene, remember? I tried telling you a few months ago while you were glued to Lizard Man." He rolled his eyes.

"You clean up your life Quincy. I'm just about through with this *rebellion* of yours."

Quincy laughed. "Ohhhkay Dad. Thanks for the heart to heart."

Quincy made to leave, but Bradley grabbed his arm.

"Dammit Quincy! You are my son and you will respect me!"

Quincy broke free, his blood rushed through him and he was aware of all the anger he felt. "Get off!" Quincy rubbed his arm. "I'm going to my room now, kindly excuse me. I've had a very long day."

Quincy started to walk up the stairs to his room when he heard his father yell.

"You have an eight o' clock curfew! Excused only by work!"

Quincy stopped mid-flight and looked at his father. Both men were silent. Quincy looked at his mother who had a single glistening tear sliding down her face. He paused, and looked back at his father before mounting the stairs again.

***

William waved bye to his mother as he saw Quincy pull up. "Have a safe weekend William!" Carol Denslie called from the screen door.

William put his gym bag full of garb and his sword into Quincy's back seat and then took shotgun.

"Thanks for the ride on short notice Quin. Ros sends her thanks. Ready for some excitement?"

"Got all the excitement I needed last night after at the Lipstick Trace *after party*." Quincy said sarcastically as his eyes met William's.

"After party? Oh wow, you got a shiner." William leaned in. "Looks bad, why did Alice punch ya?"

Quincy gave him a searching gaze. "Please." He shook his head. "Got this from two dudes making fun of Alice."

"Aww, you were her medicine woman in shining scrubs!" William beamed.

"You want this ride to Roslyn's place or not?"

"Oh I do! I do! I'm gonna meet her Mom today." William said proudly. "Maybe her brother too."

"Oh, yeah. That's right dude. I didn't tell you the best part about last night." Quincy turned up *Back in Black*.

"Ooh, did Alice kiss you?" William sat on his hands, swaying excitedly from side to side as Quincy drove on.

"Well, yeah." Quincy smiled and looked at Will. "She did do that."

"That's fantastic! Is there more to the story?"

"Of course, my stories are rarely short."

"Did we sell more demos? Oh oh oh! Did we sell a T-shirt?"

"You wanna hear this story?" Quincy killed the radio.

"Silent as the gravy." William zipped his lips.

Quincy scrunched up his face. "Anyway. Your madness aside, my parents think that I'm on a highway to hell."

"No, this is the way to Roslyn's." William said quietly.

"They think Alice & me are engaging in immoral sexual activity and are convinced that all three of us are going to be dead or strung out before were thirty."

"Huh." William blinked.

"Yeah. Wrong thinking there. Oh…also, I have an 8PM curfew, isn't that precious?"

"I don't get it. You haven't done anything worth that."

Quincy nodded. "Apparently sound reasoning dilutes with age."

"They'll cool down maybe, I could come over and try to well…I don't know." William offered.

"Nah, don't want you getting too involved in it."
"Okay. Well, anyway. We're supposed to merge here." William motioned to the right.

They drove on for a short while, the silence stretched on at sixty miles an hour. William wished there was something he could do. Finally, a thought popped into his head. "Hey! Stay the night at my house! That'll brighten up your day…sometime…next week." William frowned. "It sounded like a good idea in my head."

"Eight o' Clock curfew. Though you could probably stay at my house, and if not, I'll just sneak you in. Easy enough."

William winked at himself in the side mirror. "Yeah, that'll work. We got stuff to talk about."

"We got the time now, what's eatin' ya?"

"Nothing is eatin' me. It's just so cool, or it's been cool these last couple weeks. We've both got awesome girlfriends." William remembered Roslyn's kind face and sighed happily. "Roslyn's such a great girl." He smiled. "So totally rad and different from any other girl I've dated." He said whimsically.

Quincy snorted. "So how's she different from Alice?"

"I'm not trying to say Alice was lame, I'm just saying we've shared so much already, and she's fun, and pretty, and interesting! She's like you! Only a chick!" William furrowed his brow and paused. "Yeah….a chick."

Quincy took his eyes off the road for a second and slowed. "You don't sound sure."

"Well…its'…she's a chick. Just…well, she's got AIS."

Quincy held up his hand. "I don't know what that means…?"

William nodded. "Right, well, I know you bombed Anatomy, but this'll hopefully make sense. Um, AIS is a…a thing where you're all female on the outside and stuff, but you have dude chromosomes."

"That's…pretty messed up man."

"Nah." William waved the comment away like a fly. "It's cool as can be. She doesn't have periods, or acne, and she smells super good all the time."

"That last part comes because of AIS?"

"Dunno! Can't be a bad thing though!"

"Well, sounds pretty cool then, I take it back. She got girl parts?" Quincy smiled mischievously.

"Yeah, everything exterior, nothing interior I think."

"You confirmed that?"

William looked at Quin seriously. "No, I have not engaged in sexually immoral entertainment." William held his head high. "Stuff like that is your turf." He grinned.

"Oh ho! That is a low blow!" he laughed. "Might have to get you back on that one."

"You gonna hide my shoe laces again? Cuz you know I have no problems being barefoot."

Quincy shook his head and grinned. "Don't you worry about it."

William grabbed the stub of his ponytail. "Dude! This is our exit!"

"Alright, jeesh, I'm moving, I'm moving."

Quincy pulled into Roslyn's driveway and stepped out of the car, and William rushed out, his bag slung around his shoulders.

Roslyn walked out to meet them, and she ran over to William.

"Good morning." She said, kissing him lightly.

"Hiya Roslyn." William returned the kiss.

"Jeez.... there's too much sweetness going on here." Quincy said.

"Aw, do you want to kiss William too Quincy?" Roslyn asked, moving William to face his friend.

William looked like he had just been sucker punched. "Um, that's cool, but no. I don't think Alice would approve."

"Nah thanks, I'm not into kissing guys. William apparently is, but I'm not." Quincy grinned.

Roslyn's smile momentarily broke. She eyed William, and then turned her focus back to Quincy. Roslyn pushed hair from her face and let William go. "Yeah, I also noticed how he said 'Alice wouldn't approve,' instead of saying something like "Eww...yucky, I don't kiss dudes." Roslyn's voice had gone high, and her hands were on her hips.

"I could be perfectly capable of kissing Quincy if I so chose, but I have you." He nodded.

Quincy smirked. "Good seeing you again Roslyn, I'm going to head back. You two have fun today."

Roslyn waved him away. "Go, go."

"He's going." William shrugged.

William took her hand and walked with her inside.

"How was the drive up? Did you two talk a lot?" Roslyn asked, closing the door behind her.

William shifted his bag from his shoulder and sat it down by the door. "Um, we talked a little yeah."

Roslyn nodded. "Well, my Mom is in this way. Eli's not home. Come on, I'll introduce you."

As William walked through the house he marveled at how hip everything looked. He saw pictures of David Bowie, Roxette, and his jaw dropped as they turned from the hallway and into the kitchen. In the pass through was a picture of Boy George with his arm around a woman slightly resembling Roslyn.

"Wow!" William froze and looked up at the picture. "Are you for real?"

Roslyn laughed. "Close your mouth Willy, you're starting to drool."

"That's Boy George...and is that your Mom?"

"Yes it is, I met Georgie at one of his after parties."

William turned to see the woman from the picture walking out into the kitchen. "I'm Joelle, you must be the boy whose run off with my daughter's heart." She extended her hand, and William didn't feel worthy to shake it.

"You're wow. You've met him." William couldn't seem to make his tongue work.

"Your boy seems a bit slow of speech today; you didn't tell me you were dating Moses."

Roslyn shook her head and patted William's shoulders. "He loves the glam rock. He also loves makeup. Don'tcha heartthrob?"

"Oh I do." He nodded his head. "I'm William, William Denslie. And it's great to be meeting you."

"Roslyn tells me you've got a band. Do you? A band of ruffians?" she laughed, and sat down on a barstool.

"Aw that's just Quincy, he got into a fight the other night. Nothing big though, he just got a black eye."

"Well that's good, ain't much of a show unless there's a scrap." Joelle looked to her daughter. "You going to be taking him up to fair with you?"

"That's the plan." Roslyn scratched William's back.

"Well, you two ride safely; don't be afraid to hold onto her William."

"Okay." William blushed.

Roslyn took William's hand. "Time to go, I'll be home Sunday night Mom."

"Alright dear. Take care William, nice to meet you." Joelle got up and began to sort dishes.

The ride to the Renaissance fair didn't seem to take long today, maybe because William was holding onto his favorite girl, or maybe it was because Roslyn had been speeding.

Roslyn hopped off the bike and reached into her saddlebags to get her change of clothes.

William put his pink helmet onto the handlebars of the bike and rushed to catch up to Roslyn. "So, what do we have going on this weekend? Isn't it supposed to be Thieves Guild theme?"

"Yeah, it is. People might try to pick pocket your nuts this weekend, might want to look after them."

"Oh I will, nobody but honest payers will touch them."

"You're so easy." She rolled her eyes.

"Aww that's not how I meant it, I'm not a boy toy."

"That sounds like it could be a good song for your band."

William had to agree. "I think you're right, I could start writing it tonight before the bonfire."

"I'm gonna get changed. Don't miss me too much." She walked away, and William supposed it was time for him to get ready.

William came out of the bathroom he had recently occupied and felt the sun pelting down on him.

"I think it's time to buy a hat." He walked to the women's restrooms and yelled in. "Hey! Roslyn, you still in there?"

No reply came from the forbidden realm. "Hmm. Must have gone on without me. Ah well, I'll find a hat and meet up with her."

He felt his change purse jangling at his side. He started dancing with the coins.

He saw a woman with an open shop and knew this was the place. "Hail my lady. I am in need of a grand hat! It must have a feather. Those are my requirements, what have ye?"

"Look over there, got plenty." She said, almost bored.

William tried on a few different hats, some pointy and some that were simply ludicrous. He finally decided on a tan colored one with a large black feather. "How much do I owe thee?"

"Twenty-five." The merchant said.

William shrugged and opened his purse. "Here ya go! Thanks!"

He danced off, watching his shadow with its' crazy feather shape. "I love it!"

William wondered where Roslyn had gone, he had walked the fairgrounds twice now, and still there was no sign of her. He walked over to the tent grounds and laid his belongings inside it.

***

The day passed by, and around dinner time the flap to his tent parted. William had been lying on his cot reading a book. He got up and put his glasses onto a small table he'd brought along. "Roslyn!" He waved her into the tent.

"Hi Will." She said.

"Sit down with me, I'd wondered where you'd gone to earlier, I couldn't find you."

She was wearing a purple top and a velvety looking skirt. William stared unashamedly. "I was off in the woods, taking a walk." She sat next to him.

"Could have asked me to come with you, the woods can be dangerous for an unarmed gypsy like yourself."

Roslyn wasn't smiling, and it sent a chill down William.

"What's wrong?" he asked, silliness abandoning him.

Roslyn frowned, and William could see her damp eyes, only now did he notice the redness. "What did Quincy mean earlier?"

William furrowed his brow. "I don't understand."

"'William is apparently into kissing guys.'" She looked him full in the face now. "What did he mean by *that*."

William hadn't caught it when Quincy said it, but now that chill was all over him. He realized in a second the hidden meaning behind that comment. "Oh."

Roslyn raised her eyebrows. "Yeah. Did you tell him about my AIS?"

He looked at Roslyn, and felt the words catch in his throat. "I did." He felt that this wouldn't be good. He hadn't meant to let it slip out.

"I'm sure Quin didn't mean it in a mean way." William tried to smile, but Roslyn's hurt face wiped his face clean.

"Do you know why I don't tell people?"

This feeling was unlike any he had known, the guilt permeated him, and he began to feel sick. "Roslyn, I didn't mean to let Quincy know, I really didn't."

"I don't tell people because of comments like those. It hurts William."

"I'm sorry, I shouldn't have said anything, but it was kind of an accident."

"You made that joke last night, and at the time I thought it was cute, but now I see that it made you think it was okay to joke like that." She shook her head. "I suppose I'm partially to blame, but it's still on you, William. I had trusted you with that information."

"I know you did, I know! I felt special that you had come to trust me like that, it made me feel good."

"Well, I don't think I'll be capable of trusting you for a while."

He tried to wipe a tear away from her cheek, and it nearly made break when she pulled away.

"Roslyn…" he frowned, kneeling close to her, "don't get upset please. I really am sorry."

"It's too late, I'm already upset."

He knew it was true, one look at her and he felt his heart breaking. "Okay okay, Quincy knows, but I'll just tell him not to bring that sorta joke up again. He doesn't think sometimes; he doesn't mean any harm."

"*You* don't seem to think sometimes either. That I had told you about my AIS and my secrecy about it not even a week ago, and then your best friend knows about it. That he would just so nonchalantly joke on it makes me deeply upset. Is he going to go around joking like that in front of everyone? Believe it or not, I don't want everyone knowing my business like that."

"Okay, well, just …I won't say anything again. I promise."

William's stomach was somersaulting. He could barely stop from shaking; he didn't like how this felt.

Roslyn shook her head. "I'm sorry. I can't look at you right now and say 'okay, that'll be fine' because I don't know if you're the guy I thought you were. You seemed to realize how important that was to me. So, I'm going to go now, and I'd appreciate you giving me some time."

William felt as though he had been hit by a train, and as he watched Roslyn leave his tent he felt as though he would never be well again.

***

The clouds rolled in on Saturday morning, and William awoke to the sound of the *drip drip drip* on his tent. He rolled over and looked at his small portable clock. It was nine a.m., and he remembered with what sorrow he had gone to sleep.

"I've gotta do something, gotta buck up! That's what I should do." He put on his old hat, not wanting to get his new one ruined in the rain, and left the tent.

William sloshed through the mud outside his tent, and stopped by his boss's office to pick up his ration of nuts. With his satchel heavy and heart full of hope, he walked the grounds of the fair. William approached a fair skinned girl selling flowers. She had daisies in her blonde locks and a generous bouquet held in her hands.

"My Lady, I am in need of your services. Might ye run a red rose to the Gypsy's Ocarina stand? For trade I shall give thee a bag of nuts, complimentary, like." He held out a bag of sugar coated almonds.

"I can do that." The girl took the nuts and made off towards the front of the fair, she unknowingly carried William's hopes with her.

He spent the day trying to catch glimpses of Roslyn. He would tell himself to go see her, but a new type of fear had taken hold of his heart. She had said she wanted time, and he just didn't know what that meant.

As the clouds finally parted and the day became warmer, William thought it might be time to try his luck. He walked past Roslyn's stand, wearing a tentative smile which was ready to morph into a full grin the moment he felt it was safe.

Roslyn looked up from her Ocarina she was painting, and saw him. She looked away and started painting again with a frown on her face.

William couldn't take it, he just had to try. "Roslyn. Oh Roslyn." He said, walking over to her stand, hands held out in open surrender. "This is driving me nuts, it really is. What can I do to make it better?"

"You can leave, I asked you for time, and you've not been giving it to me. Sending flowers isn't going to make this better. Neither is stalking me all day."

William's hopes crashed like waves against rocks, and he sulked off, suddenly not feeling up to selling nuts anymore that day.

He retreated into his tent and sat his satchel down. Sitting crossed legged, he took his rapier off, and laid it next to his satchel of nuts. He ripped open a pack of them and started eating; they gave him a little ray of happiness in the day. He didn't stop after the first one was empty.

At every fluttering of his tent flap he looked up hopeful, anticipating that Roslyn's beautiful face would peek in and he would find happiness again. Each time, he was disappointed.

William couldn't remember a time when he felt sadder, and it felt so wrong. Renaissance Fair was supposed to be one of the happiest places on Earth.

He zipped up the front of his tent, no longer wanting to suffer the disappointment. He went to bed early that night, and when the morning came he felt no better. He packed up his belongings and walked to the gate where fantasy met the real world.

He looked to see if Roslyn was at her stand, and he saw it completely empty, save for a sign saying "Closed for Sunday." William took out his cell phone and waited for Quincy to answer.

"Hello." Quincy sounded sleepy.

"Quin, can you come get me please." William asked, tracing lines in the dust surrounding the payphone.

Quincy took a moment to respond. "Yeah, of course." The line was silent. "You okay man?"

William looked over to Roslyn's stand again, before he felt tears start to trickle down his cheeks. "No, dude, just hurry please." William said, hanging up the phone. He looked out at Roslyn's usual parking spot and saw it vacant.

***

Quincy walked out to the porch to check the mail on Wednesday morning, and was surprised to see a small package with his name on it. It smelled of perfume and he immediately thought of Alice. He rushed back up the stairs into his room, ignoring his father's demands to slow down, and tore the package open.

Inside the parcel were chocolates, and Quincy punched the air. "Yeah!" He shouted. He opened a chocolate and began to eat one happily. He remembered his first date with Alice, the drive in; and wondered if she had purposely purchased this gift over all the others. He would have to remember to buy her something thoughtful too, maybe a good movie, instead of a lame drive in one.

He heard the phone ring, and his excitement mounted. *Alice!* He thought, and jumped over his bed to pick up the cordless. "Hello?" he answered.

"Quin. It's me. What rhymes with forlorn?"

"Denslie?" Quincy didn't recognize the sniffly voice coming through.

"Who else? Donut man?" William responded.

Quincy flashed back to an earlier time and felt odd. "Why do you want to have a rhyme to forlorn?"

"I'm writing a new song. It's called *I'm a broken Boy Toy.*"

Quincy sighed. "Are you still not talking to Roslyn?"

William whimpered. "I tried calling her again yesterday. That'll make the eighth call."

"Dude, one day soon here you really need to tell me what you did to make her so mad." Quincy said.

William didn't respond, and Quincy had to wonder if he had killed the phone. "Dude? You there? William?"

"I'm here. I just don't want you to worry about things man. Maybe torn is a good rhyme."

"Dude, I am not performing a sappy breakup song."

"Of course you don't want to, you and Alice are madly in love, I daresay you are exchanging gifts and saliva on a frequent basis. Oh Quincy, love is a tempest tossed sort of agony. Enjoy affection while you can my friend."

Quincy rolled his eyes. "Jesus man, do I need to put you on suicide watch?"

William exhaled. "No, you don't dude. I'm sorry to worry you."

Quincy felt badly for William, and couldn't think of anything he could do. "Dude, it'll get better. I think Roslyn's crazy for you."

"She might have been, had I not been such a fool."
"A fool? You? Never. You're a pirate! Remember?
William Denslayer? Scourge of the Seven Seas?" Quincy
smiled.

"No, I'm just a horrible person. I can't understand
why you like or trust me Quincy, I may one day break your
heart just as I did Roslyn's." He sighed.

"What did you do? Tell me now, or stop this
melodrama dude, I could walk downstairs if I wanted some
of that nonsense."

William sounded hesitant. "Well, I'm gonna tell
you, but only because I've got to tell someone. I hate that it
has to be you, but who else am I gonna talk to."

"Could try Alice." He suggested.

"No, not about this. I don't want to."

"Well, out with it then." Quincy urged him.

"I told you about Roslyn's AIS. Then you made a
comment about it to her."

"Were you not supposed to say anything?" Quincy
put down his chocolates, suddenly feeling nervous.

"No, I wasn't supposed to say anything. That's why
she's mad, she doesn't know if she can trust me again."

Quincy looked at his picture of the three of them,
and he felt guilty. "It's my fault then, the reason you're so
sad. Damn dude, I'm sorry."

"I don't want you to beat yourself up over it pal, I
messed up. I've got to fix it." William said.

"You tried sending her flowers?" Quincy suggested.

"Doesn't want flowers. Tried it at Ren Fair. No way
Jose."

"You tried going up to her house?"

"I took a bus the other day, she wouldn't answer the
door."

"God." Quincy felt like he had stolen Christmas.
"Let me know what I can do to help man."

"Think of a good rhyme for forlorn?" William asked weakly.

"Anything you need Will."

Quincy hung up the phone and sat on his bed, never remembering a time where he had felt so low.

***

Roslyn had been missing Will these last few days, and early Wednesday afternoon she began to really think about whether she had been overly harsh with him. The flower Will had sent her last Saturday was on her desk looking as lonely as she felt.

Her phone began to ring again and the ID showed as Denslie. She went so far as to place her hand on the phone and was about to pick up when her door opened.

Eli was standing there looking peeved. "Ross, if you're going to play hard to get can you at least put the phone on silent? I promise, he won't know the difference."

The phone stopped ringing and Roslyn nodded, turning it to silent. "I'm sorry Eli; it's bothering you isn't it?"

He shook his head from side to side. "What's getting to me is you. One minute you're okay, the next you're in here crying. Mom's even getting worried about you."

Roslyn walked over to her chair and sat down. "I'm going to be fine, I promise."

"Do you realize how much happier you were when you were with the guy?" Eli walked into her room, his lanky arms swinging at his side.

"He made a mistake, he violated my trust Eli."

"And you don't think I ever did anything to violate your trust? You still like me."

"Well I don't have much of a choice but to love you, you're so silly and pitiful." She smiled briefly, her brother was a trip.

"Come on, I've never met the guy, but isn't four days long enough for him to suffer? He's not Dad, Roslyn; I don't think he meant to hurt you like that."

Roslyn was truly thankful that Eli was so insightful; he seemed to always know how to put things into perspective. "Alright, little brother; I'll give him a break. Next time he calls I'll answer."

"I'm glad for that. I'll be just down the hall if you need to talk."

She nodded and looked out her window. "I did leave him without saying goodbye, which was just a little bit harsh." Roslyn bit her lip and tried dialing William's number. She felt that maybe it was a sign when it returned a busy signal. Disappointed, she hung up.

***

Quincy heard his phone ring at a quarter to eight on Wednesday night. "Hello?"

"I'm at the backdoor, let me in."

At hearing Alice's voice, he felt a surge of excitement. He knew sneaking her in was definitely off limits, but still, he crept on silently, becoming one with the wall as he slid to the basement and let her in. She had her hair back in a ponytail and was wearing a cute camouflage top and shorts. "Mission accomplished, Sir." She said, kissing him quickly.

"What are you doing here?" he laughed.

"We'll talk in your room; this basement is no man's land." She let him lead her up the stairs.

Once they were safely inside Quincy's locked room Quincy felt safe. He turned on the music so their conversation wouldn't be heard.

"Aren't you the little rogue agent." He said, admiring the camouflage outfit she was wearing.

"It was a dangerous mission, but I had to accept it. I had to see you." She was glowing.

"I'm glad you're here." He said, drawing her in for a kiss.

They stretched out on his bed and whispered as the sun went down.

"So Will & Roslyn are really having problems then?" Alice asked after a lull in conversation.

Quincy felt like he could fall asleep with her right next to him. He stirred and nodded. "Yeah. He said things to me that he had been told in confidence."

"That's a shame, they're so cute together." She said.

"Not nearly as cute as you." He said.

"I love my Quinnie, even with your lame come ons."

He smiled. "When do we need to sneak you out of here?"

She wrapped her arms around him. "My parents are under the impression I'm spending the night at a friend's house, I neglected to mention the friend was you." She grinned mischievously.

"It's a good thing my parents don't tuck me in." He smiled. "This is kind of exciting isn't it?"

"I thought it would be. Will your parents work in the morning?"

"Both out by nine."

"So I'll get plenty of time with you. Good." She laid her head on his chest.

"We're so doomed if we get busted." Quincy shook his head.

"You worry too much."

"I don't worry enough." He sighed, stroking her hair.

"Okay, what's wrong?"

He grimaced. "I messed up really bad; I'm responsible for Will & Roslyn's argument."

He explained everything carefully to Alice, who listened silently. "And then I said '*Apparently Will doesn't have a problem kissing guys*'."

"Wow." Alice leaned against his headboard. "That sounds pretty bad."

"I know. I really wish I hadn't said it."

"You realize by telling me you might have just made it worse?"

Quincy nodded. "Who else was I going to go to with something this serious?"

Alice kissed him. "Stop worrying for just tonight. I'll figure out what to do with William."

"But it's just *so* important." Quincy ran his hand through his hair.

"Well so am I, treat me like it." She frowned. "I snuck over here for us Quin. I missed you."

"Of course," he nodded. "You're right, and I'm sorry I shouldn't have…"

"Don't be sorry, just hold me tonight." She snuggled into him and he felt happy for the first time since he'd talked to William."

***

The next morning William was sitting in a pile of crumbled papers; pens were hanging out behind each of his ears. He heard a knock on his door and his first hope was that it could be Roslyn. His first thought was soon proven incorrect. He was seriously surprised when Alice walked into his bedroom.

"Your Mom let me in." she said, answering the unspoken question in his mind.

"Oh." He nodded sadly, shrugging his shoulders and clearing a spot for her to sit next to him. "Sorry it's so cluttered, I've been writing a new song." He sniffled and hoped his empty tissue box wouldn't lead to questions. "You wanna hear it? It's great." His voice cracked.

She sat cross legged across from him. "No Will, I'm not here for that."

He nodded and pointed at her clothes. "You special agent today Miss Green Beret?" He rhymed out of habit.

She frowned. "William, you look like a wreck." She put a hand on his knee.

"Oh no, I'm cool." He flashed back to a memory of a happier time. *Who says cool anymore?*

"I seriously doubt that."

He sighed. "I made Roslyn really mad." His throat felt dry, and he couldn't quite remember when he'd last drank something. "I've just been sitting here trying to figure out how to make it better." He held up his fingers and counted off. "I tried sending flowers. I tried apologizing. I called her over and over. Nothing I've done has made any difference. She won't return my calls."

"Last night Quincy told me the story, and I'm sorry you're hurting." She inclined her head.

William's jaw dropped and his hands went to the ceiling. "He told you!? Oh no! Oh no!" he shook his head from side to side. "That might make it worse, oh man, oh man, why?" he held his head in his hands.

"Do you want to know what I think would help the most?" Alice lifted his head up and looked into his eyes.

"I don't think comfort food will do the trick Alice. Do you know that I ate a whole satchel of sugar coated almonds last Saturday?"

Alice shook her head. "William, William. What am I going to do with you?" She scooted over and gave him a hug.

He was glad Alice was here trying to help him; he hadn't had much contact with anyone in a few days. "What do you think will help? Please tell me, Maharishi Mendell."

"There's some of that silliness." She smiled appreciatively. "What I think is this: It's great that you and Quincy are so close. It's wonderful that you and he can share everything. Nothing is more important to a relationship than intimacy. But, Will, you didn't respect Roslyn's trust. There are things that you need to keep from Quincy sometimes for both of you to have a normal relationship. To put it bluntly, you either want to be with Roslyn, or my boyfriend."

William only now saw the jealousy in Alice's eyes, and he was responsible for it. "Oh Alice, I'm so sorry. Really, I am. How can I help, I want to make it better?"

"It's not only you doing it, Quincy is also upset over how badly he screwed you that he's barely been paying attention to me."

"I didn't realize how much this was affecting you both." He sucked his bottom lip. "It rains on the whole town though, doesn't it?"

She nodded. "I want to be happy, and I want you and Roslyn to be as well."

"I need to figure things out then, I guess." William scratched his head.

"Stop thinking William. If you want her, you need to go for it. She won't wait forever. Don't do a clever presentation, don't get crazy dolled up, just go for her." She got up. "Quincy and I are both here for you, but remember what I said."

He got up and hugged her. "You're both the greatest friends I've ever had. Thanks for the advice, and really, I will sort this out. I just need to know what I feel first."

"Do you love her?" Alice put her hands on his shoulders and stared into his eyes. She waited for him to respond.

He couldn't hold her stare any longer.

"If you love her William then don't let her just go like this."

"I've never been really in love before Alice, I don't know if I am now."

"Well you know what you need to figure out then."
She kissed his cheek. "Call if you need us." Alice said as
she took her leave. Though Alice was gone her questions
lingered in the air like her perfume. William decided it was
time for a drink.

***

Quincy was awoken by a shifting in his bed and a pair of
curious eyes stared at him. "Morning Quin." Alice said.

Quincy blinked several times to get the sleep from
his eyes. "You know; I usually have a thing with people
being so close to me when I'm just waking up." He touched
her cheek. "Not with you however."

Alice touched her nose to his. "That shows promise
for us then."

"How long have you been awake?" He asked as he
got up and wondered the best way to go about changing
clothes.

"About two hours, I waited for your parents to leave
and I walked over to Will's. Figured it was about time I
gave him some female advice."

Quin took his clothes back to his bed and clumsily
changed under the covers. Alice giggled, her laughter
filling the room. "Where did you learn that maneuver?"

"Summer camp. All the cool kids were doing it."
He shrugged and tossed his old shorts her way.

"Afraid to get changed in front of me are you?" she
teased him, trying to lift the blankets.

"No! Stop that!" he laughed and held firmly to his
end of the covers.

"Oh you're nothing but a bore Quincy Abrams!"
she waved him off.

"Okay, I'll be exciting." He said passionately.
"Let's play chicken or brave." He grinned. "You game?"
"What's that?" she asked, her eyes narrowed.

"Another great summer camp game."

"Doesn't tell me anything."

"We start off fully clothed. I ask you if you're chicken, or if you're brave. If you're brave, you remove a piece of clothing. If you're chicken, you skip a turn. Skip twice, and you lose."

"So basically, we end up with our clothes off or we lose? I've got you beat." She smirked, looking defiant.

"And William called you repressed."

She raised her eyebrows and sneered. "When, and why?"

"Stop stalling. Chicken or brave?" he asked.

"Brave. I hope you feel so too." She ripped the covers away from him. After the blanket was on the floor she unlaced her shoes. She carefully placed them around his neck and chuckled. "Your turn, chicken or brave?"

"Shoes really shouldn't count, but whatever." He said as he removed the shirt he had just put on. "Chicken or brave Allie?"

"Brave." She smiled.

Quincy watched with eyes wide as Alice lifted her camouflage shirt over her head. Once it was free of her ponytail she tossed it at him. It covered his face and he could no longer see. The trance was broken by the darkness, and he began n to feel unease set in.

Alice remained in her bra and shorts. "Chicken or brave, Quin?" She seemed victorious as Quincy fought to form words.

"You're beautiful Alice."

She tapped her hands against her knees. "Now who's stalling?"

Quincy knew what he wanted to do, but he didn't feel this was the right time for it. He stared at Alice unashamedly and it took all his will to make the right choice. "Alice, I love you, but this can't happen here. It was stupid of me to suggest this."

Quincy's door swung open and the two teens spun around to see Bradley Abrams standing in the doorway.

Quincy felt his heart plummet and he was only able to throw Alice her shirt back.

Bradley was red faced and his eyes narrow slits. "Both of you get decent. I want you gone." He said pointing to each of them. Alice stammered while she put her shirt on hastily, and Quincy watched as she left the room quickly.

Bradley remained in the doorway, silent and solemn.

Quincy's mouth was dry, and he found it funny that his hands were so moist. He waited for the explosion that was sure to come. He waited and waited, as his father's eyes burned a hole through him. Finally, he could stand no more.

"It wasn't what it looked like, I promise." Quincy sounded timid, and he hated it.

"What type of fool do you take me for?"

"Listen, I know I say a lot of stupid crap that isn't true, but I give you my *word*, nothing was going to happen."

"Your *word* means nothing. You have gone behind my back and God alone knows what else you've done."

"Dad, please. I was just about to…" Quincy felt hot behind his eyes.

"I could tell what you were about to do, were it not for the call of a concerned neighbor you'd have gotten away with it too."

"I know how this must have looked, honestly though, Alice & I—"

"I don't care what you and that little harlot were about to do. You are out of the house." Bradley gripped the doorknob so hard it made his knuckles white. "You've got half an hour, get your shit, and get out. Or I'm calling the cops on you for trespassing." Bradley slammed the door behind him and left his son on the verge of tears.

Quincy sat in his bed in disbelief, heart stinging from the injustice of it all. He moved in a daze as he walked around his room. It slowly sank in that he was no longer welcome within these walls. The thought of his expulsion seemed both liberating and heartbreaking. He grabbed his binder, his CD's and his hamper full of clean clothes.

He couldn't hold back the tears as he picked up his photo of his two best friends. Quincy was grateful the band gear was still in Woody, it would save him a breaking and entering charge. *Trespassing! What a joke!*

Quincy hauled his hamper and backpack down the stairs, where Bradley waited for him with his hand outstretched. "You may have your key back if you ever choose to follow our rules."

Quincy shook his head and passed his key to his father. "You don't even have a clue who I am, and that's what's so tragic." Quincy said as he turned away from his father and into the cool air of a world less angry.

Quincy placed his stuff in Woody and laid his head against the steering wheel. He reached into his pocket and pulled out his phone. He hit the number two and waited.

"This is William."

"Dude, I'm coming over, I need help." Quincy shook and couldn't stop his voice from doing the same.

"I'll be here man; you don't sound too good."

"I've been better."

***

Quincy arrived at William's house and walked up to the porch where William was waiting. He sat down next to him and shook his head. He didn't quite know how to tell the story, it seemed so awful. "Dude, things got really messed up just now."

William took a pen from behind his ear and started rolling it between his hands. "Tell me about it."

"Guess things have been bad for both of us." Quincy sighed. "That's karma I suppose."

"No." William cleared his throat. "I mean, tell me about it. What happened?"

Quincy let out a single laugh. "Right. Well." Quincy wondered how best to go about phrasing all of it. "I'll just be open on it man, I'm not gonna hide anything from you."

"I appreciate that; it usually helps me to get a full idea of what's happened." William rubbed his nose; Quincy saw it was a little red just like his eyes.

"My Dad walked in on Alice & me." Quincy looked over to William, and hoped that William wasn't going to smack him.

"Sex*ual* imm*orality.*" William enunciated distinctively.

Quincy frowned. "We were playing chicken or brave."

William weakly held a finger up in the air. "That is a fun camp game."

"Yeah. Well…wait…didn't know you went to camp."

"4-H! Duh Quin! I told you this." William shook his hands in the air like he was trying to climb the clouds.

"You starting to feel better? You seem more energetic than you have in the last few days."

"Kind of," William looked out at his lawn. "I'm getting feelings sorted. Enough about me, go on with your story."

"So, Alice had her shirt off and my Dad walks in. Looked like hell incarnate, man."

"And her shirt was off?" William asked, his eyes as wide as saucers.

"Yes. It was. I was just starting to say that 'hey, maybe we should quit, I don't think this is such a good idea.' Then my Dad walks in."

William put a hand on Quin's knee. "And her *shirt* was off?"

Quincy sunk his head and looked at William. "Is this getting through? Yes. Her shirt was off. We were on my bed. Dad walks in. I suffer heart attack."

"Okay, I've got it. You've sure brought her out of her shell. Good work Quin!" He patted his friend on the back

"Yeah. Well I'm just lucky I didn't get her out of anything else, like her top, or I might not be standing here."

"So what happened next?"

Quincy picked at a speck of chipped paint on the steps. "Dad kicked me out.

William's shoulders slumped. "Oh no, that's terrible."

"Enh. I'll get over not living there, but it sucks that I'm not presently living *anywhere.*"

"Don't think anything of it man, I'd bet my Mom and Dad would let ya stay here until you get some stuff figured out."

Quincy grimaced. "Does that mean I have to watch all those weird seventies shows of yours? God, I hope I don't pick up your vocabulary."

"No, I mean, you could sleep in your car. As Roslyn said, you do have quite the backseat." William smiled, and then realized what he had said. "Ah man." He whistled sadly.

"Still no luck with your lady?" Quin asked.

"No. I've tried calling her, but every time I do her phone is busy. It stinks man."

"Sounds like it, I'm sorry for my part in it dude." Quincy steeled himself for what he was about to say. "You know, that was my clever attempt at getting back at you for the sexual immorality comment. I didn't even think about how Roslyn might have been affected by it. I'm sorry."

William whistled low and followed it by an exploding noise. "Well, I'm figuring some things out like I said. I'm bad for her, I know that, anyway." William kicked his feet outward. "You want me to talk to my parents? I am sure they wouldn't ask too many questions about *why* you were kicked out. They'd be a little hypocritical if they came down on you for your sex*ual* imm*orality*, they've told me stories about their rebellious age."

"That must have been an enlightening experience."

"I'll go talk to them, come on in." William said getting up.

Quincy looked out to his car, with all his stuff clearly visible in the windows. He sighed, and walked into the house with William.

As was typical, Quincy smelled sandalwood incense as he entered the living room, the multi colored bean bags were vacant. There was music playing in one of the rooms, and Quincy recognized a sitar from the song and assumed it to be Sergeant Peppers Lonely Hearts Club Band. The house was cool, which felt refreshing against Quincy's hot face.

"Mom! Dad! Where'd you go?" William walked into the kitchen and opened the pantry, tossing Quin a granola bar. "Here man, this'll help ya." William took a strawberry one for himself.

"Down here son!"

William motioned for Quin to follow him downstairs, and Quincy just shook his head. It was something about the Denslie's basement that just made Quincy laugh. It must have been the dyed rugs and beaded doorways.

Robert "Robby" Denslie & his wife, Carol were at opposite ends of the pool table, Carol was lining up a shot, her long brown hair getting in her way. Robby was bouncing his stick up and down on his shoes.

"Hi Quin, nice to see you again." Robby waved with his free hand.

Carol didn't break her gaze, and she cleared her throat. "Eight ball, side pocket."

Crack. As the eight ball rolled towards the forecasted pocket Robby looked exasperated. He went over to a green board and added another hash mark to a long line of victories.

"It was a good battle honey." Carol said.

"It was like Vietnam all over again. That's what it was."

"Yep, course we both lost then." Carol said, sipping on a can of cola.

"Mom, Dad?" William said, as he sat down on a barstool. He motioned for Quincy to come over too, and Quincy decided this was probably a good time to eat his granola bar.

"Hi Quin," Carol said, just noticing him.

"Another winning game Carol?" Quincy asked, smiling as best he could.

"Well, guys. I've got a favor to ask."

"Are we about to run you up to Roslyn's place? Did you two finally make up?" Robby asked.

"No, Dad, not quite." William bit his lip. "You remember that story you guys told me about what happened after the concert at Hilltop Village?"

Carol and Robby both laughed, seeming to grow younger before Quincy's eyes. "Yes, I recall the night." Robby said.

"Well, it kinda just happened to Quin." William held out his hands in a surrender sort of pose.

"Hmm." Carol sat on the edge of the pool table. "Were you thrown out for murder? Or drugs? Or abetting a felon?"

Quincy swallowed his bite and shook his head. "No not at all. I've never done anything like that."

"It was sex*ual* imm*orality.*" William grinned feebly, stealing a look at Quincy.

"Do I have permission to kill your son? You know, with us being on the topic of murder?" Quincy asked.

"I'll say no to that, someone's got to get the house once we're gone." Robby said, stepping over to Quincy and William. "Do you need a place to stay for a while?" Robby put his hand on Quin's shoulder.

Quincy felt a smile creeping onto his face, a sense that maybe not everything was going to end badly. "Sir, that would be very nice indeed. Thank you."

Robby smiled. "You don't need to worry about too many house rules, just try not to set the house on fire. I trust your judgment; you're Will's best friend. Just follow his lead and you'll be okay."

Carol came over and stood next to Rob. "You're welcome to stay; we remember how it can be. Just promise me that you'll try to get on good terms with your parents again. You're young, they're not so much. Don't leave the gap so wide that it's irreparable." She smiled kindly.

Quincy looked at the Denslie family, and felt better. "Thank you, I am very grateful."

"Come on, let's get some stuff moved into the guestroom, you can help me work on my new song." William said excitedly, tossing his granola wrapper into a tie-dyed painted waste bin.

***

Alice had just made it back into her house; her heart was still racing as though it was seconds away from death. Her parent's cars were not in the driveway, so she thought she would be safe. However, due to recent events, she decided to do a thorough search of the house. All rooms proved vacant, and the telephone didn't show any missed calls. She doubted that Quincy's Dad would call. That sort of thing would actually take a modicum of caring, which she knew he did not possess.

Finally feeling as though she could breathe normally, she went up to her bedroom. She locked the door behind her and pulled out her cell phone. She felt horrible. She had been trying to maintain every bit of caution, but she had missed Quincy's Dad. She hadn't lock the door when she came back in to his room.

"I really hope Quincy's okay...." She turned her phone on and checked for new messages; she had missed all of Quincy's calls, five of them.

She found one text message, and no voice mails. She opened the text and read. *Got kicked out, no key. Can stay at Will's. Call me. Love, Q.*

Alice couldn't help but feel cheated once again. She was of course grateful that Quincy had somewhere to stay, but of course, it was with William. She hit dial on her phone and heard it ringing.

"Alice!" Quincy answered sounding out of breath.

"Quincy! God I'm glad you answered." She paused. "You're out of breath, what are you doing?"

"William & I are in the spare bedroom."

"Well, that's just great. I hope you enjoy yourselves." She said spitefully, and she wasn't quite sure what had made her say it.

"Ha ha. Funny joke. Are you okay?" Quincy asked.

Alice found herself smiling, she was glad he hadn't caught her venom. "Yeah, I'm okay. Hearts still racing, but I'm okay. Are you?" she released her pettiness and focused on him.

"I will be. Will's parents are letting me stay for as long as I need."

"Do they know what happened?"

"Will says it's a non-issue, says they've done their fair share of rebellion."

"Quincy, I'm sorry I didn't lock the bedroom door." She said, as she heard silence on the other end.

"It's alright, I'm sorry I brought the stupid game up." Quincy replied.

Alice listened intently. "Is he singing Tiny Dancer again?"

Quincy laughed, sounding more at ease with every second. "Yeah, you know Will."

Alice looked up at the photos of all of them. "Yes, I do. I'm glad they're helping you. I think you were going crazy in that house anyway."

"I was. This could help."

"Can you tell William thank you, and to disregard what I told him earlier? Tell him, it's good that he has someone he can go to. Tell him I'm sorry?" Alice twirled her hair, and she sensed curiosity in the silence.

"I'll tell him…yeah."

"Don't worry about it, Quincy, I promise, it's nothing. It was me being stupid and selfish. I love you. Get your stuff unpacked. Call me later. I'm going to get a shower."

"I will do that, and I love you too. Talk to you later."

"Bye, baby." She said, and she got up. She felt like a hot shower would do her good.

***

Quincy was just coming out of the bathroom, drying his hands on his pants as he walked back to his new room. He opened the door and light flooded his eyes from the window. It was starting to feel like he could actually live here, his room was a good size and he had a nice double bed, so plenty of room to stretch out at night.

Quincy liked his room, but one thing he never expected to see in it was William crying. He was sitting cross legged in the center of the room. Quincy was shell-shocked as his eyes fell upon his binder adorned with metal bands. His private journal, in the hands of someone not him!

"WILLIAM!" Quincy's mouth was wide open, a perfect landing bay for any suicidal flies.

William looked up, his face red and tears practically streaming down his face. He shook his head and just held up his hands; over and over he shook his head. "Quincy." He licked his lips, and stared down at the binder. "This...is..." William sobbed "This is so good!" His lip trembled comically.

Quincy started chuckling despite his efforts to be angry.

"Quincy, this is *exactly* what I feel right now! It's sooo good! I mean, this part right here: *"My heart soars like a bullet, upon reaching its apex it falls like my dreams. My only dream is of her, and my only breath is for her, and my only desire is her. My existential squandering of hope is meaningless without her affection."*

Quincy turned red. He was reading *The Alice Entries*. "Um, dude. That's kind of a personal journal; you really shouldn't be reading it."

"It's just so dark, and so deep, God man, did you love Alice when you wrote this? *I awoke today, and felt it might be a good day to die, for her hand wasn't in mine! Maybe tomorrow, tomorrow will be my day, my dreary forecast predicts shower after shower, a shower I'll spend alone!"*

Quincy was shaking his hands, turning towards the door and closing it. "Dude! Quiet! I don't want everyone hearing that!" he made to steal the journal from William, but William leapt up and stood towering over Quincy on a desk.

"She tears my soul apart with her accusatory eyes, she seems to know my thoughts but not my heart, oh wise wonder when will your affections rest on me?" William

held the journal up like it was the most sacred book ever. "Quin! Do you realize what this is?"

"Yes! My private thoughts, on private matters, concerning people private to me!" Quincy thought on how he might seize the book from his friend, not wanting him to read further.

"Did you love Alice when you wrote these things? Tell me by God, or I will preach this book like it was the book of life!"

Quincy rushed over to the open window and latched it shut. "Yes! Alright!" he rushed to William and jumped up to rip the journal from his hands. "I loved Alice when I wrote that! What is the big deal about it, man? That's my book!"

"It can be your book again! I have learned the wisdom of Mister Q & A! I at last have realized the reason I've been so miserable! I realize why I've been tossing words like a baseball player tosses balls! I've understood at last what has been hidden from me!"

Quincy snatched the journal and clutched it tightly to his chest. "Well do tell then BILL!" Quincy frowned, patting his journal as if it were a dear pet.

William hopped down off the desk and proceeded to open the window. He swung it open wide and stared out at his street as a king looks out upon his kingdom. "Attention world and all who dwell within it! I am William Denslie, and I am in love with Roslyn Lyden! This is the dénouement—that's French by the way! French! I have become a man and taken a woman to my heart! She dwells within and never shall she leave!" he beat madly upon his chest and screamed joyfully.

Quincy stared in open-eyed wonder at his friend who he was sure had gone into the depths of true madness. "William, step away from the window please...please?" he wondered if he should approach.

"Quincy Abel Abrams! You!" He turned, grabbing Quincy by the collar of his shirt, and stared into his eyes.

Quincy could smell strawberry breath, and could see William's left eye twitching. "Dude, you're too close!"

"You can never be too close! Quincy! I love Roslyn! And tomorrow she shall know it! By your words you have liberated me from my red-walled prison of pumping blood and captured emotion! Your words have changed my world! You are my hero!" He shook his head from side to side and kissed Quincy square on the lips. "Come with me my friend, we must have BAND PRACTICE!"

Quincy stood swaying on the spot as William raced out of the room. "Weirdness has settled on the town, and the dogs of confusion have been let loose." Quincy wiped his lips off with his sleeve, putting his journal under his new bed. He hoped that William wouldn't try searching for it too much; the journal seemed to have a very strange effect on him.

Quincy timidly walked out of the room and peeked into William's bedroom. His friend was on the phone talking animatedly, his head lolling back and forth as if he was having a fit. "Alice! You must come over at once! Bring a lemonade mix and your guitar string shredding fingers! I need your every skill tonight!"

William was hopping up and down on his bed, his face beet red and his tambourine shaking wildly in his hand. Pens had fallen out from behind Will's ears and his hair had taken on an unkempt kind of glamour.

"No Alice! I am not mad; I am in love! Now is the time for action, we must rehearse! For tomorrow, we take our show on the road! We perform at the gates of Lyden's Keep and shall not return until we have a Queen for this Fairy King!" His eyes grew wide and he twirled in the air. "I want my wings back! And those pants! Bring them also!"

"William, dude…I don't even understand, but I'm behind you."

"That you are!" He said, pointing at Quincy. "Alice, get here soon!" he snapped his phone shut and leapt from the bed. He put his arm around Quincy.

Quincy removed Will's arm. "Maybe not so much right now man, I'll permit you the kiss, but I'm not going any further. Alice might get jealous, so might your lady."

"That was a kiss of brotherhood! Of kinship! Come now Quincy, to the basement!"

***

William, Alice and Quincy were all in Moore Ning Wood, cramped up tighter than sardines with all the band equipment. The horizon seemed to be on fire as the sun blazed its final rays for the day.

William was concentrating entirely on his Positively Passionate Purple lipstick application. He had nearly torn off the drop down mirror more than once trying to put his lipstick on evenly. His fairy wings kept hitting Quincy who drove on, seemingly wary of William in this new state of his.

"Come on Quin, faster man!" William said tapping his foot on the floor.

"I will not get pulled over for you, dude, so chill out! We're going to get there tonight, I promise!"

"William, here, for God's sake." Alice said, rummaging in her purse. "Take this," she held up her mascara. "Keep it, use it. It'll make your eyes prettier."

"Woo!" William exclaimed, doing his eyes up. "You guys ready for this man?" He did his best Gene Simmons tongue impersonation, and applied his mascara.

"Dude, I still don't know how you fit into those pants. They leave little to the imagination." Quincy commented.

"These pants are magic. Just like fairies! With them I can't lose!"

He pulled out a scrap of paper and ran through the lyrics to his recently completed song. He knew nothing could go wrong, yet he was still nervous.

"Will, you sure about this? Pledging your love to Roslyn?"

"I have never been more certain about anything! My forecast predicts sunshine and warm winds!" William surreptitiously looked at Quin who had started to smile.

"DARNIT Quin! This is our exit! Go! Go!" he waved his hands as if doing so would make his friend turn the wheel faster.

Quincy let out a small scream. "Eeek! Fine man! You should drive next time! I'm not cut out for this, I'm a simple drummer, when are we going to get a driver!"

"Once we get to 147 fans, I've told you! It's the magic number!"

"How that makes any sense I don't know!" Quincy wailed, his head was shaking madly.

"Quincy, please get us there safely, I'm too cute to die." Alice begged him.

As Quincy slowed the car down on the main road William began to feel slightly nervous.

Roslyn's house came into view just over the hills, and William was filled with something he could only rationalize as courage. He exhaled mightily and nodded. "Let's do this." He said.

The three of them emptied out the car, setting up as quietly and quickly as they could in front of the window William indicated.

Alice had brought her acoustic guitar and Quincy had just finished putting his drums together when the last light of the day escaped them.

William fought to maintain his optimistic attitude and motioned to Alice. The first chords of her guitar broke the night silence, and William listened as Quincy played softly.

William watched as the curtains in Roslyn's room stirred slightly, whether from wind or her, he knew not. As the light from her bedroom broke the spell of the darkness, William began to employ his tambourine.

> *"Once upon a night at ten, I stared up at my Roslyn*
> *Her curtains parted, and my heart started.*
> *Beating like a tribal drum.*
> *I've got no excuse, and I've got no gum,*
> *To give to you, but I've gotta say one thing that's*
> *true*
> *I'll try to put this better than the Crüe*
> *Be my composite, I'll be your absolute value*
> *I've lost six days and happy rays and I've searched*
> *my soul*
> *Took some time to realize it's you that makes my*
> *number whole*
> *I can't stand math, and I can't stand to miss*
> *The only girl I long to kiss*
> *Rosalyn! Oh Rosalyn be mine! Come outside and*
> *end my whine!"*

William watched as Rosalyn stepped out onto her balcony, looking more beautiful than William had ever remembered. He kept playing his tambourine and kept on with his song.

> *"I'm a broken boy toy and I have no joy*
> *So long as we're apart!*
> *I've felt forlorn since I earned your scorn*
> *And now I want your love*
> *Please Maid Roslyn be my missing glove!*
> *No more nuts or plastic guillotines*
> *If you'll be my butterscotch Jelly Bean!*
> *Missed you like mad and I've been sad*

Please come down from there!
Cuz I'm a broken boy toy, a pitiful lad!
But you can make me fair! You can end my song!
Such simple words, three syllables, and I'll pervade
the night no more!
Cuz I know that you're the one I've been waiting
for!"

William looked up and saw a smile on Roslyn's face, and he couldn't remember the rest of the words. Alice and Quincy played on, and he would have to thank them later. He climbed up the lattice that led to her. He had a horrible fear of heights, but he was motivated by a cause much greater than fear, true love was feet away from him.

"Roslyn." He climbed onto her balcony and knelt at her feet. "Lady Roslyn, I grieve, for I offended you so horribly." He clasped her hand in his. "Please, forgive me."

Roslyn looked angelic in the slowly spreading moonlight, and William felt his heart beat against his ribs.

"William, your song...was ridiculous." Roslyn looked him over. "Quite like your outfit." She laughed pitifully.

"I knew if the song didn't get your attention the outfit would, it was my backup."

"Been trying to call you." She lifted him up so that he faced her. "I was hard on you, and I'm sorry too."

"Roslyn, these last six days have been dreadful, I can't imagine what you've felt, but I know I never want to be the cause of it again. The thought of you not liking me anymore, it nearly destroyed me." He said dramatically.

"William." She moved hair from her eyes. "You're being dramatic."

"No I'm not! I'm being honest. I was so sad; I was even crying. But I finally realized why I was so torn up. It's cuz I love you, and by hurting you, I hurt myself."

Roslyn looked down at Quincy and Alice, who played on. "They both know don't they? About the AIS?"

"They do. I wouldn't lie about it, not to you. They know, and they don't care. They like you, because you make me happier than I've ever been."

"And you love me?" she asked, peering into his eyes.

"I love you more than air that keeps me alive. I love you more than my heart beating. I …"

"STOP STEALING MY LINES YOU CRAZY HIPPY!" Quincy yelled up.

William laughed and was happy to see Roslyn doing so also. "Yes. I love you." He knelt again, and kissed her hands.

Seconds passed, yet each successive one was like another six days to William. She knelt down, and stared eye to eye with him.

"You're not going to hurt me again, are you William?"

"I would sooner kiss Quincy again." He said.

The guitar stopped playing, and William grinned devilishly. "Sorry Quincy! That was for the kissing guys comment!" William shouted down, and he heard Quincy cursing quietly.

Roslyn covered her mouth to stifle her laughter. "You kissed Quincy?"

"I did. And let me just say, kissing you is so much nicer. You've got supple lips, very lovely. His are all hard and…by God, Alice," he called down. "I don't know how you do it; he doesn't seem to be a good kisser."

Roslyn positively burst out in laughter at that. She stroked his wildly styled hair. "It's not that he's a bad kisser, you're just used to me." She leaned in and placed a kiss on his lips.

"That had better be kissing I see up there, otherwise I won't be able to endure this gloating smile Alice is giving me!" Quincy called up.

William & Roslyn broke apart, and each was smiling. "I love you too, William."

"That means the world to me." William smiled, glad that he could once again be happy. It was more than his happiness though, he realized, because he could give the happiness he felt to another. He drew Roslyn in and held her close to him, not caring that a lanky boy had just come to the window with Joelle. Not caring one bit that all music below him had ceased.

Happiness had taken hold of William's heart. He had found his Gypsy Queen who made his Fairy wings flutter. The night air was cool as it started to rain. Tomorrow it might be sunny, but for now; they savored happiness in every dark refreshing drop.

Book Four
Frostbitten

December 2004

Quincy sat on the warm hood of his dead car in bitter contrast with the wind that bit at him. The December winds were brutal today. Quincy picked at a spot of rust that felt like cancer as his fingers ran across it. He adjusted his coat and looked through the windshield. He saw Alice reclining in the front seat, her light blonde hair strewn across her face.

William was drawing on the fogged up windows as his girlfriend Roslyn read her biology book. Quincy met eyes with William who smiled reassuringly back at him.

Quincy exhaled, his breath appearing as great white puffs in the light of the orange setting sun. On one hand, they were just off the exit ramp and a hotel could be seen. It was within walking distance and could at least give shelter for the night. On the other hand, they probably wouldn't make it to their last show of their winter tour. Vinyl Confessions wouldn't be happy with it, but Quincy thought them to be a very pompous group, hardly even considered pop.

He looked at the rusty spot again and cursed. "There will be other tours." He hopped off his car and walked to William's door. He opened it and knelt down.

"Well, Will, it's dead. Engine won't even turn or some shit." Quincy looked at the drawings William had rendered on his window. There was the Sunflower Heart band logo Lipstick Trace had adopted.

William drew a headstone on his window. "Wood died as he lived." William paused dramatically. "Pitifully."

Quincy held his slapping hand back as he would soon need William's help in pushing his car and didn't want him upset. "Just…help me get the car pushed into that hotel parking lot. It'll be dark soon and we can at least stay there until we get a ride back home."

Roslyn put a bookmark on her page she was reading. "Wake your woman, I'll help push."

As Will & Roslyn exited the car, Quincy opened up Alice's door. He put his hands up to her cheek which made her jump.

"Cold!" she jerked away from him. Wiping the sleep from her eyes she righted herself in her seat and assessed her surroundings. "Did your car die?"

"No, he's taking a nap." He improved upon the truth.

"I told you to get it looked at before we left, would you listen?" She rolled her eyes and got out of the car. "What do you want me to do?"

"Push please, Miss Infallible." Quincy responded.

William, Roslyn & Quin began pushing the car towards the hotel with Alice at the wheel. It took them a few minutes, and despite the cold they were soon a little sweaty.

Quincy didn't like the fact that he hadn't listened to Alice, and liked even less the fact that she had been right. "Stay here guys, I'm going to get us some rooms. Can you guys watch the car until I get back?"

"Yes Q, I'll make sure nobody hijacks it." Alice saluted him.

Feeling all kinds of happy, Quincy took out his credit card and put it in his coat pocket for easier access. As he approached the desk girl, he wondered to how uncomfortable she must be. She looked like she had better places to be, and kept glancing up at the clock. Her nails rapped a spiteful melody on the counter and her bubble gum popped with a ridiculous intensity.

She eyed Quincy as he approached and her eyebrows formed a V as he came closer. She stopped rapping on the counter and flashed the best pseudo-smile he had ever seen. Her red lipstick was almost too bold for a desk job. "Hi, welcome to the Roadside Rest. How can I help you?"

Quincy compared her customer service skills to his, and realized that perhaps his needed refinement. He could tell she hated her job, but she seemed happier in her speech than he ever had. Taking a mental note, he began. "I need a room for four this evening please."

She typed rapidly on the computer in front of her, her eyes moved across the screen like a pair of salsa dancers. She emitted a low hum and shook her head. "I'm sorry we don't have any rooms with double beds. I have single rooms, that's the best I can do. It'll be fifty-nine dollars after tax for each."

Quincy ran the numbers in his head and it occurred to him that he and Alice would be sharing a bed. He found himself smiling a little bit at that thought. "Okay, that's fine. It'll be plastic." He handed her his card which she carefully inspected.

She asked him for his ID, and he dug it out of his wallet. The hotel, he noticed, wasn't actually so bad. It had some vending machines and had cable, he saw, from the brochure on the front counter. She handed him his two magnetic room keys. "I'm Diana, if you need anything, let me know." She touched his hand lightly with hers as she returned the card to him. The touch gave him pause, and her eyes met his for the briefest moment. It was a shame, because Alice walked through the door at that time.

Alice hadn't noticed him, he suspected, but still, a feeling of guilt latched onto him. He smiled remorsefully at Diana, and walked off to join the rest of his group.

"Looks like we'll be sleeping in separate rooms tonight guys...and girls." He added as an afterthought, catching a glance from Roslyn. "Couldn't get the same room with double beds."

"That's fine with me Quincy I didn't wanna sleep in the same room as you anyway. It'd make cuddling with William exceptionally awkward in light of your latent lust for him." Roslyn stated.

Quincy stopped breathing. "Yeah. Whatever you just said. Go for it." He put his hand on Alice's shoulder and started to walk out towards his car to pick up their basic living essentials.

"You go get our stuff..." Alice said distantly, "I'm going to call home and let our parents know what's happened." She paused, catching Quincy's glare. "Well...not yours obviously, but I'll at least let the rest of ours know."

"Yeah. Appreciate that." Quincy said, as he walked off toward the car. Diana's bubble gum popping and finger nail tapping had resumed.

***

Alice held a brief conversation with each of the respective parents. The Denslie's & Ms. Lyden were the easiest to deal with. When it came time to talk to her own parents, Alice had to do a little truth modification.

"Yes Dad, I understand if we sleep in the same bed you'll give him a new reason for being sad." She laughed. "Of course, of course you were kidding." She hung up the phone on her father feeling rather okay about things. She stepped back into the lobby. Her eyes fell upon the desk girl, and Alice recalled the longer than necessary hand touch she had seen the girl exchange with her boyfriend.

Alice took the stairs back up to her and Quincy's room and found their backpacks sitting on the bed. She sat on the chair next to the sliding glass doors that overlooked the abysmally small patio. The night was fast approaching, and her mind wandered back to the desk girl and Quincy. Her lip curled with a touch of malice and she realized that her imagination was still her worst enemy.

Quincy walked out from the bathroom with a goofy grin on his face. "Room smells like potpourri, doesn't it?"

Alice made herself smile.

"Yeah, sucks about Wood though, he added."

"Well, if you'd listened to me about fifty miles ago you mightn't be in this situation right now, eh Abrams?" Alice used his surname purposely, knowing it'd be like a little dagger under his fingernail.

Quincy sat on the bed. "Yeah, I know you were right, it's just a stupid guy thing. Stubbornness, you know?"

"So Roslyn's Mom says she'll pick us up tomorrow morning. She's got the biggest car out of our parents.'" Alice got up and sat down beside Quincy. He smelled grungy. "You need a shower, you kinda smell like ass."

Quincy laughed. "Sorry! Next time I'll drive and you can push, would that be okay, Princess?"

She grinned, pleased that she was getting to him. "And another thing, getting a shower might help you with that little slut downstairs too. She might seem sour on the outside, but I'm sure with a little flirting she'll be all over you tonight if you wanted."

Quincy stood. "Sorry, what?"

"You and her, I saw what was going on between you." Alice felt her face flushing, and didn't care to research the situation much. Maybe it was her jaded nature or past that made her automatically suspect her boyfriend of treachery.

"I will tell you if anything ever happens, she was just handing me card back. She was a little touchy, but that's nothing worth accusing me of flirting about."

"I seem to think it is. I know men, and that little touch probably sent you reeling didn't it?"

"You seem to be going really stupid over a five second feel." Quincy crossed his arms. "What is this really about?"

"This is what it's really about Quincy."

"You want me to go downstairs then? Cuz honestly, I was easily admitting to you right back there, that I was wrong and you just seem like you didn't even hear me.

"Seems like you just wanted to rip me a new one for the passing touch of some random chick. She touched my hand for a bit longer than a standard second...so what? Jeez, I didn't do anything with her. Unless you want me to? Let you have a really good reason for pissing you off?"

Alice walked up to him, stared in his eyes for a 'bit longer than a standard second' and landed a solid hit in his jaw.

"What the hell!" he exclaimed in total surprise, his eyes were wide and his hands flew to his face to massage his jaw.

"Seems to me you deserved it." Alice said, as she stalked off and locked herself in the bathroom. She slid down against the door and sat cross legged in the strangely fragrant bathroom. Her tears came quickly, as did Quincy's departure from the room as made apparent by the slamming door.

***

Roslyn heard the exchange between Alice & Quincy quite clearly. It was rather difficult to concentrate on her Biology book when you could hear two normally good people venting and raging just next door. As Roslyn heard the door slam, she once again bookmarked her page and got up. "Will, I'm going to see if Alice needs anything."

"How do I turn on this water faucet? It doesn't have any knobs." William replied.

"Lift it up sugar." She said, as she closed the door behind her. She heard his cry of enlightenment. She knocked gently, certain that Alice would be listening for the slightest sound that Quincy was returning.

"Who is it?" Alice called out.

"Not Quincy." Roslyn responded. She heard Alice getting closer to the door, and heard a small click from beyond.

Roslyn came in and saw Alice in the light. Her cheeks were red and her fists were clenched. She looked so little to Roslyn in the dim light of her hotel room. "What happened, chicky?" Roslyn asked, sitting down on the short chest of drawers.

"We had a fight, Quincy and I."

"I doubt anyone in the hotel or five-mile radius would argue against that point." Roslyn said, tilting her head.

"Did you see Quincy when we first came in the hotel? He was flirting with the counter girl." Alice shook her head. "And they were looking at each other and just…ooh if he thinks he's going to cheat on me with some drop out ditz."

"Alice, are you sure of what you saw?" Roslyn waited, allowing Alice to ponder over her simple question. Roslyn knew precisely well what she had seen, and had a good guess as to what would have happened had they not entered at that time. Nothing.

"He was being flirted with, that is undeniable." Alice said, storming around in little circles.

"You're gonna fry a microchip Alice, sit down or I'll tie you to the bed and tell William what a great time we had."

"Well what would you do in my stead, had you seen him being touched like that by some strange flirtatious chick?"

"Probably would have waited the space of an hour to see if he was going to bring it up to me first. Course, there is the more realistic option that he didn't think anything had actually happened and he was just going to let it go."

"Did you *see* how guilty he looked when I walked in? It was like he had his hand in the cookie jar."

"Alright, let's suppose you're right about it, what all happened before he stormed out?"

"I punched him. Plain and simple, I was just so furious!" Alice huffed.

"Now see...to me, it makes me wonder how much trust you have for your boyfriend. Did the process cross your mind that maybe he actually is loyal to you and wouldn't hurt you?"

Alice bit her lip and looked up at the ceiling. "Of course it crossed my mind."

Roslyn smiled and stared down at her hands. "Okay, so no, it didn't cross your mind. You jumped to a conclusion that would cause the most drama."

"That's not it at all! I just hate feeling like something was happening behind my back."

Roslyn smirked. "Why? What makes you care so much?"

Alice got up again, and Roslyn shook her head, signaling her to remain seated. "I care so much because...ugh!"

"Remember express yourself please or I can just leave you with your misery and unevaluated thoughts."

Alice stared up at her, eyes straining to remain open. She looked close to a breakdown; she was scratching on her arms and pursing her lips. "I care *so* much because... he's stupid. He's a jaded metal wannabe. He's so down, I'm so not. He's got a spiteful tongue and a hateful disposition, but underneath it all, he's a good person.

"I hate myself for being a bitch, and I know I am, trust me I do...but I've been screwed over before by guys and I just can't bear the thought of getting screwed by him because crazy as it all sounds, I think I'm really in love with him."

"Isn't that what you two mean when you say 'I love you'?"

"Of course I tell him I love him, it's what boyfriends and girlfriends do. But when I've been saying it to him lately, I really think I mean it."

"Okay, one...never say it just to be saying it. That's just...so perverse I can't even begin to justify it. Two, if he's been under the impression this whole time that you love him, and not romantic love, you might want to make sure you rectify that upon your next meeting. That is the kind of thing boyfriends should know."

"Did I ruin what Quincy & I have?" Alice held her face in her hands and sobbed gently.

"I think what happened was, your *beginning* to love Quincy, felt an unusual amount of jealousy over some chick showing minimal attention to your man, and you immediately revisited your own painful past. You gotta understand Alice, cuz Will & I already do; you are the only girl Goth Boy sees."

Alice chuckled weakly. "Yeah. Maybe."

"Also...your hitting him was a shit bag move. Don't be a shit bag, Alice. I'm gonna go, Will's probably flooded the bathroom wondering how to turn off the water faucet." She started towards the door.

"Thank you." Alice said, and she turned on the lights in her darkening hotel room. Roslyn closed the door behind her, as gently as she could.

***

"I just can't believe she punched me is all." Quincy sighed, as he stared at the blank television.

"Well, you did say you kinda liked it. But that's beside the point. Wonder what made her go so loco?" William took off his shoes and socks and sat Indian Style on his bed.

"I wish I knew man." Quincy said as he heard a knock on the door. "That'll be your lady I presume." Quincy got up to let her in since Will had just gotten comfortable.

Roslyn inclined her head slightly as Quincy let her in. "Give Al a little bit before you talk to her Q, think she's got some things to consider. Time will help this one. You can stay here though if you like. It's getting really cold outside."

Quincy considered staying in the comfortable room, but his heart was displeased with the thought of comfort at the moment. "No thanks, the cold will do me good." He said dramatically.

Quincy crossed the highway on foot into the field of grass stretching out before him. It was beginning to snow; little diamonds fell from the sky and landed on his nose. He was feeling less than excited about going back to see Alice, she'd been so vindictive. "God, just fix this. Because I don't know if I can." Quincy realized this was the first prayer he had said since moving away.

He eventually reached a chain link fence that overlooked the expressway. He sat down and stared out at the passing cars, headlights speeding along like supersonic fireflies. The wind blew his hair across his forehead, and he became acutely aware of a crunching noise behind him.

He exhaled and reached down and stuck his hands into the accumulating snow. Someone lightly sat down right beside him, and he recognized the smell of Alice's shampoo. His hands still felt warm despite the snow's cold affect.

"You love me, Quincy." Alice began, and Quincy wondered how she was struggling to make her voice steady. He could hear the scratchiness in it like a warped record. "Have you ever questioned it?"

Quincy didn't turn to face her; he kept his gaze straight ahead on the expressway. "Of course I have. I would be a child to not do so."

"You know me Quincy, where I've been. What kind of person I still struggle not to be."

Quincy remained silent, knowing that as the silence stretched on, her chances of remaining silent would dwindle. He could always count on Alice to keep talking.

"I don't want to make something out of nothing, but I do want to make sure nothing affects our something. I think I hurt you earlier, and I want to talk to you about why I did. Can you listen to me?" He felt her hand reach down and grab one of his, placing it firmly on her knee.

"I won't interrupt you." He said. "But if you're going to hit me again, let me know in advance."

"See? That was part of it. Quincy, I am pretty certain of the fact that even though I've made tremendous strides, I think I'm always going to be a jaded bitch when it comes to guys.

"I don't think I'm ever going to give you the fair chance you deserve. You tell me you love me, and I say I love you. But up until the last few weeks, I don't think I've actually been *in love* with you."

Quincy let his silence remain as he turned to look at her. She was staring at him, waiting to meet his gaze. He turned away and waited for her to go on.

"I'm going to hurt you, if I haven't already. Because I'm actually falling for you Quincy, and I guess because I've always been taken advantage of and then abandoned…I am afraid to trust what I have with you. I saw that chick thing touching you today, and all the feelings I've been developing lately just came into perfect clarity."

"So seeing another girl touch me makes you want me more? Well that's an interesting relationship dynamic." He laughed.

"I can't tell if you're being serious or not, but I still am. I feel like I haven't been honest with you since we started dating. Not completely anyway. I mean. I do love you, and I am in love with you now, but what I thought was love before wasn't really.

"And I have to make sure you want to be with me, because I'm a horrible person, nothing is going to change that. I'm always going to want my way, and I won't admit you're right even if you are. I can't guarantee I'll always be kind to you, or not punch you when I'm super emotional."

"Awesome." Quincy said. "So I was right about you all along." He said, turning to look into her eyes. He wanted so desperately to see her clearly right now.

"If you just said that, you weren't paying attention to a word I said." Alice got up, tossing his hand off of her.

"And if you leave now, you might not ever get to be proven wrong." He grimaced.

"I don't want to talk to you anymore if you're not going to listen to me."

"Should I go flirt with the desk girl in the mean time? Could it help out your desire to stick around?" He said caustically.

Alice whimpered quickly, not more than a whisper, but Quincy heard it. "Fine." Alice said as she walked away.

Quincy felt a weight fall onto his heart and it held him fast as Alice walked away from him. He turned around to see if she would look back. She never did.

In the dying embers of a day where time had been spent, Quincy felt the chill overtake him as he leaned back into the snow and let it cover him completely.

***

William watched the whole exchange from his hotel window. Judging from Alice's body language on her walk back William decided that perhaps he should put his shoes back on.

"I'm going over to Quincy." Will said, kissing Roslyn goodbye. "I'll be back soon, I promise."

"Do what you have to Will. Just do it well." She said, as she once again picked up her book.

Will picked up his thin leather jacket and walked out into the hallway. He heard a door open, and he turned back for a second to see Alice gazing at him through a crack in the door. Will felt that they were exchanging thoughts like radio waves. She was clearly broadcasting on AM, Angry Mode. He raised his eyebrows and shook his head at her, for the first time feeling pretty disappointed in her.

"Quincy loves you Alice. You shouldn't ever forget that." He called to her, as she shut her hotel door with an air of exasperation.

Will shook his head and walked towards Quincy. He touched Quincy's shoulders with the toe of his boot. "Quincy? You still got a heartbeat under there?"

Quincy turned his head to look up at William. "I think I'm still amongst the living."

"Well, that's good. You should come in from there, you'll catch your death of cold then I'll have to be accountable for your final expenses. It would totally sink the Lipstick Trace budget."

"That would be a tragedy to rival your face." Quincy said scathingly.

"I'm serious, get up." William said, kneeling down and grabbing hold of Quincy's arms. "You made me a promise once where you and Alice are concerned. Now I expect you to get up, and fix things."

Quincy groaned.

"Or are you going to promise something, then go back on it?" William asked. "Because if you are, I'm going to have to punch you too…and then go to confession over it."

"You're a really bad motivational speaker William." Quincy said.

"Please?" William said, beginning to shiver. "You've got to be freezing, get up."

Quincy sighed, and allowed William to help him to his feet. "She drives me nuts man. And the worst part about it is, she doesn't even know it."

"I got a good solution for you then Mr. Love. Go tell her. Unless…that is, you were wrong about your obsessive litanies. And you just want to…I don't know, give up."

"Can I think about that for the next eight hours please? I'll sleep on the floor."

William considered him with a resigned sigh. "Yeah, come on up. Though, you wanting to spend the night on my hotel room floor as opposed to with your girlfriend is a little hinky Q."

"Yeah. Maybe it is." Quincy said, as he walked back to the hotel.

***

Sunlight filtered through the window of the hotel. Quincy rolled over on the hard floor and felt a lump in his throat. His sinuses were like an over packed can of sardines. He looked out the window and saw Roslyn's Mom's car with its trunk open. He was alone in the hotel room. His head was still a vault of ideas that had been collected in the lull of last evening.

He put on his coat, and decidedly marched over to Alice's hotel door. He knocked on it, timidly at first. When he was ignored, though he heard movement from the other side, he knocked harder. "Alice, let me in."

Alice opened the door and retreated back into the room. She sat on the bed and stared at him as he entered. He shut the heavy door behind him, and turned up the heat.

"Alright, let's be clear on a few things, Alice." Quincy's voice sounded like a frog's croak. He sniffled and sat down in front of Alice.

"You look…you sound awful. Did you sleep in the snow?" Alice asked, her hand reaching out to touch Quincy's forehead. "Here, sit with me."

"I wouldn't mind, thank you." He said, sitting beside her. She looked as timid and tiny as Little Miss Muffet surely did as the spider approached her. He smiled at the thought, and reached for her hand. "I'm here for you, and for the maniacal relationship we have started, Alice. I don't care if you're a bitch, or completely domineering, and perhaps just a little bit sadistic."

Alice's unkempt hair fell in front of her eyes, and Quincy tucked it behind her ears affectionately. "How can you love someone who is so cruel to you? I am never going to completely trust."

"You will, I'll leave no room for doubt." Quincy sighed heavily. "I have never had one thing easy; everything I've ever done has been a struggle. Fact of the matter is, I'm alright with an uphill battle, because it makes the easy times that much sweeter. So give me hell, punch me daily, and spit in my face. Just be sure to throw in a few nice moments too, and I'll be cool with everything else."

Alice sat, silent. Her hand trembled in his, and she looked up into his eyes with certainty. She let out a small whimper which transformed into a little cackle. Her cheeks were red and her eyes were like saucers. She looked quite crazed as she lifted his face up with her free hand. He started to smile, and it was then that she slapped him for all he was worth.

"ACH!" He screamed, as he began to rub the spot where her palm had hit. "What the f—" Then her lips were on his.

He barely had time to draw breath between assaults and was soon thrust backwards onto the bed. His head landed on her pillows and between jabs to the ribs and tongue lashings his heart was swimming with emotions. Before long, their hotel room door opened, and William entered. Will's eyes sprung wide, then, he turned on his heel like a military officer, walked out and slammed the door behind him. Alice withdrew from her realm of exhilaration.

Quincy stared up at her, her cheeks were still red, but her face was also a little sweaty at this point. She began to laugh, a healthy laugh though. He reached up and caressed her cheek. "There now...see? That's kind of what I was going for."

"We could have done that all last night if you'd only listened to me about that devil cursed car of yours."

Quincy, certain that he should admit defeat in order to save his own behind, agreed. "You're absolutely right. That car was a piece, and I will start to save for a new one immediately, my little cupcake."

She slapped him affectionately on his face. "Good. Let's get our stuff, we have to get back to town if we're going to wrap presents before Christmas Eve dinner at my parents."

Quincy was stunned. "Jesus, it is Christmas Eve isn't it?"

"Has been for a few hours...I just hope I don't catch whatever it is that you've got."

"Ah this?" He drew his sleeve across his red nose. "Don't worry about it, it's probably just from lying in the snow for about an hour last night."

"If I don't punish you, you punish yourself I see?"

"Yeah."

As they stood to leave, he drew her in for a final kiss before closing the door to the first hotel room they'd 'shared' together. Alice and Quincy walked hand in hand down to Roslyn's mother's car. William and Roslyn were waiting for them. Roslyn in front, Will in the back seat.

Alice took the seat next to William, and Quincy got to crunch himself into the back with all of the band equipment. "You two doing better then?" William asked in a whisper.

"We're better than ever. Thanks for asking man."

"If you're better than ever, why did I see you crying a few minutes ago Quin? You didn't look too happy in there."

Quincy smiled knowingly at Alice, and inclined his head the most miniscule amount.

Alice slapped William square across the face and burst into laughter, pleasant laughter, as William eye's nearly bulged out of his head.

Roslyn's Mom spoke up. "She's damaging your merchandise honey, best see to that one."

Roslyn looked back into the car and stared Alice down. "Unless you plan on giving me a new one for Christmas, back off him. I would hate to have to beat up your man meat."

The hotel faded into the distance, as did Quincy's car. He would call to have it towed, and, felt a little bit of regret as it faded into nothingness. It was his first taste of freedom; there was always a future full of freedom just waiting on him.

Quincy watched Alice in an animated conversation with William, and a bit of mischief found its way into Quincy's path. He reached towards Alice's neck and pinched her quickly. Her screech was the sweetest sound he'd heard all day, and it completely made up for spending an hour in the snow, frostbite and all.

**Book Five
Skin Deep**

September 2005

Alice Mendell had lime green paint on her patched overalls. Her hair, now down to her waist, was held back in a long ponytail so she wouldn't get an unintentional dye job. Lipstick Trace's first CD *Less Mic, More Jive* was playing in the other room, quite loudly in fact. Alice hoped that Quin's new neighbors wouldn't mind. They already made a comment about 'loud college kids', and was hoping that she could help Quincy's neighbors warm up to him more. Sunlight filtered in through cream colored curtains and tiny dust particles floated lazily in the air.

Quincy Abrams walked into the room, carrying another roller paintbrush. He walked up to Alice and kissed her, while his hand and the rolling brush layered her backside with green.

"See if I kiss you again." She took her brush and slapped his face until he looked like a lime.

He wiped the paint from his face and patted her on the shoulder. "Thanks for helping me with the renovation. I appreciate it."

"I wasn't about to let *this* apartment be painted in black and trimmed with red. God only knows if you'll put your little skull head garlands around your windows. You'd get away with it now, but if I do end up moving in, keep in mind that this'll only be the beginning of the renovations I'll make."

Quincy sat on a bar stool and swiveled around, looking at his new office room. "I think it looks good, I can start moving stuff in here now."

"Stuff." Alice sighed. "Your technical term for everything."

"I didn't coin the word, but I won't hesitate to use it." Quincy snickered.

"Will and Ross'll be over soon; they just texted me. Said they have more apartment warming gifts for you."

"If they got me another base drum I'll be happy." Quincy walked around the room, opening the door to a closet. "It smells like wood." He laughed. "I miss that car."

"I'm kinda glad it's gone, your new one suits you much better." Alice walked over to a window and peered down at his red sedan. "Much more comfortable. Oh look, there they come now." Alice said.

Quincy smiled, and walked to the front door to unlock it. William looked rough with stubble across his face and a cake box in his arms. "Hey buddy!" William sat the cake down on a fold out table and clapped Quincy on the back. "How's the new digs?"

"Doesn't look very healthy does he?" Roslyn reached out and held Quincy's chin with the hand not holding a bottle of grape juice. "A bit green all over. Has he been feeding himself again Allie?" Roslyn leaned on William.

"I've still got the paintbrush if you want some color on those pale cheeks Miss Lyden." Quincy nodded, holding his hands out for the drink. "And thanks for this, it's my fav."

"So, Quin, I was thinking. And this time I think I've got a good idea." William tugged at his friend's shirt sleeve. "Let's stop renovating the place for today, and go do something incredibly boss."

"Are we going to finally get your hair dyed purple Will?" Alice asked.

"Not today! Maybe tomorrow, or at the next show!" "Today, we should all go get our first tattoos. He pumped his fist in the air. "I've thought about it for a while…"

"Half an hour…" Roslyn broke in.

"...and as a professional band with a full length CD, we need one at the very least for each of us. Otherwise how will people take us seriously?"

"I take you seriously." Quincy smiled.

"Aww thanks Quin." William grinned, white teeth illuminated by the sunlight that once again shone through the window.

"I think that could be fun actually. I'd like to get one." Alice stepped forward and wrapped her arms around Quincy. "What do you think? You up for a little pain today?"

"My whole life is a torrent of pain, assuaged only by the numbness I feel from the deepest sleep. God surrendered my soul to the devil, and I've become his playground."

"Didn't you try that line on your parents once?" Alice asked.

"Yep." Quincy bent to tighten his shoelace. "But I was actually quoting..."

"I knew you were quoting," Alice pushed him softly. "Quincy just heard his *poem* has received an A by his professor. He's pretty excited over it."

"Way to go man! That's totally awesome." William high fived his buddy. "All the more reason to celebrate!"

"Well, let's go then." Quincy said, making sure he had his wallet.

"I think I'll get changed first...if you don't mind. I for one won't walk out with green all over me."

"Your box of *stuff* should be in the bedroom!" Quincy called after her, and he walked with Will and Roslyn out to the front steps. He breathed in the early Fall air and leaned against the cool brick of his new place. "It's nice; I think I'll like it here." Quincy commented.

"I hope you do; we'll get the tour when we come back. I wanna check out your patio." William nodded.

"It's good, I've got some room for the dart board and grill."

"So what kinda tattoo are we gonna get?" William asked.

Quincy shrugged and looked to Roslyn.

"I'd tell you to get something hideous and embarrassing, that way you'll always have something to talk about at after parties." She suggested.

"How about the heart and flower symbol off the album?" Alice said, coming out of the apartment and locking the door behind her.

"I'm all over that, I could see myself with our sign." William reached out and grabbed Roslyn's hand.

"That's actually pretty appealing," Quincy agreed.

"We'd be like the Corps! All having the same tattoo!" William clapped his hands. "That's it, I'm doing it." William announced.

"Alright then, let's break the skin." Roslyn grinned as they all walked out to the driveway where her bike and Quincy's car waited for them.

"You lead the way dude, we'll follow." Quincy said, stopping to open Alice's door.

"Righteous!" William said, strapping on a frosty blue helmet and taking the reins of Roslyn's bike.

William kicked the bike to life and Quincy watched as the Roslyn & Will pulled out. "Alright," Quincy said, turning on the radio and smiling devilishly to Alice. "Should it be on my rear end?"

William sat on the patched and padded bench and watched his three friends smile encouragingly at him. His artist returned with a tray of colors and slender packages. Will's heart was thumping like a wild rabbit's foot.

"So, you'll be doing me?" Will asked, and he could almost see Roslyn's crooked little smirk.

"Chest tattoos usually mean you take your shirt off." The artist replied.

"I'll take it off, but can I at least know your name first? Will asked, lifting his shirt over his head.

"I'm Peter." He ran a copy of the band logo off a nearby machine.

Will laid his shirt down. "Like Brady?"

Peter scowled. "No. Like a dick."

Will heard Quincy stifling his laughter, but Roslyn & Alice made no effort to hide their own.

"Hmm." Peter stood in front of William. "Ain't got much nipple do ya?"

William blushed, as Peter put the trace on his right breast. "Does this look right to you?" Peter readied his gun.

"Doesn't look left for sure."

A smile crossed Peter's face. "Then let's start."

Will was surprised that it didn't hurt more. He had expected terrible agony, at least the pain of a bee sting! But he was quite comfortable. "You know Peter, I asked a rabbi about tattoos and he said they were a violation of God's law."

Peter shook his head incredulously.

"Will, every word you say is a violation of God's law." Quincy said.

"And you're not even Jewish." Alice piped in.

"Good thing, too." Will peered down at his chest as Peter dipped his gun in ink.

When Will was finished, Roslyn went next. She had volunteered to take Quincy's place, as he wasn't yet ready.

"Will I be tattooing your chest also?" Peter asked hopefully.

Roslyn watched as William grew wide eyed. "I think you had more than enough fun on first base playing with my boyfriend's chest. I wouldn't want you getting too excited; those are nice pants and I'd hate for you to ruin them on my account." She said smartly, as she got positioned on the bench. She raised her shirt up to just above her belly button. Taking her hand, she pointed to a spot close to the line of her pants.

"There?" Peter asked.

"Absolutely." Roslyn replied.

He held out his hands uncertainly. "Just to put it out there," he said as he readied a new needle. "If you ever have kids, this might not look the same afterwards."

Roslyn grinned. "It won't be an issue."

William smiled, and the secret knowledge. Was shared amongst Quincy & Alice. Peter shrugged, terribly out of the loop.

"It's your body." He said, putting his outline on Roslyn's flesh.

Alice got hers just above her bust line, and with every successive pass of Peter's gun, Quincy's face got a bit green, William noticed.

At last, Quincy's turn came. "I want it on my hand please."

"Since I'm a songbird of sound advice today, I'll say visible tattoos can inhibit job opps. I'll do it; I just don't want angry parents in here. Kid got a 666 tattooed on his wrists once when I first started. He had a faked *release* form from his parents. Got in some shit for that one."

Quincy scoffed. "I'm 20, I live on my own, my father is the devil, and my Mom didn't know when to stop buying me cartoon crotch huggers. Trust me, I'm good."

Peter nodded and set to work. "It's odd, all you guys getting this symbol. But, whatever."

"We're in a band! Lipstick Trace." William stepped forward shamelessly. He put his arm around Roslyn. "Well, except for Roslyn here. She's our talent agent." He took out a bright yellow flyer from his back pocket. "Come see us some time, we always play this club."

"...Thanks?" Peter said as he walked them to the front of the shop and totaled them up.

Alice's tattoo was the cheapest. "A discount for the enchanting view." Peter commented.

Quincy escorted Alice out with his right hand, once outside he couldn't control himself.

"That guy was a *dick!*"

William smiled. "You mean; he was a *Peter.*" William corrected him.

***

Quincy spent the next few days making his apartment feel like his old room. The music helped, like it always did. "There are blank spots on these walls where AC/DC posters should be. I really should go back and rescue them, presuming they've not been burned." Quincy spoke to himself, this habit had been growing on him in this last year.

He heard keys turning in their slot, and went out to see Alice. She carried two brown bags with her, full to the brim with groceries. He smiled.

"Is there really early blizzard coming?" he took a bag off of her hands.

"I've got yogurt, popsicles and two or three coffee blends." Alice said, sitting her bag on the bar table and methodically putting each item in its newly appointed spot.

"Sweet. I can always use more caffeine."

"Mr. Cineplex Manager, you." Alice tossed a can of green beans at him.

Quincy rolled his eyes. "Someone needs to make sure teenagers aren't screwing in the back rows."

Alice grinned, then her smile faltered. It did not escape Quincy's notice.

"What was that for? My jokes that bad?"

She folded up the emptied bag and stuck it in her recycling drawer. She sat down on a barstool and opened a can of lemonade. "Saw your Mom." Alice let this bomb fall through the air.

Quincy blinked, willing away the itch that wouldn't be sated. "Really? She never goes out." Quincy recalled. "Like…ever."

"Yeah." Alice's resolve cracked like a hardboiled egg.

"Well, what did she say?" Quincy asked curiously.

"She didn't recognize me at first. She wanted …." Alice paused, collecting herself. "She asked how you were." Alice held her head steadily, and looked at Quincy carefully. She watched his eyes, for in them she saw everything.

"That's strange." Quincy played with a paring knife.

"Loneliness can do that to people." Alice licked her lips. Uninvited silence crept into the room.

"Quincy," She reached out for his hand not holding the knife. "Your Dad…" she saw his eyes darken, "Your Dad left your Mom."

Quincy stopped playing with the knife, and blinked. "What?"

"I'm sorry baby," Alice said compassionately, "he's been gone for the last few months."

Quincy coughed, and shook his head. He moved like a broken needle on a record. Back and forth, yet not really going anywhere or making any comprehensible sounds.

"I'm sorry, to tell you." She said.

"Don't be. Nothing he does really surprises me anymore." Quincy said. "Didn't show up for my graduation, doesn't give a damn about anyone but himself."

"I really wish I could say something that would make your words untrue, but she looked really bad Quincy. I can tell she'd love to see you." Alice got up and led him to the barstool next to her, before he wore a trail into the hardwood.

Quincy was a little surprised to feel the back of his eyes burning, of all the things his father had ever done, he had never expected him to abandon his mother. "It's just like…where is the structure in life?" he said, looking up at Alice.

"It's not so big a deal," Alice quickly took that back. "I mean, it's not *not* a big deal, I just mean, it happens to people. People fail and sometimes things get taken for granted."

Quincy felt himself shaking. "That's why she was out." Quincy swallowed, feeling like he was forcing cotton down his throat. "Because she's alone now."

"She's got to be missing her son. Didn't you always say she seemed more in touch with you than your Dad?"

"Seemed to be more, but she rarely acted on it."

"At least she was there in May." Alice said, looking at the picture of Quincy in his long black robes and hat.

"Rituals. Meaningless rituals and traditions. Yet why am I bound to them? Why do they matter so much to me?"

"Because. You care. You kiss every kiss like it's your first." She grinned uncontrollably for a second. "Not that that sorta thing is bad. But, you treat every day like your last one, and you want to be remembered for your integrity and faithfulness."

Quincy smiled briefly. "Yeah." He turned his face away from her. "I just, feel like the world has passed me by, and I'm the only one abiding by the true things."

She shrugged. "What does it matter what the world does, so long as you're happy?"

Quincy stood up and stared out the window. "Because I am the seed of my father and his traits are in my blood, and I don't want his shadow to fall on me."

"I don't see your father in you." Alice said.

"It's because he hides behind my eyelids, he lunges into my laughter, and I can't stand it. I will not be him." Quincy said.

"You won't be." Alice frowned.

"Every fear in me has that basis, that root." Quincy turned on his heel. He seemed to be battling so much within himself. "I'll go see my mother soon, Allie, I promise." Quincy said. "Excuse me a minute."

"Sure." She took a drink from her lemonade.

Closing the bathroom door securely behind him, and making sure the lock was engaged, Quincy sat upon the sink. He could almost hear his mother's voice echoing through the years, telling him not to break the sink. "If I am my father's son, and he didn't have the resolve to keep his word, am I that much better than him? Can greater things be expected of me?" Quincy questioned himself, staring down at the small diamond he had pulled out from his pocket.

***

William was sitting comfortably in The Keen Bean on a plush chair drinking his favorite iced coffee. He was reading a copy of his Introduction to Philosophy book. Darryl, his manager, came out with a fresh tray of fragrant scones. "Weren't you off an hour ago Denslie?" he asked, placing the scones in their display cases.

William lowered the book. "Indeed Sir, I was, I'm just meeting Roslyn here after she gets outta class."

Darryl nodded.

"Boss?" William asked tentatively.

"Employee?" Darryl said, wiping his hands on his pants.

"You know I'm in a band, right?"

William's bearded and bemused boss nodded. "You wanted to invite me to a show, right?"

William sat up. "You know you're always invited. But what I really wanted to know, was if you'd be willing to let my band's CD be sold here. You see, I tried going to music stores but they said they didn't support local tragedies. I'm not sure what they meant, but I'm sure it was a misunderstanding." William grinned.

"Yeah, well go on Buffalo Bill, what do you suggest?"

William's lip twitched slightly. "Well," he tried to remember everything Roslyn had suggested to him about sales. "You buy some of our CD's, and we split the profits 60/40."

Darryl considered it, twisting his fingers through his brown forest of chin hair. "Alright, forty percent is good for me, that'd be no problem."

William blanched. "No I mean, you're doing us the favor, you could have the sixty percent if you wanted it. Course, I'd be okay with paying you less." He flashed his pearly whites.

"And I'll be happy to pay you less if the CD's bomb." Darryl extended his hand and shook William's.

"Sir, there are two things that I know beyond any shadow of a doubt. 1: The sixties are over, and the good guys lost. 2: Lipstick Trace is going to change the world."

Something in Darryl's smile made William think he was believed. William took out his backpack and removed ten CD's. Darryl handed him sixty dollars from the drawer and placed *Less Mic, More Jive* on the counter just above the sparkly sugared scones.

William left the coffee shop smiling as he saw Roslyn roaring through the parking lot.

***

Roslyn was lying on her bed that evening, listening to her lecture from earlier that day, when she felt her phone vibrating. She rolled over wearily, Will knew not to call her for at least another hour. But when she saw Quincy's number on her caller ID her interest peaked. Smirking, she removed her earphones and answered in a low, throaty voice. "Lady Lyssa's pleasure line, how can we spice up your night?"

"Aw jeez," came his response. "I was looking to talk to a guy…."

"Ass." She rolled her eyes.

"Yeah, I know." He sighed.

"What's up? Will isn't here."

"I know he's not, I wanted to talk to you."

She waited through his hesitation. "Well, what can I do for you?" She asked, sitting up in bed. She listened intently as he explained about his Dad, his voice was stronger than she would have expected. She knew Quin could be overly emotional at times. She took a deep breath when he finally fell silent.

"I'm sorry about this, first of all." Roslyn said gravely, as memories of her failed father came to her mind. "It's tough. How are you holding up?"

"Alice left a little bit ago; she was good about helping me…"

"Yeah, I bet she was." Roslyn grinned.

Quincy cleared his throat dramatically. "But I honestly don't think she can relate to the situation like you can. You know her Dad."

"Well…" She shrugged. "Quin, I'll tell you. I don't think there was anything you ever could have done to change the man. He was the loser. Not you."

"I always thought it had been me, I still wonder if, like…"

She shook her head and switched the phone to her other hand.

"Quin, listen. I spent years trying to figure out my excuse for a father. Trust me. He's the one who messed up."

Quincy was quiet.

"You've grown up a lot since I first met you, and it all started when you got the boot from that hellhole you were in. You've got your life together, and I don't think your Dad ever did."

"Roslyn, do you think that...I'm a completely different person than who my Dad is? Like, I won't make his same mistakes?"

Roslyn considered his question, suspecting some other meaning behind it. "If you scorched your hand by putting it on the burner of a stove, would you do it again to see if it feels the same?"

Quincy laughed.

"I didn't think you would Quin. And I don't think you'll make his mistakes, you are your own person."

"Well, I ... yeah." Quincy stammered. "Thanks Roslyn. I knew you'd be able to help."

"I'm gonna go now, but, does Will know this yet? Should I be the one to tell him?" She asked.

"It's up to you. I'm going to go to bed, it's been a tiring day."

"Alright, talk to you later." She hung up the phone and considered the conversation. It didn't come to her what Quincy was truly worried about, but that didn't stop her from hypothesizing obsessively. She only minded not being able to read him like a book.

***

Quincy sat outside his old home until his feet began to tingle. He shook them awake and with a deep breath, he exited his car.

He approached the door and laughed. The welcome mat always had been misleading to him, he wondered if he could ever feel welcome here.

Closing his eyes, he knocked on the door and waited. He saw the curtains flutter in the window next to him, and seconds later, the large wooden door opened before him. Like the smell of lilac rushing to meet him, the memories of the last year grabbed him by his shirt collar and bombarded him with emotion.

Denise Abrams appeared before him, and there was such a reassuring calm about her that Quincy lost the words that he thought he was going to say. He gave all he had left to offer. "Hi."

She looked him up and down, frowning slightly as she immediately saw his tattoo, yet still she seemed happy.

Quincy said "Hi," again, not quite sure he had made himself loud enough, and not wanting to make her think he was being rude.

At once, her arms were around him, and Quincy felt his heart race at the unexpected outpouring of emotion.

Releasing him, she smoothed out his hair. "Come inside?" she asked He felt awkward, to his right was the room where the dreadful TV had been...he paused and reflected on his thoughts. *Where the TV* had *been.* The room was now occupied by a set of exercise equipment.

Once they were in the kitchen, Quincy sat down at the table and realized he could rest his elbows on the table. No longer was it being used to house coffee tins and varied refuse. "It looks so different in here, so...clean..." he was awed.

"Your *father's*" she said the word distastefully, "absence has made a genuine difference." She said.

"I can tell." He leaned back in his seat. "Why did he leave?"

Denise didn't answer immediately, which made Quincy feel guilty. His question had come suddenly, selfishly, and he began to regret asking it. "It's just...I was always alone, and at least you two seemed okay...not really happy, but at least okay."

"Your father and I are different people; I think we always have been Quincy." She said, sitting down.

"I wonder why you married him then." Quincy tried to remember the last time he'd had this long of a conversation with his mother; the concentration made his head pound.

Denise shook her head and clasped her hands. Perhaps unknowingly her attention fell to Quincy's hand again.

"What is that?" She tentatively reached out for it.

"This is my tattoo." Quincy said with pride.

Denise frowned. "I hope they were clean."

"I don't want to sound like an asshole..." Quincy shook his head. "But where was this concern when I needed and wanted it?"

Denise frowned. "I'm sorry Quincy, no matter what happened with your father and I ... I was always trying to protect you from..." Denise rubbed her hazel eyes and Quincy still noticed the tears that she was trying to stop from coming out. "...I was always trying to protect you."

"I protected Alice that one night just before I got kicked out."

Denise blinked hurriedly and nodded. "I know; I think it scared your father." She said quickly, her face flushing.

Quincy shook his head, not understanding how or why it would have so scared *Bad Brad.*

Denise pursed her lips. "How *is* Alice?" Denise asked, steering the conversation away from Brad.

Quincy couldn't help the smile that came onto his face. His mother genuinely seemed to care. How he would have loved this interest years ago!

He looked at his tattoo and then at his mother. "I think I'm going to marry her." He admitted, and his mother was the very first person to whom he had confessed this secret ambition.

"You're so young Quincy." She said after a painstaking minute. "Are you sure?"

"From the very first kiss, I've known."

Denise smiled. "Well, she is a very lucky woman, I've not told you this, but I'm proud of who you are. I could see it for years now; you've always been smarter than your age."

Quincy's thoughts were washed away like driftwood as he heard these words. It was the truest expression of love he'd ever received from his mother. She was proud of him.

When he didn't respond she faltered, her gaze broke. "Have you asked her parents yet?"

He shook his head. "I'm resolved to do that next, today is the day."

His mother looked at him, and Quincy truly saw her for the first time. She had changed so much, she held her head up and spoke strongly, so much different from before. "I'd like to have lunch with the two of you, Quincy; I think it would help me into this idea of you getting married."

"Just as soon as she says yes." Quincy said, and the ring box in his pocket had never felt more right.

***

The day seemed to pass unnaturally fast, and Quincy wondered how he was going to broach the subject with the Mr. & Mrs. Mendell. Quincy hopped onto the stoop outside their house and with a great breath, he knocked politely on the door.

He had left his mother's house feeling uplifted and secure in himself. She was *proud* of him, and therefore, he was not someone to be ashamed of. In fact, the Mendells' were the luckiest people because their daughter was going to marry a wonderful guy.

All of these happy thoughts were precariously balanced on whether or not Alice actually would accept his offer of marriage.

Brenda opened the door and seemed surprised to see Quincy.

"Hi Br...Mrs. Mendell." Quincy decided formality would be best.

She grinned slightly. "Hello to *you*, Quincy." She said, adding emphasis to her own formality. "Come on in." she said.

"Thank you." He grinned anxiously, listening for the sounds of Alice's father.

"Alice isn't home yet Quin, she's still in her last afternoon class." Brenda mentioned, straightening a picture in the hallway that Quincy had just absentmindedly set off center.

"I understand that, and it's actually you and your husband I want to talk to." He was right on it now, he could feel the secret rushing to his lips, and he could see himself asking the Mendells' for their blessing in his decision.

Quincy wasn't expecting to see Brenda frown. "I'm sorry, but it's just Alice and me right now, he's away on business."

Quincy stopped suddenly, frowning from the sudden news. "What? That's not...no. I'm sorry. He can't be gone."

"I drove him to the airport," Brenda laughed, looking at Quincy with concern. "Are you feeling alright? You look pale."

Quincy sat down, right there in the hallway, and slumped his head back. "Oh cruel fates, how long will you toy with my mortal shell and feeble mind?" Quincy despaired aloud.

"Okay, what's wrong?" Brenda said, sitting down beside him.

"Brenda," Quincy abandoned formality and regressed into his naturally quick tongued ways, finding it far easier. "I want to say this plainly, because I can't wait for Daniel to come back."

Brenda got up and motioned into the living room for Quincy to take a seat, he groaned as he did so.

"What is it?" She asked, her hands crossing her chest. Quincy could tell she was starting to get concerned, her face was becoming far too tight; the laugh lines that usually resided around her mouth were pulled taut.

Quincy put up his hands openly. "I want to marry your daughter. What's more than that, I want you and Daniel to approve of it." Quincy said quickly, all the words falling from his mouth like water off a mountainside.

Brenda inclined her head, and her lips parted.

"I also haven't asked the question yet, to Alice I mean, to marry me. I want to make sure that you and Daniel are okay with it. I think it's important that you two are in on the situation and know what I'm hoping for. I'm not always going to be a manager at this movie theater, I'll be able to provide for her, and really, I can."

He thought back to all his journal entries. The emotions clenched his heart so that no blood could course through his veins. He felt light headed and very nearly fainted. He leaned back in his chair and tried to control his breathing. He closed his eyes so he wouldn't see anything. He was too afraid to look into Brenda's eyes and see rejection. All he heard was the chirping of birds and a low crunching noise. The noise persisted, and Quincy's curiosity eventually overtook him. He opened his eyes and saw William sitting in the kitchen, chewing on a long piece of green celery.

"Hmm..." Will said, looking at Brenda and then back at Quin. "Ya know, I can come back and talk to Alice later Mrs. M." William said, nodding quickly with those bright brown eyes of his. William hopped off the kitchen chair he was occupying and paused as he walked past Quincy.

He patted Quincy on his shoulder with his free hand, and stared deeply into his friend's eyes. "Quin, I'm just gonna say, you might want to slow down when you finally ask Alice for her hand in marriage, I know you very well and could barely keep up with what you're saying.

But that aside, I hope she accepts your offer. And," he nodded his head towards Brenda, "with Brenda's permission, I would like to take on the role of Daniel Mendell in his absence and speak to you as a father."

William stuck the celery stalk into his mouth and puffed on it as it were a cigar. "Now you listen here, son, and I say 'son' in the strictest sense of the word. You want to marry our daughter, you want to take those little hands that used to reach out for me from the depths of a bassinette and cried '*da da, da da*' and put a ring on one of those little fingers. You want my wife and I to give our daughter away to a man who might break her heart and leave the pieces scattered under the fridge next to the bread crumbs and dust bunnies. Is that what you're trying to say, *Son*?"

Quincy rose from the sofa. "William. I think now is a good time for you to leave." He pushed William toward the door.

William loudly protested. "I will not be kicked out of my own home, I have a mortgage to pay off, and my very favorite pair of shoes are still in my closet! You'll pay for this you young hooligan!"

Quincy bolted the door and with his face redder than a beet, he turned back to Denise. She was trying to hold back the smile on her face, but it wasn't working. "I really do want this to be serious." Quincy said, his confidence nearly broken.

"How do you plan on proposing to my daughter?" Brenda asked, placing her hands on Quincy's shoulders and peering into his face.

Quincy knew it all by heart. Every step he would take was rehearsed and every word that would come from his lips would be perfect prose. "Brenda, I give you my word that there will be no other man in this world who could love your Alice more completely than I could as a husband. William mentioned those hands of hers, and I would hold them in the winter to keep them warm, and I'll assure you, her happiness will come before my own."

"You're both very young, how can you be sure this is what you will want in a year?"

Quincy shook his head. "I could as easily quit breathing as I could quit loving Alice."

"Well," Denise breathed heavily. "I think you mean what you say, and for that, I will give you *my* blessing. I'll talk to Daniel; I don't see him saying no to you, not with how happy you make our daughter."

Quincy heard the words coming from Denise, those longed for words of approval, and he even laughed now, having remembered how silly William had acted.

Quincy had the permission to get every happiness deserved to him, and he was not going to stop until it was all accomplished. He knew where Alice would be later tonight, and he knew how to set his plan into motion.

He thanked Denise profusely, and then left the house, certain to start his plan right away. With trembling fingers, he pulled out his cell phone and dialed Alice, the shrill dial tones burrowed into his head and he couldn't wait until they were overtaken by the sweet voice that eased the sorrow of his soul.

"Hello?" she spoke.

"Hey! It's me. Can I see you tonight? I want help with something."

"Sure. What's up?"

"I need your help on something; um…" he realized he had just repeated himself. "I'm writing something, and I want your opinion on it. I want to know what you *think* of my proposal." He grinned at his own boldness.

"Sure, I'll be over at seven seventeen." She laughed.

"Weirdo. I'll see you then."

Quincy hung up the phone and jumped into his car, as he drove away from the Mendell's, he was struck by an absolutely brilliant idea. An idea that was beautifully his, and he had no doubts that it wouldn't come to fruition.

Quincy was singing in his car and was nearly swerved into the emergency divider when he felt a pair of hands, cold hands at that, close around his ears.

Screaming profanity to make a sailor turn in shame, he wrenched around to see two chestnut eyes staring at him incredulously.

"Quin! You're gonna pop the question!" William said, hopping into the front seat as Quincy passed by a state trooper.

"Hells bells, Will, sit the hell down and strap in!" Quincy peered into his rearview to see if he was being pursued. Fortune was on his side.

"Dude. Like, you're taking the plunge, tying the knot, flipping the pancake!"

Quincy shook his head. "Flipping the pancake?"

"Would you prefer to put a bun in the oven?" Will asked, fastening his seatbelt.

"Not quite yet, but my unruly spawn will surely drive you nuts." Quincy couldn't help himself from smiling directly at William.

"You seem hopeful." William said, smiling back.

"All my happiness hangs on her response, my friend." Quincy sighed.

"So you're gonna ask her when?"

"Tonight. My Mom's gonna come over and help me cook something up special."

William's eyes bulged and he tugged at his long hair. "Your *Mom*? Like...your mother?"

"Yeah, that woman who owned the waterslide I slid down when I came into this world. Her."

"That sounds pretty...unusual when you put it like that."

"Flipping. The. Pancake. I shall say no more."

"Man. You're proposing to my ex tonight, and your Mom, who disowned you, is helping you cook up a five course meal. What's your papa up to?"

"He left her. My Mom that is, not your ex." Quincy gripped the steering wheel.

"Man. That's…heavy. Did he have another chick?"

Quincy shook his head. "I don't know. From what she was saying to me, it sounded like he was only staying with her so he wouldn't have to pay child support…" Quincy felt his cheeks grow hot.

William had nothing to say to this, or rather, he did, but his lips couldn't form the words. His lips flopped around like a fish out of water.

"Yeah. I'm going to treat Alice so much better than he treated my Mom and by extension, me."

"Well, I guess your Mom is doing okay, then? She's not like…crazy over him leaving?"

"She's plenty pissed, but she's had some time to cope with it. For me, the wound is still bleeding."

"Maybe you should put some Alice ointment on it, could sting a bit at first, but it'll help in the long run!" William slid his seat back and put his feet out the window.

"I'm going to propose to her tonight. Yes. And remember Willy, you're gonna be my best man, so try and get some sort of halfway decent speech going. We're gonna cut the cake to Cherry Pie. It's going to be great."

"You've got quite a bit planned already, wonder what Alice'll think."

"I do not care about all that, I have ideas on what I'd like, but as long as she says yes, I'll be happy." A thought struck him. "How the hell did you get in my car?"

William held up a duplicate of his car key. "It was in Alice's room; I couldn't help myself."

"Umm…why were you in my would be fiancée's bedroom?"

"Well," William grinned sheepishly. "Her bedroom door was open, and I saw her spare keys lying around the floor, and I didn't want them to get swept up...so I sorta moved them, meaning to put them on the dresser, but then I heard a knocking on the door and got distracted. So then they ended up in my pocket."

"Hmm. Well, alright, I'll buy it, I'm in a good mood."

"Good enough mood to drop me off at my place?"

"You realize it was two blocks from Alice's house right?"

"I do."

Rolling his eyes, Quincy pulled a U turn. "I'm in a good mood, but don't test me Sir."

"If Alice says yes can I test your patience?"

"If Alice says yes, I'll give you all my Maiden CD's."

William blanched. "No thanks."

Quincy grinned and dropped his friend off at his house.

***

William smiled as he walked into The Keen Bean. He was happy because of a few things this morning. The bells on his ankles were louder than the bell above the door that jingled as he walked in. Secondly, he was happy because it was such a gorgeous day so far. Surely, tonight would contain romance at Quincy's apartment, if all went well.

The early risers were still sipping on their steaming mugs of "mud" and many of them looked perplexed at the continual jangling of bells long after the door had closed. William put a dollar in the tips jar as he waited at the counter; the smell alone was enough for a tip. Will motioned for Darryl, who seemed hesitant to come over and see him.

"What's shakin', Denslie?" he asked.

Will scratched his chin, liking the morning stubble that was still very much present. "Ya know, I was wondering just that. How many of our CD's have we sold already? Because, uh, I've got more…about…twenty?" He looked into his satchel. "Yep. Twenty extras."

"Actually bud," Darryl said, wiping off the finger prints Will was now leaving on the glass display case, "we haven't sold a single copy yet."

Will frowned. "Bummer. I mean, obviously these cats aren't the demographic." Will said, waving at the bald eagle's sitting behind copies of the Daily Times.

"I'm sorry man." Darryl said.

"Well, I'm not gonna give up yet. Do me a solid?"

"Lay it on me." Darryl said, tossing a used rag into the sink.

"I know we've got this Muzak stuff playing, well, pretty frequently. Maybe we could play less Muzak and instead play *Less Mic, More Jive* during happy hour? Could get some exposure and I mean, this is *our* investment you know. I want us to succeed." Will leaned across the counter and stared at his boss.

Darryl shook him off. "Remember our little talk Denslie, no physical contact unless you can commit."

Will rolled his eyes. "Ross & I aren't swingers…I'm sorry." He said.

Darryl sighed. "Well, at the very least I will play your demo for you…"

"*Full length Compact Disc…*" William corrected him quietly.

"…tomorrow right after school lets out."

"Thank you so much!" William clapped his hands. "How could I ever repay you!"

"Well, Kevin called off. I need a swinger of the payroll type this morning."

Will nodded. "Sounds fab to me!" he said, walking behind the counter to scrub his hands, happiness overwhelming him.

***

Alice realized she was awake by the smell of rich coffee brewing downstairs. She didn't think her Dad was supposed to be back so soon, but the coffee couldn't be brewing for any other reason. She lazed about in bed, peeking at her clock from underneath her covers. She was rarely permitted to sleep in and was surprised to see that it was ten AM. She had definitely slept in today. She rolled out of her bed, careful to roll out on the right side of her bed as she considered the left side of the bed to be horribly unlucky.

She stretched and listened to her bedsprings creak in protest to her movements. She went over to her chest of drawers and pulled out a pair of pink and white socks, deciding that pink would be her color of choice today, pink and black.

She was rummaging in her drawers trying to find her favorite t-shirt from The Runaways. She saw a flash of gold and white and grew curious. She pulled out what turned out to be the skirt of her cheerleading outfit. She looked for the top of it, and having found it, she proceeded to lock her door. She smiled at herself for the idea, but had to know.

She put her old school colors on and looked at herself in the mirror. The look didn't seem complete, and she wasn't sure why, until she looked at her hair. "Alice dear, you're going batty in your old age." she picked up a hair band from her desk and put her hair back. "There you are now, that looks alright."

She turned around to admire herself, when she realized that her skirt was a little more *comfortable* than she had remembered it being. She grinned wryly and nodded, feeling very happy that she'd lost a little weight since high school.

Growing bored with looking at herself, she switched into her t-shirt and black denim pants. She opened her door and walked down the stairs to the kitchen, where she saw her father and mother talking in quiet tones.

"Hi Dad, didn't expect to see you back this soon." she said, kissing him on his stubbly cheek.

She noticed just a glint of something unknown in her father's expression, a shade over his eyes so to speak. Whatever it was changed so fast that she thought that she had imagined the whole thing.

"Hello honey." he smiled a bit more enthusiastically than he might have normally. "Did you sleep well?"

"I did. Slept a bit longer than I thought I would though. When did you get into town?"

"Just this morning, I caught a flight back last night. I rescheduled part of my meetings, I can get away with it."

"Seemed unexpected." She went to the bread cabinet and put two slices of bread into the toaster and sniffed deeply as the smell of toast filled the room.

"A few things seemed unexpected recently." She heard her father say, yet it was so quiet she wondered if he'd actually said it.

"Did you say something?" she asked.

"Your father is just mumbling Alice." her mother said, opening the butter dish and sliding it over to Alice's place at the table.

Alice poured herself a glass of orange juice and sat down at the table to eat.

"So what are your plans today, Alice?" Daniel asked.

"Well, I'm going to head to the park a little later, get some shots of the little leaguers for a school project. I'm going to help Quincy tonight with a paper of his." she took a bite. "That's pretty much it for me, just a normal day. What about you?"

Her father put his cup of coffee down. "Your mother and I are just going through some old things." he said, his eyes going to a box on the counter top.

Brenda walked over to the box and picked up an old photo album. "You always loved cameras and pictures Alice." She smiled, and opened the book. "Here you are in first grade. You couldn't leave the house until you were sure your pig tails were even on each side." Brenda laughed.

Alice looked over and nodded. "Yep, I was a pretty strange child."

"You had your moments." Daniel laughed.

Alice grew uneasy, feeling like there was some heavy vibe in the room. "What's going on, did someone die?" she asked fearfully.

Her parents looked at each other, and said nothing.

"Aunt Lora, she's okay?" Alice asked, automatically choosing the sickliest of her relatives.

"She's fine, honey." Daniel said, but he didn't go any further.

"You guys just seem, preoccupied today, both of you." She finished her toast.

"We're fine, it's just sometimes surprising to realize that you're in college and growing up." Brenda said, holding her husband's hand.

"Well, yeah… that shouldn't be anything new." she laughed.

"Sometimes it just hits us hard." Daniel shrugged. "You and Quincy. He's doing well in school? He's on the ball, right?"

Alice took a bite of her toast and nodded. "Quincy's great."

"How long have you two been dating again? It doesn't seem that long." Daniel questioned again.

Brenda gave him a furtive look. Alice noticed.

"We've been together for over two years now Dad, what's up with all the questions?"

Daniel shook his head. "Just, being your father honey." He lowered his head a little.

Brenda cleared her throat. "Well, we're going to head to the mall honey. Need to do some shopping."

"Alright, pick me up something nice." she grinned.

"Anything for you sweetie." Daniel said, finishing his coffee. He got up and kissed her on her head before walking into the other room.

***

William had just left his final class of the day when he felt his pants vibrating. "Ooh!" he exclaimed, reaching into his pockets for his tiny flip phone.

"Hello, this is not Bill Denslie." he said, readjusting his satchel over his shoulder.

"Denslie, this is Darryl. You got sixty seconds?"

"Hold on, let me do the math." William looked at his bright red plastic watch, and saw the little mouse inching slowly towards the cheese hour hand. "I do. What's shakin' Dangerous Darryl?"

"Denslie, I'm going to lay it out for you like this, your CD is a hit. This flock of teenies came in today, heard it playing, and ate it up. I'm out of stock."

"For real?"

"No, for fakes. Of course for real cracker brain. I need more copies, can you drop any off like, five minutes ago?"

"I was in class five minutes ago…"

"It means I want them now. Can you deliver?"

Will looked into his satchel and saw several of his *full length CDs'* surfing around his notebooks and art supplies. "Signed, sealed delivered, boss man."

"I took the liberty of raising the price to fifteen rocks."

"Really, now?"

"Really."

William stopped walking to smell his favorite patch of tulips growing in the campus gardens. He breathed deeply and thought of the luck he had stumbled across. "Darryl, it seems fame has found me at last."

"Well tell fame to help you find my establishment. I want a new pair of shoes Denslie, and the *Less Mic, More Jive* CD is gonna buy 'em for me. Be here in twenty."

"That's more than sixty seconds!" Will declared, sensing that Darryl was about to hang up.

"Time is money! Anyone telling you otherwise is selling something!" Darryl said, and William heard the phone disconnect.

William considered what Darryl had just said, and marveled at it. "But, we are selling something." William paused.

"Oh well, I'm feeling pretty good right now." William said. He picked a dandelion out from amongst the throng of tulip and placed it behind his ear. He hadn't planned on going by his work today, but then, he hadn't planned on making money either.

He opened his phone and dialed Quincy, he had to know about the development. William listened to the phone ring and waited for his buddy to answer.

"I'm up to my eyeballs in spices WD40, this had better be good." Came Quincy's unique 'hello.'

"Spices? Why, aren't you tasty enough?"

"I'm cooking dude, remember proposing to Alice tonight? What's up?"

"Ooh, what are ya having? I'm feelin' pretty hungry."

"Food. Talk to me, remember the busy innuendo?"

"Alright, catch this."

"Hands are full. Lose the hippie slang."

William heard a pot clatter in the background and smiled appreciatively, Quincy sure seemed to be making an effort. "So you know how I sold our CD's to Darryl at work?"

"Don't remember that conversation, no."
"Alright, well, I did. Made a few bucks initially, well now he's just sold all of them. He wants more. From what it sounds like, we're the hottest thing since glam rock."

"We *are* glam rock you dweeb."

Quincy did sound more receptive to the progression of the conversation, so William pressed on. "Anyway, man, this sounds like a good time to get a show going, if we're as popular as it seems, we'd make some serious coin."

"Yeah sure, I'm down for any night but tonight. Unless Alice says no, in which case I'll be booked all the rest of my life, seeing as I'll have killed myself in a ritualistic fashion using gardening supplies and kitchen knives."

William heard a woman shout Quincy's first, middle, and last name and his jaw dropped. "Is that your Mom?" William asked.

"Sorry Mom, really...I won't 86 myself, I promise. And yes, my Mom is helping me out. Did you really think I could orchestrate something this complex on my own? Please Willy, I'm a failure in the kitchen."

"Well, that's cool man." William nodded.

"My failures are cool. Great man. I love you too."

"Look up man, Gods happy for ya, it's a beautiful day. I'm going to the Keen Bean to drop off some more of our CDs', you woo win and wed Miss Mendell and I'll handle the easy stuff. Good luck buddy!" William said, hopping onto a ledge and balancing himself as he walked across it.

"Thanks man, good luck with um... breathing or something. Whatever the heck it is you're doing now."

"I'm walking on a pseudo balance beam."

"Right. That." Quincy said, hanging up.

"See ya man!" William said, speaking to the dial tone, then shutting his phone.

***

The light of the setting sun illuminated the blue van that was driving towards the horizon. Quincy's mother had just left and his apartment smelled of Rosemary and chicken. Quincy felt pretty pleased with this only being one of his first actual attempts at cooking. His forearm wasn't stinging nearly as much as when he had first burned it on the skillet.

It was almost seven seventeen, so cautiously Quincy lit two black candles and sat them in the center of the table. Just as he finished putting the food out there was a knocking at his door. He nearly upset the salad dressing in his surprise. With a calming pause he gathered his thoughts and checked his pocket for the tenth time to make sure the ring hadn't run off.

He walked to the door and reflected that tonight would either end in his ultimate happiness, or be his undoing.

Swallowing the ball of cotton that was in his throat he answered the door and saw Alice before him.

"Hey." She said, greeting him with a kiss.

"Come in. Dinner's ready."

Alice walked in and removed her pink windbreaker. "Dinner?" she asked. "Nice." She said nodding her head. "Who's delivering?"

"Nobody." Quincy said, putting her jacket into the closet. "I cooked, as a thank you for helping with this paper." Quincy smiled as Alice sniffed the air appreciatively.

"Quincy...my God. You trying to get me to spend the night?" Alice stared at all the food.

Quincy grinned. *If all goes well, you'll always spend the night.* "Well...my paper is written to be a persuasive piece." He pulled out her seat and motioned for her to sit down.

As the candles burned lower Alice & Quincy began to talk.

"Well, I am pleasantly surprised." Quincy said, wiping his mouth on a napkin, proud of himself for not wiping it on his sleeves.

"In that the meal wasn't poisonous?" she took a sip of her soda.

"Well, that." He nodded. "It was also good."

"You'll need to cook for me more often." Alice placed her glass down in front of her.

Quincy knew that dinner had been his safety zone, and his heart pumped blood through his system, mixing with the adrenaline flooding his body.

"So, um." Quincy began awkwardly. "My paper."

"Of course. Bring it here. If I can just get my lethargy to wear off, I'll be able to read it.'

"Okay." He began. "But you have to let me know right away if it persuades you to my way of thinking or not."

"I will give it the attention and response it deserves." She laid her head upon her arms. "And am I ever one to deny you my opinion?"

"Well this would be the time...knowing you." He grasped his hands together and walked towards his office. He opened his desk drawer and pulled out his proposal. The golden script was set on a silver matted paper, and decorated with stars and moons.

"Today is our day." Quincy said, looking into his drawers one last time, and noticing his richly decorated journal. He lifted it and pressed it to his lips. "Today is our day." Quincy whispered. He left his room, and admired Alice as she sat at the table, still lounging comfortably.

"Here." He handed the proposal to her. "Please read this, Alice Mendell." Quincy said, and as his hands grasped the decorated paper, Quincy's control of his happiness left him. His heart was in her hands. With a single word, his heart would be broken, or forever made whole.

He watched her face disappear behind his words, and he went to one knee. He opened the silver glittery box, within which, shone a silver band. Its diamond glittered in the light of his fluoresce light bulbs.

Quincy watched, as slowly her eyes focused in on the paper. The seconds passed with the speed of a geriatric drag race. Quincy knew that she had read it all, for her eyes had stopped moving left and right. He swallowed, as she lowered the proposal, ever so slightly.

Her eyes grew wide as they flashed in comprehension. She saw the ring, and her lips shook as she met his gaze. "Quincy…" she said, watching him intently.

Quincy began to recite from memory every word that was written on the proposal.

"Say yes, or I will kill myself.
It may seem melodramatic, I know.
But before you say yes, take this slow.
This is a memory you can't keep on a shelf.
I'm on my knees, and when you look up
You'll see my eyes, tearing up.
If you say no, know that I
Seriously, honestly, will die.
And then you'll have that over your head.
Imagine walking down the street, hearing what's
said.
'Oh Alice, I hear your boyfriend's dead.
Yup! He keeled when him I declined to wed.'
Marry me, cuz I'm not that bad.
A little cynical, but as Will says, that's rad.
But all the same, it's your choice,

All I'm waiting on, is the sound of your voice.
Marry me Miss Mendell, it's all I require
To stay in this life, and out of hellfire."

Alice was shaking her head, and Quincy's thoughts panicked. He tried to untie his tongue, while simultaneously attempting to hold his hands steady under the crushing weight of Alice's ring.

"Quincy…" Alice said, her voice low and her hands clasped at her stomach.

He heard the refusal in her voice, and prepared himself for the worst rejection he'd ever experienced.

"Your eyes weren't watering." she said.

He was taken aback by this. He heard his neck pop as he tilted his head up to meet her gaze. "What?"

"Your eyes weren't tearing up when I looked at you."

Quincy couldn't believe what he was hearing. And so, he chose to shake his head until reality shifted to a more favorable one.

He felt hands upon his cheeks, and knew they couldn't be his own; his hands were far too sweaty now. The lips on his forehead also couldn't be his, because he couldn't remember a time where his own lips had been there. And the couplets of "yes" sounding in his ears surely were the most wonderful words he'd ever heard.

***

The next twenty-four hours were a rush of emotions for Alice; she bit her nails as she stood outside the door of her parent's house, staring down at the ring shimmering on her hand. She knew the reasons for the previous day's questions when she saw her father and mother. The real reason for her father's flight home became clear to her as soon as Quincy and she walked into her home.

The two men talked in quiet tones in the other room as Alice and her mother talked about the previous night. There was relief when Quincy & her father exited the den shaking hands. Yet the most palpable emotion was anxiety as she heard about her plans for the very next evening.

"Dinner with your mother?" she looked at Quincy. "I'd absolutely love to." She smiled outwardly, while inwardly she was unexpectedly nervous. She'd heard the story on how Quincy's mother had improved since Bradley left, but still…. Quincy was very jaded over the way he'd been treated while in their home. How much more so would his mother, be having lived with that man for so long?

***

Quincy and Alice waited at the restaurant until Denise Abrams walked past the host stand. Quincy looked at himself, he felt pretty sharp. It wasn't a five-star restaurant, but still, his button down blue shirt and slacks made him feel fancy. He had caught himself staring at Alice's diamond almost as often as he found himself smiling. His mother walked over to the table, waving awkwardly.

Alice stood up, wearing a lovely blue shirt and a black skirt, Quincy was smitten. He smiled and hugged his mother when she came to join them. "Mom, this is Alice, my fiancée. Alice, this is my mother Denise."

The two women embraced and sat at the table, their waiter came right at once to bring them drinks. Quincy felt that a man could have the best service in the world if you had a dead president talking for you. His theory was proven correctly by the prompt service they were receiving.

"So you're the lucky girl are you?" Denise asked, placing her purse at her feet and sitting up in her chair.

"I am." Alice smiled, placing her hand on Quincy's.

"Well, I've heard Quincy talk about you, and though I'm sure he's honest enough, why don't you tell me about yourself? We haven't had much time to get acquainted."

Quincy smiled a little, knowing that Alice was battling her modesty right now. He could see her thinking of how to make herself not appear conceited, and he took silent amusement in it. Relief for Alice appeared in the form of their food arriving.

The conversation grew easier as their meals disappeared. "So you're in this band of Quincy's, also? I guess that means you also have one of those…ink stains on you?"

Alice nodded. "I do." she grinned uneasily.

"Well, at least you had the good taste not to put it right on you, yours is covered it seems."

"Oh yes. Definitely covered up."

Quincy felt himself giving over to laughter as he waited for his mother to ask where the tattoo was, when he heard a raucous laugh erupt from behind him. His good mood dropped at once as 18 years of memory washed over him and covered him in a black dread. His fears were confirmed as he looked up into his mother's eyes and saw them turn to ice.

He let go of Alice's hand and peered around. He bit back the bile that was rising to his throat. There was his father, wining and dining a woman at least ten years younger than him. She was dressed in a revealing dress and his father seemed determined to will the dress right off of her. Bradley hadn't become aware of his son and ex-wife sitting so closely to him, or if he did, he didn't show it.

Quincy turned back, and his expression was grim. He knew that the ease and joy he had recently been feeling were chased away by the demon sitting behind him. Alice grabbed his hand, and he became aware of how cold he had become. Shivers were cascading down his back and racing to his toes.

"Quincy, honey, it's fine." Denise said, seemingly sensing her son's emotions.

"It's not." Quincy said. His lip began to twitch slightly, as he heard his father laugh again, calling out loud for another refill.

"Quin, come on, let's just get the bill and go." Alice began to say. "We're finished anyway."

"Is that the woman he was cheating on you with Mom?"

Denise said nothing, and Quincy took it as a yes. He handed himself over to his emotions, which were boiling over the pot and sizzling on the burner. He placed his napkin on the table, and got up. He regretted making Alice look so afraid, yet he couldn't stand for this. He hadn't seen his father since finding out about his infidelity; Quincy was a torrent of anger.

He walked over to the table and loomed over his father and the woman with him. "Hello, Bradley." Quincy said, his hands shaking at his sides.

Bradley looked up and comprehension became apparent in his eyes. The woman with him stopped laughing and stared up at the uninvited stranger. "Bradley, who is...

"I'm his son and that's his ex-wife sitting at the table over there. Did he tell you he had her living in fear for eighteen years? Or that he's an emotional abuser? Or maybe that he..."

"Quiet down, Quincy. This is a nice restaurant." Bradley grabbed hold of Quincy's hand, and Quincy reeled backwards.

"Get your hands off me. Or this whole restaurant is going to hear what I have to say." Quincy whispered shrilly.

"That wouldn't be a smart move, *Son*... course you never were one for brains."

Quincy ripped his hand out of the clutches of his father, and stared at the woman accompanying him. "Trust me, he's not worth your time."

"And you aren't worth mine." Bradley said, standing up and coming eye to eye with Quincy.

"You don't rule me anymore, you're nothing to me."

"You treat me with respect, I am your father." Bradley said, reaching out and trying to grab hold of Quincy's shoulders.

Quincy wrenched away and, emotions overtaking him, swung out at his father. He felt his fists connect with skin and it was then that he heard a crack in his joints. Quincy punched him again this time in the stomach. Bradley Abrams fell backwards onto another table and cursed loudly. Quincy heard Alice and his mother from behind him gathering up their things and they were quickly at his side urging him to leave.

Quincy's vision cleared and he saw a no nonsense sort of man swimming through a sea of tables towards him. *The manager no doubt.* Quincy thought. He took one last look at the waste of woman sitting in front of him, and took one last look at his father.

Quincy shook his head, and with piercing clarity he realized he was free of the spell his father had cast over him for all those years. The grief and doubt were gone, and all that was left was bitter understanding. "You know what..." Quincy said, rubbing his stinging hand quickly. "...I never wanted you either."

Quincy left his father on the floor, and he took the arms of the two most important women in his life and left the restaurant. The no nonsense manager man beat Quincy to the exit and turned him around. "You can't come into my restaurant and cause that kind of commotion. I have to ask you to never come back here, Sir."

Quincy snorted. "That's fine. I don't much like your dress code anyway." Quincy turned around and held the door open, leaving eighteen years of abuse far behind him.

***

William, Roslyn, Alice & Quincy were sitting in the bean bag covered basement of William's parent's house discussing the events of the day.

"So they threw you out?" William asked, bug eyed and curious looking.

"Well, we were on our way out anyway." Alice said, leaning back on Quincy's chest.

"Well good job on whacking that failure of yours Quin, wish I'd had the opportunity more than once," Roslyn said smiling, her hands laced in Williams.

"I'm past it now, it's pretty awesome." Quincy sighed, kissing Alice on the top of her head.

"We've set a date, by the way." Alice looked at William and Roslyn. "We're not having a great big wedding. Quincy and I just want you two there, and our parents."

"Your parents can come too." Quincy said, nodding at William and Roslyn. "Your folks put up with me enough over the years to be called family."

"Groovy man, I'm sure they'll get ya a nice wedding gift. Maybe some bean bag chairs of your own." William said.

"And, Will, I still want you as my best man." Quincy said, hopefully watching his best friend.

"And I want you as my maid of honor, Roslyn."

Roslyn gawked at Alice. "You guys have the date down, the maid of honor and best man chosen…who's officiating?"

"We were actually hoping Eli would." Alice said.

"*My* Eli?" Roslyn raised her eyebrows.

"Yes, *your* Eli." Quincy said.

"Well, yeah, I could see him doing that. Seems that online degree will actually be used for once." Roslyn commented.

"Good, good. It'll be legal and everything?" Quincy asked.

"Legal in all fifty states, he'd likely do it free for the two of ya. Provided he can come to the reception."

"We don't see a single problem with that." Quincy answered for himself and Alice.

"I've got one question for ya Mr. Q & A." William said.

"Ask it, but I've got something to tell you also." Quincy said, scratching his chin.

"Do I have to cut my hair?" William asked.

Alice laughed, and shook her head.

"Whew, that's good. I'd hate to lose this shag." He laughed. "What do you have to say Quin?"

"As of two weeks from now, you'll no longer be able to call me Mr. Q & A."

"Oh? How's that? And two weeks? You two aren't letting any moss grow." Roslyn shook her head.

"Alice & I have talked it over…" Quincy kissed her head again. "I'm taking the Mendell name. The line will end with him." Quincy nodded his head and watched his friends.

"I think that's a good idea Quincy." Roslyn admitted.

"Wish I'd have thought of it." William said sadly.

"Why, you don't like Denslie?" Alice asked. "I'm sure you'd make a great Lyden." Alice grinned after she saw Roslyn do the same.

"Nah, I just mean it would have been this great thing to suggest to Quin. Ah well, I suppose I'll have to get you something super great since I couldn't give you that idea."

The room grew comfortably quiet and the incense they had started was burning low. "So I can be the best man huh?" William smiled happily.

"I wouldn't want anyone else to do it, dude." Quincy said, getting up from his bean bag chair.

William got up and shook off his pants, though nothing was parting company with them. William grinned and looked down at his friend. "That'd be boss, man. I'm down with it."

Roslyn went over and sat down beside Alice; the two of them exchanged words, hugged. Quincy and William watched the exchange, not saying a word, knowing they didn't need to.

***

There was a single row of white wooden chairs in the field of wildflowers. Two thick candles burned upon a table, at the center of which rested a pillow with two silver and gold wedding bands. There was a trail leading up the hill to a graveyard of antiquity, the well maintained gravestones stood as witnesses to the ceremony of life and love about to unfurl below. Quincy Abrams stood boldly in the face of stirring winds; his hair that he'd worked so hard to get fixed blew across his forehead.

He could just make out a white and pink dressed figure making her way towards him. At her side walked a man in a white shirt and black slacks. Quincy smiled nervously, and caught a reaffirming smile from both his mother, and Alice's. The two mothers sat side by side next to Mr. & Mrs. Denslie.

Quincy got a poke in his side from his best friend, his *shag* pulled back into a tight pony tail. William was dressed in a brown suit that his father had likely used in his *heyday* as William would have called it. Quincy smiled at his friend and gave William a quick hug. "Thank you William, really man, I never once thought I'd be friends with a hippie like you."

William grinned. "Come on man, now's no time to get emotional. Your Mom hasn't even started crying, don't you start before she does. You didn't even put on good mascara, so you can't cry…it wouldn't be right." William clapped his friend on the shoulder.

Alice came into better focus and Quincy' smiled. She was the most beautiful woman he'd ever known and as of today she would be his.

Eli Lyden stood with his hands folded over his Bible, and looked as though he was in the most comfortable position conceived. He was clean shaven and his short haircut had no difficulties with the rampant breeze.

Eli cleared his throat, and Quincy took his place. Daniel was walking arm in arm with his daughter. Quincy stepped to meet them as they stopped in front of the row of chairs. He watched as Daniel kissed his daughter's hands. Daniel stepped forward and extended his hand to Quincy, who couldn't help but to hug his soon to be father-in-Law. "Thank you, Dad." Quincy said quietly, his chest felt like it was full of canaries.

Daniel nodded, and coughing just a little, he took Alice's right hand, and placed it in Quincy's. "I love you, Alice."

"Love you too, Daddy." she said from behind her veil. She watched as he stepped away, and then her eyes met Quincy's. He felt his heart flutter upwards as he knew that those eyes would always meet his at the beginning and end of every day.

Quincy and Alice stood in front of Eli, who smiled at both of them, and waited for his sister to take her place beside Alice. Once they were in place he began, speaking clearly and purposefully, as if he had done this all of his life. He opened his bible, and began.

"Friends and family, we are here to celebrate the union of this woman and this man. From their first tears to their first steps, right to this very moment, you have watched them grow and mature. You've shared in their happiness, and lamented at their distress. Share with us now their ultimate joy as they have each found their soul mate.

"Alice Mendell, you have written your own vows to Quincy, when you are ready." Eli said, closing his bible and stepping back slightly.

Alice breathed and her eyes were locked on Quincy's. "Quincy Abel Abrams, I take you as my husband. To love, to honor and to listen to my every whim. As this candle burns, so burns my love for you. I will cherish you all the days of my being. My love for you will endure through sickness and health. May your patience and longsuffering endure through the sickness, as I'll likely be driving you crazy. Will you take this ring, as a symbol of my devotion?" She held out his band of silver and gold, the metals as entwined as their fates soon would be.

"I do." he smiled, his voice sounding insubstantial compared to the beauty of the words she had just spoken to him.

She, smiling, placed the ring on his extended finger and smiled at him.

Eli, motioning at Quincy, nodded. "And you Quincy, have prepared your own vows for Alice. When you are ready."

Quincy reflected on how long he'd spent on writing the vows. It hadn't taken him any time at all to write them, for what were the vows but that which he had written since he'd first moved to this town and caught sight of Alice. He cleared his throat and gazed into Alice's eyes.

"Forever, I pledge myself to us. My honor, loyalty, love, and devotion are yours. I will be at your side while you sleep at night, and cradle you in the darkness. When the mornings are too much to meet, I will lift you up and my love for you will illuminate the chambers of your heart and mind. I love you, and there is no greater joy for me in life but to do so. I give myself completely to you Alice Mendell. Please accept this ring as a sign of my unyielding and irrepressible love for you." Quincy reached back and took the band from William's hand and held it out to her.

Alice, silver tears gliding down her cheeks as well as Quincy's now, extended her hand. "I will."

"By the power vested in me by the authority of Desalle Ministerial Universities and Colleges, and the state of Nebraska, I pronounce you husband and wife. You may kiss the bride." Eli said, nodding to both of them.

Quincy raised Alice's veil and gazed at those lips he'd dreamed of for years. Their lips met as their souls had over two years ago when they first dated.

Eli's words brought them back to themselves as he declared. "Gathered friends and family, it is my pleasure to present to you, Mr. and Mrs. Quincy Mendell!"

Quincy took Alice's hand and, together as he had dreamed of, they took their first steps as husband and wife. William and Roslyn were not far behind them. As the midday sun reached its apex it shined down upon the circle of friends, as different as could be yet singularly united in love.

William and Roslyn shared a kiss under a nearby Sycamore as they had done at the Corline County Renaissance fair last summer. Beneath the trees branches cameras flashed and pictures were taken. An exuberant happiness filled the field of wildflowers and it had no intention of leaving.

William took Roslyn into his arms and peered into her eyes. "You know, this is a good color on you." he said, touching the soft cherry red fabric. "It would look beautiful on you on our wedding day." He said bravely, his tongue dryer than sandpaper.

Roslyn turned as red as her dress and gazed at him. He knelt down and looked up into her eyes.

He brought out a small clay ocarina, one of Roslyn's own. He began to play a happy little tune that filled the air. Roslyn watched him as he played and kept saying how beautiful it sounded.

He took her hand and pressed his lips against it. He stood up, and watched her carefully. He reached up into a low hanging branch, and pulled out a tiny ruby, suspended on a chain of silver. William smiled as he remembered his sad little necklaces sitting at home, not quite necklaces any longer. He held out his hands and placed it around her neck. It reflected sunlight in the most beautiful way.

"William!" She whispered to him. "I do hope you spent so much time on their wedding gifts! It's not my wedding day, I don't need..." she stopped.

The very last gift he had for her came from within his coat pocket. It was a skillfully carved wooden ring, intricately designed with tiny creeping vines and small leaves. He smoothly slid it onto her finger. It felt cool in contrast to Roslyn's hot hands; yet the ring was a perfect fit.

Roslyn's eyes nearly popped out of her head as the seriousness of his proposal came upon her. "William!"

He smiled. "It's from the tree at Ren Fair...the one we always sat under. I waited for a tree branch to fall from it. I couldn't bring myself to snap a live branch off of it. I carved it just for you."

Roslyn covered her mouth and leaned against the tree for support. She fingered her new necklace and brought her ring finger closer to her face to admire the details. "You are for real?"

"As real as fairies." He ran his hands through her hair, kissing her head and waiting for her response. He didn't want to steal Quincy's thunder, really, he didn't. He just couldn't think of a more perfect place to propose to the woman he loved. He found the answer 'yes' in every moment of passing happiness under that sycamore tree.

"Well, we'll simply have to be married at the fair."

"Aye. It'll be the finest shindig Corline County will ever have the opportunity to see." He whispered to her.

The two kissed as Quincy and Alice walked to their limousine, neither party needing anything else save the company of their soul mates. Neither party cared that a reception was being held., Will and Roslyn not caring that it would probably be considered improper to be late.

This was the better end to their story. Today was the first day of the rest of their lives, and as Quincy had so often said, today was their day.

About the Author:

Chad McClendon is an author who grew up in Silver Grove, Kentucky. When not writing, Chad is solving technical support issues and turning his callers into characters. You can find him online at www.cmcfiction.net

Acknowledgements:

I would like to thank my family who has always supported my writing dream. Lipstick Trace would be nothing without the groundwork of David Bowie, and a dear friend from high school, the individuals who helped shape William Denslie. Thank you to everyone who said this would never happen, you provided much motivation over the last 30 years. This, and every book, is the realization of a dream—and these words mean my dream lives forever.

Social Media Links:

Website: http://www.cmcfiction.net

Facebook: https://www.facebook.com/cmcfiction/

Twitter: www.twitter.com/cmc_fiction @CMC_Fiction

Made in the USA
Charleston, SC
15 March 2017